The American Book of the Dead

This is a work of fiction. Names, characters, places, and incidents are products of the author's imagination. Any similarity to persons living or dead is purely coincidental.

The chapter "Gentleman Reptile" was published in a different form in a single volume by Cloverfield Press (www.cloverfieldpress.com).

Edited by Erin Stropes. Thanks to Clifford Pickover and Tom Baum for additional editorial help.

Front cover illustration from *Confrontations: A Scientist's Search for Alien Contact* by Jacques Vallee, used by permission.

Cover design by Cathi Stevenson @ Book Cover Express.

The American Book of the Dead

[a novel]

Henry Baum

Backword Books
www.backwordbooks.com

For Olivia

Contents

Introduction: Eugene Myers

The year was 2020. Except as I write this the year is 2008. Let's just say it's written in hindsight. 20/20 hindsight. Believe me, you'll forgive me a bad pun by the end of the book. I live in a time when violence is a religion, God is dead, and humor is something grandfathers used before the war. Fitzgerald claimed irony was dead in *The Beautiful and Damned*. If by dead, he meant reborn, he would have been more accurate, because the true age of irony didn't die for another ninety years. Somehow Fitzgerald was wrong about many things: no second acts in American lives? America was about to begin the biggest second act in the cosmos.

So I am sitting at a desk in Los Angeles in 2008, a young man with a new family trying to make ends meet. I am also a man of fifty, a teacher, waiting out the apocalypse. I am also a man of indeterminate age feeling sagely and satisfied. There are three people writing this book at once. A triumvirate of past, present, and future. A trinity even, but evoking the Bible is both boring and overblown. I haven't earned your trust yet.

Is this book merely the product of a young man's overreaching imagination or is he onto something? He is a deeply flawed version of myself—this is saying a lot because I am also deeply flawed. He is just beginning, as a man, as a writer. He is starting the novel with the idea that he might, finally, justify his life. The novel will take him years to complete and only parts of it are accurate. Which is where I come in. I take this flawed young man's rough draft and revise the shit out of it, a complicated form of self-criticism. He has no idea it's happening because I am like a ghost. I am both a product of his imagination and a mentor. Nobody ever said inspiration could be defined.

So if the young man in 2008 is writing this book and you—his elder—are helping him, he's not a prophet at all. Really, he's getting Cliffs Notes from the future. True and false. First, he had to bother to ask. He had to know which answers to look for. I am proud of him; he's closer to me than a son. I could not write the book for him. In short, it's a two-way street.

I forget that you don't know what I'm talking about. There's so much to cover, there's almost no place to begin. Simply, War World III happened. Great, another World War III novel. Not true, WWIII really did happen and this book comes from the future, across space and time, things now mastered, only because World War III happened and those who were left inherited not just the earth, but space.

And by the way, please don't classify this book as science fiction. File it under history, or a memoir of the future. Fiction, fine. But not science fiction. For you purists, this is not a cop-out, I am all for science fiction. But if it is considered science fiction, it will be considered a lie, speculative, which it isn't. If it is seen as fiction, it might be seen as closer to life. In the end it is not prophecy, because prophecy is a prediction of something before it occurs, and this is something that has already happened. I am less a seer than a witness.

Maybe I should start at the beginning. 2001. September 11th. It was why I started this book in the first place. I was sitting on the couch with a cup of coffee, watching the early morning news. I had spent the morning walking the dog around the neighborhood—I bought myself an egg sandwich and an orange juice, someone eagerly handed me an election flyer: I felt like I belonged to the timeless city. I was waiting on the couch to pick up my then-girlfriend who was arriving on the 9:00 train from Florida. I had forced her to leave because I saying, he's our man. Extra-sensory pretension, but that is what young writers must feed on or else wither in the doubts thrust on young, sensitive men—the feeling, sometimes, that every cell on earth is female. So I stayed home with the baby, taking care of her as best I could. Which isn't to throw into the mix that I was a bad father. I was a good father. I could fly into brief rages when she wouldn't leave me alone. Normal human anger, right? Or the hypersensitivity of a future genius? I was still clinging to self-aggrandizement—what other defense did I have. Why do I mention this? Because out of this environment came this novel, and out of the novel came Other Things.

Let me get to the plot of the novel I was proposing. A writer uncovers the secrets of the UFO conspiracy, secret societies, and life after death, all of which lead to World War III spearheaded by a fundamentalist Christian president. In short, everything that eventually happens.

All in all I was not such a good man to be around. Everywhere I saw both the potential for God and the potential for apocalypse. I believed UFOs were everywhere. I believed in the imminence of war. I believed that humanity was primitive, ignorant, past saving. The book was causing my marriage to fail—a form of personal apocalypse. I didn't know which came first, my dissolving marriage or my obsession in the dissolving world.

Everything wasn't dire. The book was coming easily, usually a good sign. I felt like I might be onto something. It turns out I was channeling these ideas. In the hierarchy of inspiration, channeling is somewhere below divine inspiration and somewhere above blind luck.

Before this becomes unintelligible, I'll cut ahead. The Myers family (my name is Eugene Myers) was living outside Los Angeles. I was teaching a college creative writing course. I'd written enough by this point that I got a job teaching a course in autobiographical fiction (irony!) Not a great school, and the position didn't pay much, but it was a job. Still trying to write, still plugging away. At 25, struggling as a writer was romantic, at 50, irresponsible. My life at the time should be some proof that my young self wasn't embellishing. If he was being dishonest, he would have made me a success. But I cannot deny who I am: a moderately successful writer who can barely pay his bills on a professor's salary and is still trying to write that one novel that will allow him to die satisfied.

What can I tell you about the world today? The death of art is a good way to talk about the death of the world. When I was in my twenties, the 19th century was just one century away, lingering like a god behind us, a giant monkey on our backs—Dostoevsky, the Brontës, Flaubert, a modern Bible. The 20th century was much less imposing. For all the war, technological breakthrough, etc. the century ended in an artistic fizzle. Regrettably, the 21st began with the same fizzle, which never ended. It turns out that fizzle was the sound of a wick burning out before the great dynamic explosion of war. People had stopped trying, as if they had been struck with some tragic premonition. It's all going to die, why bother? A kind of rational apathy that is only undepressing in hindsight. Instead of a great economic depression leading up to a war, there was a great artistic depression, which is *almost* to the world's credit—that art had any impact at all. The past masters seemed clued into a greater light, but with God dying there were fewer clues. And it turns out that the lack of good art is as bad a thing as poverty. It fucks with the basic ether.

They say that every generation romanticizes the one that came before it, unrealistically. But for us it really was the last decade. The world really did suck more than it ever had. You cannot imagine the alienation one feels when witnessing the world fall apart. Longing for the times of McDonald's and bad movies, to bring back those you hate, is a complicated mental process, especially for a born misanthrope. Misanthropy was supposed to fade with age, wasn't it? Only if the world improved with age as well, which it didn't. Misanthropy wasn't just a product of envy, condescension, vanity, and immaturity, but survival. While we lived in a world of rational apathy, we thought I needed the space to write a novel. I wept like I never had before when she left for the plane. I know now it was a kind of mourning for our unborn daughter. Proof that maybe I do have some premonition in me. I wrote a hundred or so pages, all the while hard-up and lonely and begged her back. She was living with an ex-boyfriend who had become a cult member, a follower of the Falun Gong movement. I write these details because they don't seem real exactly. Rarely does my life seem interesting enough for fiction. Perhaps on that day everybody had an equal story to tell.

Sitting on the couch, drinking coffee, wondering about the day to come. Out of the corner of my eye a low-flying wavering plane, as if struggling.

Now, this was a daydream I'd had before. Often sitting in my 3rd floor apartment with its rare view of the NYC sky, a sliver of the Empire State Building, I would fantasize that a plane was flying too low. God, it's going to crash, I would think, maybe even with a slightly drunken sense of hope—at least, then, my delusions would have some proof. Once I even heard an explosion, surprised to hear the next day that nothing happened. I knew every trajectory of planes in the sky. I hated planes. So when a plane was flying south as low as the buildings, I knew this was wrong. Something was about to be realized.

I didn't run to the window. I didn't want to see it crash. A BOOM. Oh no, I said out loud, something people did in movies, and felt slightly awkward, like I was trying to prove grief. I went to the window. The World Trade Center was out the window to the left, twin overseers of my neighborhood. Imposing, thoughtful, indifferent, romantic: New York City buildings. They always seemed like a fiction, a white smoky haze about them as if superimposed against the blue screen of the sky. They were just too tall.

A black smoking hole in building, jagged and fragmented, as surreal as the buildings themselves. Many people must be dying in there. I went out on the fire escape to watch. Felt guilty, like an audience, came back inside. Got my camera, took one picture, which I still haven't developed. Checked the news. Still interviewing somebody about a book. Another boom, a cloud of fire, and an excited shout of "Whoa" from the Chinatown onlookers. They were shocked but entertained—not despicably, I suppose. Life is boring, uniform, redundant, and this was something different. It was even magical, in the sense of seeming both fake and uncommonly alive.

I had to leave for the train station. I wasn't going to risk the subway. I hailed a cab and rode uptown with a smiling Pakistani man who spoke with an embarrassed, maybe grateful smile that this was likely an act of terrorism.

I tell this, as if it needs rationalizing, because it informed the rest of my life. Immediately, it influenced my life with my girlfriend. The following month we conceived a child, then married on Halloween—which when the marriage is faltering loses all its irony and seems like a terrible mistake. To live a mild life and then to be thrust into war, to understand in however small a way what people throughout history must have felt, gave me the kind of empathy that might only come once and can't be repeated. Also I was part of something that was the beginning of the end of the world.

Throughout my life I often felt like I was living in a shell of the better past. The sixties, the Beat Generation, the Lost Generation, punk rock—I was too young for all those things, and so the past seemed to loom over my life like a successful older brother. It's a stupid, lonely, one-sided battle to be in competition with the past. Finally, on September 11th, I felt part of the consequential present—a present that my heroes may have labored through. Men who had gone to war and lived to write about it. The irony was that I would eventually live through the worst war of all. And so all that time I spent lamenting the valuelessness of the present was wasted time, even if I was right. It turns out that my love of the past was a kind of premonition—I was idealizing the past because somehow I knew the future was going to be fucked up beyond recognition.

The worst part of Sept. 11 for me—beyond the tragedy, the loss of life, but I'll admit I am too self-centered to be permanently empathetic—was the fact of seeing a nightmare actually come to life. A writer's job is to believe in made-up stories as if they were true. If it wasn't so, there would be no energy to write. But this was something I'd imagined *actually* coming to life. A plane hitting a building, the aftermath, fire. And if I tried with all my soul to believe in something I was writing, I was still protected by objectivity—the knowledge that I am God of my world, and I can change it as I please; nothing is permanent. The God of our lives was doing as he pleased that day. From that day forth I had the disturbing sense that some illusions might be real.

After September 11, Stephanie and I fled New York. This might seem like cowardice, and I confess to it. But I always found New York a dangerous place: both dangerously self-affirming and self-destructive. Either way, capable of snapping. Add to that the threat of daily suicide attacks and it was enough reason to leave. A walk through Soho wasn't worth it. It was hardly worth it before the attacks.

We moved to Willamette, South Carolina on a whim. I always wanted to be a Southern writer and live in small-town South. I quickly learned the obvious—that to be a Southern writer you have to be Southern. My naiveté can be amazing. The same could be said about my time in New York. I lived in New York for ten years trying to recreate the will of past writers, not realizing that we were living at the beginning of the future and not the continuation of the past.

Stephanie quickly got pregnant, in October, a September 11th baby (called the Doomers, not the Boomers). Out of this environment—a new baby, a failed writer—I started writing a novel. The book outlined everything that was terrifying me at the time. My dreams were filled with images of the end of the world. Dozens of planes crashing to the ground a night. Explosions, broken buildings, people in rags fleeing and banding together. In one of these dreams I heard names—survivors, I told myself in the dream. I woke up and thought, "There's a book in this."

Here's where it gets confusing. I hear derisive laughter. "Metafiction on steroids," it was called. Long story short, it's the book you're reading. So where's the confusion? The book was about a writer in his fifties working on a book. In the future the book has yet to be written, even if it was written in the past. Complicated, but it solved one issue: the older writer is not aware of the book that has already been published because in his world the book has not been written. But wait—I hear people say—you've been talking as if the war has already occurred and the novel has yet to be conceived. Here's my answer: time doesn't exist. All of these different stories are happening at once. Makes enough sense to me, not to a number of detractors, including a fair number of publishers who rejected it, saying it was "awkward" or "it doesn't work." Consider this a preemptive strike because at that time I was very sick of not getting published.

Which should bring us to where I was when I first conceived the novel. My daughter couldn't live on hope for much longer. She was just born, on the day John Coltrane died, among other things. My wife was working—supporting us—as a legal secretary. I lived by the blanketing delusion that hope was as good as money. My wife disagreed, rightly. We fought daily, nightly, about money, our doubt as parents, we woke the baby, made her cry, made us cry; there was crying. Terrible times and the punchline is that my wife was working for a divorce lawyer.

The lawyer's name was Geoff Smith, a fat, deep-Southern man. Mean and gracious at once, as if Truman Capote wasn't gay. No real point in describing him, just giving you a glimpse…

So I struggled at home taking care of the beautiful 11-month-old girl, Sophia Margaret. Most of all wanting to be a full-time writer—one who had once believed that he was being overseen by writers from the past, a great harem of dead writers, also lived in a world of rational cynicism, even a rational desire for the apocalypse. Armageddon was a form of ambition, an antidote. Play Arvo Pärt's Tabula Rasa and you'll see what I mean.

I have to admit, during those years leading up to the Big One there was something electric in the air. Impending doom can be exciting. Actual doom is something else. Like the difference between drug addiction and drug withdrawal.

I didn't know we were close to the end. I was still thinking about Dickens and Dostoevsky, Mozart and Beethoven, Lennon/McCartney, as if past achievements would somehow save us. They were proof, weren't they, that the human race was worth saving? They were proof like DNA evidence is proof—irrefutable, perhaps, but invisible.

The point of this prelude is to give some backstory. I never hoped for any of this to come true, no matter how much I thought humanity deserved it. One question I hear out there—if this is so important, why spend the time to write a book? Shouldn't you send it to the president? You must be asking that facetiously. I think you know that most people won't believe me. Some will, though, and I hope to find some of you by sending this out into the world.

It does seem trivial to use a literary medium to describe the end of the world, like using a billboard to tell the news. What can I say, I'm a writer so I chose my medium. I am also making the vain attempt to sum up the end of the world, as if my far-sighted eyes are the window in. I guess I've just summed up the limitless ego of the writer. Even in the face of genocide, he tries to make a case for the beautiful uniqueness of his life. But what choice did I have in the face of the Great Oppression—the death of God, science, love and hate—except to believe in myself.

1: Gentleman Reptile

"There's something wrong with me. I'm attracted to every one of my female students. Every one. This should be illegal. And they like it, they know. Professor Myyyy-errrrs, they say. Such a sexy name I have. I didn't hang around with girls like that when I was their age. I dreamt of it. Of course. But I don't even think there were girls like this when I was in college. It's like they're always naked. I never sowed my oats, do you hear me? I married young, I thought it was a mature and literary thing to do. It would make me a man. And if I got divorced, it would also be a literary thing to do. I'd be another Mailer. But—cruel joke—I don't want to get divorced. I have failed a lot in my life and I don't want to make a legal document of my failure. So I look at every young girl and wonder what it would be like. I've been adulterous a thousand times over just by looking at them. Eighteen is too young, they should raise the age to thirty. Help me doctor, help me, I even want to sleep with you."

I was talking to Sharon, an English professor—beautiful, a lesbian since birth. Smarter than you. Inappropriately dressed in tight seventies basketball shorts. Red hair, blue eyes, her skin pouted. Imagine a playmate from *The New Yorker*. Every sane man's dream.

"You've got a problem," she said.

"Hell yes, I've got a problem. What do I do?"

"Maybe you have to sleep with one of these girls. Then you might see how young they are. Like sleeping with a child."

"Maybe it would be the most profoundly erotic experience of my life. Then what?"

"Maybe you'll have to teach her more than you think."

"In this day and age? And besides, I'm a teacher."

"You've got an answer for everything."

"It's a problem. It either has every answer, or no answer."

"It's a fairly dull problem, Eugene. Professors have always been tempted by this and many have gone through with it. More have gone through with it than been caught. And most of those who have been caught haven't been fired."

"You're not much of a help. So you think I should go through with it?"

"Yes."

"I know I'm just looking for approval. If I beat off, the problem will go away. But it always comes back, like hunger for Chinese food."

"I'm leaving."

"You're right. I'm sorry."

She looked at me with amusement and disgust, like a mirror. Then she wrote something down on a notepad, as if making a diagnosis. She stood up and stared at me intently for a moment. In her look: softness and respect and some lust. They should sell how that feels. And then she took off her top. She stood there with poise, as if I'd offered a piece of my life and she was offering me a piece of hers.

"What do you think of them?" she asked.

"They're nice," I said stupidly.

She walked around the desk, hand trailing along the edge, and sat on my lap. Sweetly, not aggressively like a porn star out to avenge her life.

It became blurry at this point. I saw flashes of her smile, her acceptance. This wasn't going to last long. "Can I *go*?" I said. My clothes were still on.

She smiled. "Yes," she said.

And I did. It was my first wet dream since I was fourteen.

And now I was fifty. I was lying in bed next to my wife. Stephanie, beautiful. The woman from the dream was my wife when I met her, at 23. Mixed with a girl who walked her fashionable dog around our neighborhood, also around 23, wore tight basketball shorts, naked with clothes on. Probably didn't write for *The New Yorker*. I wrote down the dream immediately in a notebook beside the bed, which was something I'd been doing lately. One time long ago, I dreamt the first scene of a novel, woke up, and didn't stop writing until the book was done. So I was trying to force inspiration. A quick analysis: the dream was about a more hopeful time when I was convinced of my future, but now the future was here and nothing like my faith. Mostly, the dream told me what I desired. I knew that already.

As I was writing, my wife woke up.

"What are you writing?" she asked.

I almost told her. She wouldn't take that as adultery, but immaturity. She was half-right. "A dream about work," I said. "I'm hoping it will spark a story."

"Oh."

"At least I got some pages down," I said, hopefully.

"At least."

There was terrible emphasis on the word, "least," which fueled me to write with more pristine detail the lesbian professor straddling me with worship. It's not a very good marriage.

—〰—

At the time I was working on a novel about the end of the world. One thing was true about that dream: I saw an apocalyptic amount of lust in my students' eyes. I had been wondering how to put that into words. I settled on the main character discovering his daughter doing porn online. I was the father of an eighteen-year-old so this was my worst nightmare come to life. Writing was like a prayer, a way to ward off disaster. If I wrote it, it couldn't actually come true because that would be too much of a premonition.

So which came first, my desire for my students or the novel? Both, no doubt. Writing was a form of therapy and method acting. I was trying to write a new *Lolita*, a vain attempt to shock people. Fifty years old and I still hadn't lost the urge, probably because it hadn't been done for so many years.

I should explain where the world was. This was a world Nabokov hadn't considered. The last sexual taboo had been destroyed on the 8th of January. That was the day a midseason replacement sitcom, "Stick it to Me," went on the air. It was the first pornographic sitcom. Full nudity, full penetration, full money shots, all on free prime time. Once the internet entered the television business, the networks had no choice. SITM wasn't the highest rated show ever, that wasn't the point. Pornography was on TV. Soon after, you could see girls sucking off men in broad daylight, a crowded street. TV doesn't cause violence, TV doesn't cause promiscuity, some shout. That only applies to *intelligent* people, of which, we all know, there aren't many. Most others looked at TV as if it were an advertisement for reality.

I'm not against porn. Many porn stars had interesting stories to tell, I'm sure. But for all the empowerment porn stars may have claimed, they had no control over how porn was regarded—as a joke, as loveless, as discarding human feeling. The only thing that sitcom empowered were the networks and television executives who probably raped for sport.

I would be lying if I said I didn't watch SITM myself. Everyone did at some point. It was like watching an erotic car accident. I could never claim to be a fully evolved man.

I went online to research the book—no, really, I found it angering, disappointing and arousing, which was a potent kind of fuel. Watching these beautiful, meek girls slowly emptying themselves. Thumbnails, pictures, movies, words like "Slut getting a mouth blessing." I browsed briefly, saw a link for a movie clip, "Teen Girl with Glasses Schooled in Cock" (I loved girls in glasses, just look at my wife), and clicked on it, and then there she was.

Sophia. Our daughter. I clicked stop quickly, my hand trembling. A freeze frame remained on the computer screen. My daughter was sitting in a school chair in some sort of classroom with a teacher, some man, pointing to the word "Cock" scrawled on the blackboard. I didn't have to watch it because I knew what would happen. My heart felt deeply alive and dead at once, almost like when she was born and my wife had an emergency cesarean. Like feeling your soul.

You asshole. You petty scumbag. All this time you were being playful about somebody else's daughter. But also, I had predicted this, so I was proud for a moment, before realizing that my daughter was doing porn. Mostly I was thinking, Can't I go back in time?

What does one do in this situation? I drank whiskey from the bottle in my desk. I don't drink often, but I kept it there. I stared at the picture of her on screen. It was similar to staring at the first edition of my first novel, turning it over in my hands, thinking it might evaporate. Almost as if I hoped it would disappear because my life would never be the same. I stared at the screen hoping to come to terms with the picture of my daughter. This is similar to a drug addict trying to cure himself by overdosing.

"She's still alive," I muttered to myself, as if I'd heard she was in a car accident and I needed to rush to the hospital. "She's still alive."

I kept staring at the picture. I couldn't help myself. There was something very powerful about seeing her on screen. It felt significant in a way I couldn't yet guess. Like this might solve something I had been avoiding. An important judgment. I wanted to know more. I pressed play.

"You're good to me," she said, as it ended.

To be honest, the worst thing about seeing my daughter was

that I felt something besides disgust, fear, regret—positive reactions, considering. No, there was something else—I won't say titillated (I have to be careful here, as careful as I would have to be with my wife, please be patient), but at the very least, *affected.* The best way to describe seeing my daughter in that position was not with pure sadness, but also fascination. A kind of fantastical fiction, the worst dream realized. It was similar to the way people reacted to September 11th, any tragedy. Wow, some thought, it's impressive, even moving. Watching my daughter, the porn star, was like witnessing an act of terrorism on our family. Hurtful, sickening, faith-destroying, but so ambitious in its degradation—and so personal—that I could not look away. The future was a violently fucked-up place that any of this was an issue.

—∿∿—

I wasn't sure if I should show my wife the movie. I had been so devastated. I could just tell her about it. But she would demand to see it. And really it was something she needed to see. She had a much better chance of talking to Sophia about it. Some things a father cannot talk about with his daughter. Even someone who likes to believe he's honest.

I would have to be careful with the way I broached the subject with my wife. What was I doing looking at girls online when I just happened to find a video of my daughter? Had I watched the video? This, after all, could reflect very poorly on me.

I had to wait an hour for my wife to get home. In these situations, an hour can feel like trudging through mud—and I mean that literally. I felt like I was getting dirtier by the second. I moved to the living room, away from the office. The scene was still alive on screen like a camera looking into our house. I drank the whiskey slowly. If I was drunk, I couldn't effectively defend myself.

My wife normally got home from work at five. I should have

waited at least until Stephanie had walked into the house before I told her. She didn't even have a chance to go to the bathroom, hang up her coat, have a drink. But if I have something to say, I cannot keep it a secret.

She walked into the house looking overcome, as if anticipating bad news. Sometimes it seemed like she could be psychic—at the very least she had a sharp woman's intuition. She would feel a crushing anxiety, only an hour later to be struck with bad news.

"Everything all right?" I asked her. The door hadn't yet closed.

"Yes."

"You sure?"

"Yes."

Annoyed. Get out of my face, she was thinking. I am not very good at setting up stories. Which was why I jumped into it.

"I have some bad news," I said.

"Can't I sit down at least?" she said.

"Of course, sit down," I said. But that was a lie. The ball was rolling. "I have to show you something."

"What?" As if putting up with the whims of a child.

"Please come upstairs," I said.

"OK," she gave in.

"This is terrible," I said, a pathetic warning, as we walked up the stairs, me behind her. I watched her clothes ascend: a thick, dark-maroon, flowered skirt, one of my favorites, with a black cardigan over an off-white shirt. She always looked nice when she went to work; a woman.

"Come into the office," I said. I opened the door, methodically, as if it opened into someplace that was not my office.

"What is it?" she asked, as if to say, "This better be good."

"I discovered this on the computer today," I said.

The web page with our daughter was still on screen. "You're good to me." Her eyes closed...I don't really want to describe this.

Stephanie stared at the picture of Sophia. "What is..." she said, but she knew immediately. She started crying and I felt regretful: hers was such a more honest response.

Stephanie was too hurt to even ask why I had happened to come across the video. "Leave me alone," she said and I left her in the office. I don't know if she watched the movie. The experience killed her, briefly.

—\/\/\—

When we had Sophia, I finally felt like I finally belonged to the world. I had been given a window into real passion and experience. No longer could I say that I didn't know what it was to be alive. And our daughter was beautiful, intelligent, happy. An eager artist, she loved to read, we thought we had done everything right with our daughter. So what would make her do this almost a month to the day after she had turned eighteen?

She was in the last semester of high school, but technically legal. She would be going to college in the fall at the same school where I taught, on a discount. I couldn't afford better—a whole other blow to my ego and a different story.

I sat in the den downstairs waiting for the next thing to happen. When Sophia got home from school she went straight into her room. It did not feel like my daughter had come home. Not a stranger, an imposter. My wife and I converged immediately in the upstairs hallway, without planning it, and walked silently to her door. Never in my life had I felt so much like a parent. That is, so self-righteously moral.

I knocked on the door gently, not a bang.

"Yeah," came a small voice.

I opened the door.

Sophia saw us both standing in the doorway, looking deadly. Her eyes went wide, already assaulted.

Stephanie started right in: "Have you heard of

Librarywhores.com?" she said, which sounded foolish spoken out loud, like a punchline.

Sophia looked incredulous, but not guilty. It was possible that she didn't know the site. It occurred to me that she might not even know that the movie was online at all. Which was thoughtless in a whole different way.

"No," she said, feigning disgust.

"Your father found…your father and I found some pictures of you on the internet today," Stephanie said.

Sophia was beginning to understand. "So?" she said, sounding thirteen.

"They're awful pictures."

Sophia glanced at me with a look of horror, as if I was looking at her naked right there.

"So," she said again, her only defense.

"So," Stephanie said. "I don't even know how to put this. What the fuck is wrong with you?"

My wife looked like a rabid dog that's just learned it's dying. Instinctively, I wanted to jump to my daughter's defense, "Hey, now, wait a minute." But I thought it was better if I stayed out of it.

"What…how…" Stephanie trailed off. "Explain this."

Sophia looked at me again with a "Does he have to be here?" look. Stephanie gave me the same expression.

"I'll leave," I said.

"No," Stephanie demanded. "She needs to be embarrassed as fucking possible."

The "fucks" were having their effect. Sophia was beginning to tremble, break. Part of this lecture, I now realized, was an act of sadism on our part. To make our daughter feel as bad as she made us feel.

"Sophia," I broke in. "This is a terrible thing you've done. You're smarter than this."

"It's not that big a deal," she said. "Everybody's doing it." She regretted saying that—she was smart enough to realize that it was flimsy reasoning, especially to people like her parents.

"You guys, it's just different now. This is what people do these days. It's just an activity. Doing it in front of a camera isn't different than doing it normally."

I thought she might have a point. Maybe this was progress. Maybe taboos needed to be destroyed utterly in order to not matter anymore. Just not by my family.

"It's just an experience, you know," Sophia added.

"Experience, my foot," Stephanie exclaimed. Sophia and I shared a smirk. But then I composed myself. "We're not old cranks if we think that having sex on camera isn't a good learning experience."

"Let me ask you something?" Sophia asked, poised, ready to be facetious.

"Yes," Stephanie said, ready not to listen.

"Are you against porn?"

Reluctantly, "No."

"So what's wrong with me doing it?"

I followed her logic. I was almost proud of her.

But her mother said, "That doesn't matter. I like to think in our family that we prize intelligence over ignorance. And to have sex and broadcast it for everyone to see is ignorant."

Somehow, even though at the beginning of this discussion I had never before felt more in the right, Sophia was making me feel old, out of touch. I still felt like it was a regrettable thing for her to have done. But here she was in front of us: bright, alive, lucid. She wasn't dying, she wasn't broken. Watching the video of her had been, in a way, like watching her be murdered. But it wasn't murder, it was sex. I guess I was proud that she was so confident and undeterred by us confronting her. She was the same person she always had been.

Her mother, though, was not going to budge. And I thank her for that.

"It's ugly," Stephanie said. "And I like to think that people in this family understand beauty."

"You can only understand beauty when you witness ugliness," Sophia said. She sounded so much like one of my students. "Dad has written about that same thing, you know. He even wrote a novel about a porn star."

"This is all getting too philosophical," I broke in, because I could see that we might lose the argument. "This isn't only about beauty, or intelligence, or experience, Sophia, or what I've written as fiction. It's about something just being plainly wrong. Murder is illegal for a reason. I'm sure to murder someone would be a significant learning experience, but that does not make it right. The world is disintegrating—it is becoming more of a stupid, terrible, violent place and it is better to not contribute to it. I know when I was younger I liked to write about violence, even about sexuality. But that was when violence and rampant sexuality were not so common as they are today. Believe me, Sophia, you know I'm no conservative. I just think that with the world heading where it is, it is important to fight the good fight."

"What can I tell you," Sophia said.

This had somehow become a no-win fight. I had figured Sophia would recoil in remorse and humiliation, but she hadn't. It was like an argument about grades or a broken curfew, nothing so consequential. She sat in her desk chair limply, unchanged. Which prompted my wife to say, "Sophia, do you understand, this is the end. I don't know if I can think of you as my daughter anymore. Nothing is ever going to be the same. You disgust me. As a woman and your mother and as a human being."

This crushed us all. Sophia's brown eyes got both angry and tearful. Everybody was dying. Sophia stood up and walked past us, down the stairs and out the front door, so we couldn't see her crying.

Stephanie and I stared at each other, drunk with despondency. A black shade over our daughter's room. Nothing was said. Everybody needed to be alone. We parted.

I was left alone in Sophia's room. Feminine, smelled good, clean, like fresh laundry. Sometimes I thought it might be the room of a young lesbian. There were more pictures of women than men. Marilyn Monroe, Bettie Page. I respected her love of the classics. Better big-breasted women than forgettable teenage boys. Not that I would have been disappointed if she were a lesbian, it would just be nice to know who she was. No, finding her online was as bad as could be, a murder of what remained of the innocence in my life, which I held up as evidence that the world could again be what it once was.

The air had lightened a bit with the women gone. I surveyed what had happened: I predicted something in my writing. That, or I somehow allowed it to happen by writing about it, gave her license, which was never something I wanted to face.

I didn't know what I was looking for in her room. I just wanted further evidence of who I'd created, and that she had a life beyond that movie.

On the desk, a diary. So common and gentle a thing. Old-fashioned, hopeful. We had bought it for her. There was no lock on the diary, which at this point I saw as symbolic. No lock on her diary? Of course not, this girl keeps nothing safe or sacred. This was a stretch because if she cared anything for symbolism, for meaning, she wouldn't be fucking on a computer screen, probably for money. Did it make it worse or better if she was paid?

I justified the absence of a lock as an invitation. I opened the diary and began to read.

Much of it was intelligent, thoughtful, as I knew she was. Dry, factual, mainly. There was an assessment of one of my own novels, which made me intensely proud, flattered, even embarrassed (as if she had caught *me* naked) for a brief moment, but then I remembered why I was there.

I skipped to a page toward the end. It turned out to be the most telling page of the diary, as if I still knew my daughter.

"I have to write this down. I feel so weak. Every guy I come in contact with, I just want to kiss. I wonder how women don't just want to jump on a guy and start kissing him, pulling down his pants or whatever. I know this sounds un-feminist but what am I supposed to do when I actually tremble when I see every guy? I'm talking every guy. Maybe it's because I'm young and I'm supposed to be procreating or something. I just want to have sex with every one of them. Even old man [sic]. There must be something wrong with me, cause I'm fucking horny. Old or young, I just want to have the experience."

She sounded just like her father.

—◠◡◠—

This story should be a lesson to you. The future in store is a madly messed-up place. True, 2008 is hardly different. This could happen in 2008 as easily as 2012, as easily as 1972 for that matter. The difference, perhaps, is scale. In the past, chastity was an issue, now it existed for no one. I sound like a Christian, don't I, decrying how Satan is taking the souls of our children? I think that gives a bad name to Christians. Satan—or what he commonly represents—is no good.

The reason I bring up Christianity is because episodes like the one with my family were the reason an arch-right Christian named Charles Winchell was elected president. I would have even voted for him if I hadn't sensed—like the minority—that he was a complete lunatic.

2: President Wind Chill

Charles Winchell was a diplomat's son. A born politician. He gave speeches at three years old, they said. He was many different men at once, a kind of well-received schizophrenic. Charles was his presidential name. He went by Chuck to the unions, Charlie to the ladies, and Charles at the convention. And he had a different accent, a different style of speech, to fit every name.

It was not surprising that Winchell was able to get elected. The scene with my daughter should tell you something where the world was residing when Winchell was running for president. We were in need of a dictator. The world was so uncontrollable that people were increasingly open to fascism, on the left and right, because the alternative wasn't working.

Sex wasn't the only taboo that had been broken—and by broken I mean destroyed utterly. Violence too had become so commonplace as to be—not normal exactly—but tolerated, the way one tolerated months of rain; you could complain, raise your fist at the sky, but there was really nothing you could do. Along with the casual sex came casual violence. This I will not blame on TV. The media maybe, but that's too simplistic a scapegoat. For all the media's emphasis on bad news, they were reporting on things that actually happened. Soon, there was nothing but bad news.

It began with the school shootings. I had watched the shootings become more commonplace with a sense of dread and fascination. I was as alienated as a kid could be in high school. I hated everyone, everyone avoided me. But even in my darkest rage I did not fantasize about killing every last one of them. Might have to do with my particular brand of insecurity: I believe both that I am better than everyone, and that everyone is better than me. So the school shootings to me seemed like a kind of demonic possession, religious, a mixture of sickness and ambition that was once left to the Hitlers of the world. But school violence—like Hitler—was only the beginning.

I don't know exactly when it happened. There wasn't a moment, a collective epiphany, some final act of violence where everyone said, Fuck it, why be safe? But soon perfectly normal people were walking into a Wal-Mart and gunning people down. Going postal became a pastime. You couldn't go to the market without being afraid. One of the basic tenets of sci-fi literature is to take things that are happening in the present and exaggerate the hell out of them. It's like a quantum theory of society—if something happens once, on a small scale, it can happen everywhere all the time. I mention this because it might appear that I'm using a literary device. Sure, school shootings. What's next, a shooting a day? School bombings? School warfare? Tragically, yes.

But even talking about guns and pornography is provincial. Although anything that is provincial to America seems to affect everything—to say otherwise is like saying an alcoholic father doesn't affect his children. On the world stage, things were even worse. Climate changes, many small wars over food, more terrorism. AIDS was cured, but then there were new diseases like panspermia, a virus with arms and legs that acted very much like it had a conscious intelligence, invented who knows where. The highest-grossing group was called Sickle Cell, with their album *Sick Sells*. I won't get into everything right now. I don't want to overload you with bad news.

Really, it's no wonder Winchell got elected. Try to imagine the humiliation and heartbreak. People seemed to be losing their humanity, as if in preparation for a major war.

Charles Winchell came into this environment. The world needed a change, and fast. New policies had been tried time and again, but our basic system was broken, so the planet continued to die, people's malevolence did not go away and we limped along with small progress and bigger problems. Winchell was a member of a newly created party—the Unitans—a sort of valiant attempt to destroy gridlock and divisiveness. People welcomed the new party. Even I would have voted for him if it wasn't for his creepy emphasis on Christianity, his eyes which managed to be large and beady at once, conniving and charming. He was everyman depending on who was looking at him. If you wanted a bad-ass, you got a bad-ass, if you wanted thoughtful, you got it. Of course, this was "thoughtful" to people who didn't think—I'm not sure the man read, ever, except for his Bible. But he gave the appearance of graciousness, and in that day and age that was enough. And this was not slick, former-actor, politician's-son graciousness— this was where he even got me. The man talked like a person. He sounded like a cross between an aggravated football coach, a successful car salesman, slightly Southern, from St. Louis—and also something completely original, indefinable. He actually memorized his speeches so he wouldn't look stiff and mannered. He was said to have a photographic memory. On talk shows he would say things like "Don't be stupid." He even used bad language, with a fatherly twinkle in his eye, saying, "I know we all talk like this, so what does it matter? It doesn't fucking matter, right? They're just words. We have more to worry about." His use of bad language was what got liberals on his side. He admitted that he liked women, did some drugs in college, and loved movies. I thought it might be good for the country to have a president who spoke his mind, who seemed human, no matter what his ideas. It might humanize the country. Because at the time, it wasn't as if any legislation was having any effect. People were screwing and killing each other in broad daylight. Maybe what the country needed was a good scolding by a good, hard-talking Christian. Something had to be done. If nothing else, he was entertaining.

By writing that last sentence, I am admitting partial responsibility for his ascendancy. By liking the man, I helped get him elected. I contributed to the illusion of his charm. But what did it matter when he was, basically, the only one running. The Democrat, an Asian woman, got fewer votes than a city mayor. Everyone wanted this man elected. Perhaps America had a collective death wish. A desire to wipe the map clean and start over. People had lost faith in God and country. Chuck Winchell was the best man for the job: a businessman, a preacher, a mechanic, an actor, a lover, a salesman, every American. He would resurrect "In God We Trust."

His most innocuous slogan was "Chuck is Good Luck." But the one that he threw out only so often was the heart of his campaign—the heart of the man himself. He told us that he was running on the "Apocalypse Ticket." Not literally, he said with his smirk (was it smug, diabolical, or earnest? Only God knew.) What he meant by "Apocalypse," he assured us, was that the old ways had to go. After all, the Greek word for apocalypse, apokalupsis, meant "to uncover," "to disclose," "to reveal." There was so much violence, so much casual sex, we needed a complete overhaul. Who could argue? "I'll invoke the Bible if I have to," he said. And then he would say (and this is where he charmed people), "And I won't apologize for using the Bible. Hell yes, I'll reference the Bible. Screw church and state, we've got some real problems at stake. The Bible is a book full of goodness and wisdom. As are the Bhagavad Gita, the Torah, the sayings of Confucius for that matter. Wars have started because of it, but more people have been personally resurrected. The Bible is a salve for these immoral times." Out with the old, in with the nuclear, one cynical pundit quipped. Somehow, the Apocalypse Ticket struck a chord with people. Things did need to change, boy did they, and the apocalypse was only a metaphor, right?

If only. It turned out everything the new president was shouting about was to be taken literally. The man did not have a capacity for irony. Which—*ironically*—was exactly the kind of thinking he was trying to kill with his apocalypse. The casual, smirking attitude towards violence, sex, everything. Give him credit, the man was sincere in a deepening ocean of insincerity: people had forgotten how to believe, and he was going to bring back their faith. Even if it meant killing them.

—⋀⋀—

Fast forward to the oval office, two years in.

Things weren't going as well as President Winchell had hoped. The world was falling apart and he was being blamed for it. For most of his presidency he was disliked. His initial charm had worn off. It had gotten him elected, but his election had solved nothing. No speech or town hall helped. Some said he went too far, others said he didn't do enough. This didn't match well with his personality. He'd always been a sensitive soul. A dark look from his wife could send him down for hours. In fact, he was a man for whom there wasn't enough praise in the world. One insult overshadowed everything that came before it, no matter who it came from, no matter how red a neck. So what would such a man do if more than half the country hated him? Half, Christ, he had a 93% disapproval rating.

People were just angry about the state of things, he tried to rationalize. They were afraid. He was an easy target. All the same, he didn't become president to be hated.

He needed to regain their devotion. He needed to do something permanent to help the country. What was the point of discussing another health care or education bill? They didn't do much good anyway. The world didn't just need another bandage. It needed to be baptized. The time had finally come.

Five men sat in the Oval Office. Chief of staff, VP, NSA, SOS and SOD. Gray and overweight men, none of them looking particularly healthy. It was early morning, the furniture looked like your grandparents' place. The office didn't look historical anymore, it looked old and used. The men sat in this boardroom, sunk back in chairs, as if part of the fabric. They loved their boss, but work wasn't exactly fun. It's not fun to be hated by 350 million people. More than that: the world. Even if you never read an article, the op-eds that read like obituaries, you felt it like pollution. They were as ready as Charles for what he had to say. President Winchell started:

"All right, people, we've been here two years and nothing's happened. I'm sick of it. You ever see a movie about the presidency? Nixon, Kennedy, Bush, whatever. All that slow camera movement, swelling music, as if every moment is profound, loaded with history. I think I can speak for most of us when I say that that's not how it feels. Am I right? This place is like working in an office. An office that's like a museum, but sometimes I just don't feel the romance."

He picked at a small scab on his upper right cheek. He'd been playing tennis and hit himself with his racket. The small humiliation had been reported.

"What am I getting at?" he said. "It's time to start history of our own. It's time to feel like we're part of something. And this something is going to be like nothing else in American history. We're going to change the course of the fucking universe."

He paused to make sure that his audience was listening. They were, of course. Not just because they were paid to, not because he was the president, but because they had come to adore him, bordering on worship, the way a suicidal jumper might border the edge of a cliff. They were in the business of defending him and their relationship had become like a marriage in which the country was their dysfunctional child. Even though they were a closer witness to his flaws, his temper, his indiscretions, this increased their love for him. They saw that he was human—he was one of them. But he *wasn't* one of them. He had presence. The air seemed to part when he entered the room. He was a speechmaker, despite the bad reviews. His moments of humanity illustrated just how profoundly different he was.

"We're all Christians here, am I right? Real Christians, who believe every word of the Bible. Of course, that's why I put you here. Now, I don't know why any good Christian president has not done this sooner. We all want Jesus here, right? We all want a thousand years of peace. For too long, we have been trying to prevent a nuclear war. We've had to debate tooth and nail to go to war. Vietnam and Iraq screwed us up where this is concerned. The peaceniks think this is an example of how war can go wrong. What they don't understand is it was the most peaceful thing that could have happened. It's kept another world war at bay. But that's all behind us.

"We've discussed this before, as a hypothetical, an abstract. It's always been in the back of our minds and plans, but never truly made reality. It's time for us to usher in the Second Coming of Christ. The New Testament says Christ will only come after a worldwide calamity. It's our job to make sure that happens." He turned and addressed the window, which reflected him back. "It's a shame it has taken this long. The ACLU and the non-religious have kept us from our natural human duty. It's time to test who's been bad and who's been good. Of course, we will be protected fifty feet underground. That will be our rapture. Proof that what we're doing is right."

There was a dark, calm silence. Clouds even passed in front of the sun. It had become cinematic, as promised. If there could be music, it would have sounded like the final movement of Shostakovich's 5th Symphony.

Derek Whitehead, Chief of Staff, raised his right hand and said, pragmatically, "This has been prophesied in the Book of Revelation."

"That's right," Winchell said. "We are not doing anything that is not supposed to happen. Anything else?"

"This will be the most important event in the history of mankind," the NSA said, soberly.

"That's what I'm saying."

The five of them were starting to looked pleased now, enticed. A change from the sober gravity that usually prevailed during these meetings. They all seemed relaxed, even relieved. A kind of dumbfounded joy, "Why didn't we do this sooner?" Suddenly, their lives had purpose. They'd always felt like chosen men—no matter what they did they were a part of history: they belonged to the United States government. But now they were sitting on the throne of God, the only being higher than the president of the United States of America. They were members of the final American government. They would be responsible for everlasting peace.

I do not know what this could have felt like to them. Imagine all the pride in the history of America felt in one rush. They suddenly had proof of God, they were the most important men to have ever lived, they had jurisdiction over the earth, they were absolved of any guilt or doubt, they were free. I don't know, it must have been *fun*.

3: Before War

You might read that last chapter and think it's a deranged parody of paranoia. I thought so as well. It doesn't take a great leap of imagination to call a politician a liar and corrupt, or even dangerous. Instead of referencing historical events to write my work of fiction, I invented. I was exorcising my worry by writing the novel. It is only in times of peace that you can write about war with a sense of irony.

At the same time, it did occur to me that Winchell was trying to bring about the apocalypse. There had been no direct evidence, just mountains of indirect evidence, such as his "Apocalypse Ticket." He had yet to make a speech, saying, "I am going to start the apocalypse to usher in the Second Coming of Christ and one thousand years of peace," etc. Mostly because he would have been immediately impeached, assassinated, or both. He was doing it by the book, so to speak. One world government, seven years of the Anti-Christ, the Mark of the Beast—there were a lot of rules to the apocalypse.

Aside from working on the novel, what mattered to me most was finding the person who violated my daughter. To meet the man who was holding the camera. It was evidence of something I'd created coming to life. I'll admit it, I wanted to regain that feeling—it was like participating in my own fiction. I wanted to see where that led. In a way it felt like avenging my daughter's murder. Though I knew she would get over it. People got over terrible sex the way they got over the death of a loved one, even if it stayed with them. One time with a girlfriend she started weeping in the middle of sex because it reminded her of being raped. A terrible moment, one that raped my memory, but we're both still breathing. And it's hardly the worst thing that's happened between two or more people. Or even alone.

I was compelled to meet the man. That strip of film was evidence of my failure as a father. Finding her attacker wasn't really very fatherly either. Self-involved again, I was going to avenge my failure. It was all I could think about.

I couldn't find a name or an address attached to the LibraryWhores site. It took some strength to go back there. Sophia's picture, a headshot, was on the front page. It wouldn't be surprising if the site took in videos from all over America.

Sophia lived at home and hadn't been on vacation or even a field trip in some time. The video was obviously made very recently and made somewhere in town. With no name and no address, I didn't know where to look.

My first thought was to go to her high school. Maybe he hung around the school like drug dealers or perverts hung around elementary schools. I knew it was one guy because I'd seen him in videos with other girls: I recognized his cock. This was the kind of detective work I had to do.

I went to Sophia's high school—named after a president I knew nothing about—at the end of my own school day after classes had ended, around one. I parked and walked around the school once, a collection of brick buildings and a wide expanse of grass. Most of the school was meant for recreation. I was looking for a sleazy man in a trenchcoat. Didn't find him.

And then I saw someone. He was standing by the fence behind the football goalposts. It was a big campus, old, very nice. Home of the Lions. The man wasn't wearing a trenchcoat, but he was smoking a cigarette, alone, which looked deviant. No one smoked anymore.

I approached the figure with no clear idea of what I was going to say. I hadn't really thought this through because thinking might have made me stop. He was wearing a beige button-down shirt tucked into his pants, holding a dark-navy jacket. He saw me and his mouth twitched a little bit, maybe nervous to be seeing someone out here beyond the fence. It seemed like we were the only people within miles. It felt like a desert. This remote part of the school wasn't a great place for him to be finding anyone. Or maybe it was the best place.

You can't really walk up to someone and start talking, really. I'm not a smoker so I didn't have a good in. And "Can I bum one?" didn't feel like a good come-on, especially since I had the urge to strangle him. I didn't want to owe him any gratitude.

I reached him. He seemed attractive in person, boyish to women older than him, but masculine to girls younger than him. A good combination for what he was doing. I had to remind myself that this guy could have been anyone. I so wanted to believe he was the one.

He was still smoking. I was standing, hands on the fence, gazing at the football field and the school buildings in the distance, as if looking for something. Directions, I thought. I could ask for directions.

"Is this Buchanan High School?" I asked.

"It is," he said. I couldn't place the voice. A voice that said "Take off your top" with a slight laugh, as if saying, I know this is a little bit wrong but don't worry, it will be fun.

"Good," I said. "Nice looking campus."

He nodded and shrugged and looked straight ahead.

This was about to end, just like that. I'm not the kind of person who can start a conversation out of the dark and charm up information.

"You live around here?" I said.

"Not far," he said. A slight look of annoyance, and frankly, I didn't blame him.

"Look, do you make videos on the internet?" I blurted. It felt liberating to finally say it. "I'm looking for someone who does."

He looked at me with disdain. "Videos. No, I don't make

videos. What kind of videos you talking about?" He smiled then, slightly but devilishly, as if he knew exactly what I was talking about.

"Porn videos," I said and regretted it. I had been so obsessed that I had forgotten how this looked. I was suddenly objective and realized I looked like a sweating pervert looking for action.

"I don't know what you're talking about," he said. "I have to get back to work."

He began walking away.

"It's you," I called to his back. "You're the one who does it." I started walking after him, violence stirring.

He turned back sharply. "I don't know what the fuck you're talking about. Please leave me alone."

He took a left through a door in the fence and started walking towards the school, a fearful look my way. Almighty, he was a teacher on a cigarette break. I felt like a violating idiot.

I stood by the fence for another ten minutes, as if on my own cigarette break and the air was smoke. I soon came up with a justification: what my daughter did was so ugly that it only created more ugliness in its wake; i.e. I'm a victim. Always more comforting than believing a stranger thinks I'm hateful.

Worse yet, I was back to square one.

I went back home and wrote all this out. Another form of justification. If I turn the experience into words, I have the chance to make it seem useful, even literary. Usually works while I'm writing, not so long after.

But a funny thing happened while I was writing. I was struck with the suspicion that the teacher was my man. I couldn't shed it. This might have been wish fulfillment, another way to curb embarrassment, but I was convinced it was something I needed to investigate further. Maybe I was getting a little too enamored with my powers of prediction. But what was the worst that could happen: I'd be embarrassed twice.

It seemed a little tidy that a teacher had made the video, but not impossible. You could never see his face. Anyone who could identify him by his cock alone had another set of problems.

I went back to the same spot the next day. He was there. I would have been worried about coming back to the spot where I'd been questioned by a deranged porn addict, but there probably weren't many places for a teacher to smoke in peace.

I approached him like the day before. It was just me and him. It was a nicer day, bluer.

He didn't recognize me right off. He looked at me like he couldn't quite place the face, maybe even grateful for the recognition. The sky was blue and I was wearing a light-blue shirt. The day before I'd been dressed in shades of brown, like a good professor. As I got closer, he recognized me and frowned bitterly.

"Look," he began.

"I'm sorry about yesterday," I countered. "Listen to me for a second, please. My daughter was found on a pornographic website. I thought maybe she met the man in charge of it at school. So I came looking for him. And then I saw you. That's all I am. A concerned father. I'm sorry how I came off."

He seemed relieved, even interested. A good story for his cigarette break. "I'm sorry about that," he said. "That's gotta suck."

"Yeah," I said. "So, you don't know anyone who hangs around here who might be involved in something like that?"

"Not really, no. She could have met him at the mall, the beach, any number of places."

"I know. I thought I'd try here first. She's here every day."

"Yeah, but if I was one of those guys I'd get her when she's feeling a little looser. On the weekends, when they're more ready to experiment. Besides, I don't think he'd be hanging around a high school. Odds are most aren't over eighteen. If it were me, I'd go to the community college. You see those girls? They dress like porn stars."

There was something very weird about this answer. As if he knew what he was talking about. As I mentioned before, these were sex-obsessed times, so it shouldn't have been surprising.

Still, I got the feeling, or maybe it was a hope, that he was toying with me.

"I'll check the community college," I said.

"Hell, check the university," he said. "It's not much different over there either. I'm sure you know that."

He smiled at me. What did he mean by that? I never told him I worked at the college.

"It's a college, not a university."

"Whatever. Girls seemed ready to play from every walk of life." He paused. Thought about smoking, then didn't. "It's enough to make you hate all girls, until you remember they're so good to look at."

This was him. This was the guy. What were the odds that the first person I talked to was the one, but it just hit me. His hatred, sexuality, indifference. It was him.

"It's you," I said.

"Not me," he said. "But I can understand you being really upset about this. I couldn't imagine a girlfriend doing that, let alone a daughter. That's fucked up. Shouldn't happen."

He looked me in the eyes then quickly looked away, as if the power of our different forms of regret was too much. He stared straight in front of him. "I shouldn't be saying this," he said. "But I know someone who might be involved."

—WW—

That someone was his brother. The teacher, named Joel, pleaded with me to not tell his brother where I got my information. Joel was having a crisis of conscience. "A boyfriend finding out is one thing. Happens all the time. A father is something else. Weird to think all those girls have parents somewhere."

It was just a coincidence that my daughter went to the same school where he worked. She wasn't in his class. He taught physics, my daughter didn't take physics. She'd taken one year of chemistry to fulfill a requirement and then she was done.

He insisted that I wouldn't go to the school board to get him fired. He said he knew what his brother was doing but he wasn't involved in any way. I said I wouldn't tell anyone but, of course, I wasn't sure this was true. First I had to confront the man. For what, I didn't know. My daughter was safe, she hadn't been kidnapped. At the same time, I felt like I was getting part of her back.

His brother, Frank, did indeed work outside the community college. Either that or he put an ad in the local weekly looking for models. I remembered that Sophia had taken a class at the community college to help pad her application to college. She was studious. The class was "Memoirist Fiction." Too ironic to matter at that moment.

"Just look in the back of the weekly," Joel said. "There's an ad you call and then Frank gives you the address, once he establishes you're up for what goes down."

Who was I going to get to make the call? My daughter? Not likely. My wife? Even less so. They didn't know what I was doing and I didn't want them to. They might stop me. This obsession didn't have room for an accomplice.

"Just give me the address," I said.

"OK, whatever," he said, with a sweep of the hand, as if his indifference were an excuse. He gave me the address.

I left immediately.

—⋁⋁⋁—

The house wasn't far off. It was a nice house, though not too nice. No shiny black cars in the driveway, everything wasn't glossed and newly painted. I hadn't stumbled upon the lair of a porn king. But it was nice enough that any visitors would be impressed that the owner was legitimate. It was a house I wouldn't mind living in. Off a fairly busy avenue, but on a street with little traffic. The front entrance was flanked by tall shrubs so the front door was conveniently shielded from the street. I didn't know why I was taking in all these details. I was usually only observant in retrospect. I was seeing this with pure, objective clarity. Never did I do that in my own life—the way people often did in novels, thinking reflectively about each moment as it happened. It was a strange experience—both concrete and unreal. I felt like I was entering a crime scene; that is, I felt like I was entering someone else's history and making it my own.

I rang the bell.

No answer.

I waited, doubt forming. Rang again.

Finally, I heard shuffling.

A man answered the door. He wasn't holding a camera. He looked like Joel, but older, thicker. More of a jock than a teacher. More like someone who'd abused himself, bloated.

"Yeah?" he said, sleepily.

Suddenly, I feared him. This man was capable of anything; strangling me right there. It felt like being intimidated by an infant. But I had to press forward, however thoughtlessly.

"My name is Eugene Myers," I said. "My daughter, Sophia, was on your site."

I checked for his reaction. He might have winced slightly, but mostly he was expressionless. "And?" he said.

"And I want you to take it offline. I also want you to delete every copy." I hadn't been entirely sure what I was going to say but that made perfect sense.

"All right," he said. "How much you going to give me for it?"

"Don't bother," I said. "My daughter's in high school. I don't think you want me going to the authorities with information that you're soliciting high school girls."

Still no expression. Angrier maybe. "How old is she? Your daughter."

"She's eighteen," I said reluctantly.

"Doesn't matter if she's in kindergarten, nothing I've done is illegal."

"You don't understand. I'll plaster your address all over

town. I'll send it to every newspaper in the area, every church. You won't be able to work here again."

He slackened then. He was briefly furious but I could tell what he was thinking. What the hell did one girl matter? There were hundreds of others and there would be hundreds more. Why take the hassle? "All right," he said. "But you've got to hold up your end of the bargain. Don't tell anyone about this."

"OK. When are you going to delete everything?"

"I'll do it right now. Come inside."

I hesitated, obviously. This was the sleaziest man I'd ever been close to. He seemed like the kind of guy to collect weapons. Don't forget I'd seen him have sex with my daughter. And this was where she did it. At times it was hard enough to deal with my daughter having crushes over the phone.

But I wanted to get this over with. I reminded myself that he was just a dumb, half-slept man in his house. Not a monster, not a demon. I stepped inside.

I recognized some of the front room. A black couch where the girls first sat. A half-stocked bar. Hardly any furniture in the house. This was like living a reenactment. Traveling the same route through the house as Sophia, except without a camera in my face, shyly saying, "What's the camera for?" but knowing full well. In some sense, I deserved this.

I expected standing lights, some evidence of a professional photographer's studio. All I could see was a handheld digital video camera lying on the bar. He had good business sense, I'd give him that.

"In here," he said.

The computer room was bare except for a desk strewn with bills and trash, a gray couch, and a tall TV shelf. It smelled like sex in there, like old sweat. Or maybe I imagined it.

He sat down at the desk with a groan, and he almost seemed like any businessman who was sick of his job. "Let me find the file. Should be easy." He sounded helpful, but also defeated that he had to go through this. He found the file quickly, called "Lila," and dragged it to the trash. "The file's been uploaded so

I'll have to delete it from the site. People might have downloaded it already so there's nothing I can do about that."

"Whatever you can do," I said, and felt too conciliatory. There was something perversely curious about watching him work on the computer. Even privileged. Like I was getting a behind-the-scenes tour. How I could have felt pride in light of what I was doing, I don't know. It was fascinating to me that so much power—the breaking of lives—could be achieved by one slob at a desk.

"Is there any hardcopy anywhere?" I asked.

"Not really. It goes straight from the camera to the computer. See, I'm deleting her and replacing her with a girl from next week. You know, it's no big loss. We didn't get a lot of emails about her." He smiled and snorted and looked back at me and smiled again. "That's it. Easy. I can show you the main site." He opened up the site, his piece of the world. "She used to be there," he pointed to a picture of a blonde girl, someone else's problem, "and now she's not." He looked back at me. "By the way, how did you find out about this? Did someone tell you?"

I didn't answer.

He saw my expression.

"Oh shit, did you find it yourself? Oh shit, that's funny. That's twisted."

"Cool it. You make these sites for people to look at them. I looked."

"Yeah, but I mean, were you like beating off to your own daughter?"

I saw something in his face then. I saw what he really was. It could've been a hallucination, but I saw a flash of a satanic caricature: red face, knobs for horns, cloven feet beneath the desk. The personification of a father's rage. Lasted a second. There was something else there as well—a loneliness, a fat sort of weight as this guy sat in a lonely room, a self-hatred so deep as to be unconscious, but still encompassing, the white walls of the room as gray as rain, as if light died here. It could've been just a father's hope, but it had the same effect. I pitied him a little, almost in a fatherly way, and I hated him less for doing that to my daughter. She was, after all, old enough to know better, but young enough to be easily seduced. I saw this young man as seduced as well, but by something far more permanent and damaging. Even his success seemed like a punishment.

"We done?" I said.

"We're done," he said.

Our business was over. "Good." He walked me to the door. I could feel his weight hanging over me.

"You better not tell anyone about this," he said.

"I won't tell anyone," I said.

"Really, remember," he said.

He lifted up his shirt, a long t-shirt that advertised a brand, and there was a gangster's cliché. Under his shirt, the end of a handgun stuck out of his right front pocket. He nodded and smiled joylessly, the whites of his eyes seeming as yellow as his teeth.

I opened the front door, then turned back to get a final picture of the scene. Out of the corner of my eye I saw someone in a hooded sweatshirt running towards me. I couldn't see his face, almost as if he didn't have one. I was tackled to the ground. Then it felt like a brick came down on the back of my head. My brain felt loose in my skull. I blacked out...

4: Number 1 Dream

Picture a house. Light-brown wall-to-wall carpeting so the floor looks like dirt, though it conceals footprints. That sounds grim, but it's not. The house just feels used, stained, because there's been a lot of life here. Kids' marker drawings on the wall that can only be removed with a coat of paint, the house feels cluttered even when it's clean, cracks in the wall where there was once a picture. A thread hangs down from the straight-backed chair, chair legs chipped but colored in with a brown marker if you look close enough, flowers of some kind on the windowsill, a petal falls undramatically. No nightmare, but not exactly a dream. It seems familiar.

Travel through the living room slowly and silently like a tracking shot into the kitchen. It's brighter in here, seen more daily life, less avoided. The wood tabletop of the kitchen table is slightly concave, a small TV on the countertop, kids toys on the countertop and floor, a squeak toy, maybe these are dog toys, four cereal bowls on the table. In the middle of it, a woman who is a reflection of the house. She looks part tired, part pragmatic. She's cleaning patiently. She surveys the breakfast table, ambivalently, as if she wants to keep the bowls on the table as company. She looks under the table and sees a mountain of Captain Crunch underneath one of the chairs. This didn't fall from the table, it was put there; somebody's project. She barely changes expression—pragmatic still, not exhausted. Maybe if she knew that someone was watching she would have affected a look of exaggerated bemusement, but she's alone and has no need to act. She's not the type to perform for herself or imagined people, or even God, though she's entertained the thought. So she gets to work and picks up the mound of cereal with two hands and carries it to the sink.

I hear my voice then. It must be how schizophrenics hear other voices. I'm not talking to myself as I normally do, with no lag between when something is thought and said. This is another voice—my own but from somewhere else. Eerily, like my voice is detached from my mind, saying:

"This is Miranda Goodling. 400 Riverside Court, Irvine. Remember her name. Miranda Goodling."

—◇◇◇—

I woke up on my back, woozy, the worst kind of drunk. I felt like I'd been hit in the head—no better way to describe it. My thoughts were thick and compressed. It was hard to form words. "Stephanie," I said. I wasn't sure if it came out right.

She was sitting in the corner watching TV forlornly, as if watching a story about me. She shot to my side at the sound of my voice.

"I need to throw up," I told her.

She handed me a plastic trash can with a band-aid stuck to the bottom. "They said this might happen," she said, apologetically. Her voice was as reassuring as gauze.

I threw up, which burned my throat and stomach, but cleared my head, and I realized what had happened: I was attacked and now I was in a hospital room, walls turquoise and gray.

"How you feeling?" she asked. "Do you know what happened?"

I pictured the shadowy figure who hit me, faceless like a wraith. It wasn't the same person who erased the video, it was an accomplice, waiting in the back all that time.

"I was assaulted," I told her. "On the street," I added.

I didn't want to tell her about what had happened. Like I said, I felt I deserved some kind of beating for not being a better father. I did what I needed to do, he did what he needed to do. And I thought telling her could make it worse. Pressing charges seemed like an additional humiliation, if not dangerous for my family.

"Someone dropped you off," Stephanie said. "They don't know who. It's so strange."

"It is strange," I said.

"They say you're going to be all right. It's a mild concussion. You might feel out of balance for a day or two."

"OK."

"What were you doing out, anyway?" she asked. No hint of accusation.

"Just going for a walk," I said. "Thinking about the book I'm writing. On the bright side, now I have something to write about."

—⋀⋀—

The city looked different on the drive home: more awful. The realization of what had happened was settling in. Assaulted by the man who had basically raped my daughter—if not literally, then raped her conscience. I felt forsaken. What else was the world going to throw at me? Relatively speaking, I knew I was doing all right. I had never lived through a war, been abused, sold into slavery, etc. Discovering my daughter online and then having my head kicked in was a paradise compared to many other people. But they were my problems. I stared out the window at the L.A. city—a collection of decaying strip malls, one of the least attractive cities on earth, populated mainly by people who wanted to be someone else, except for those who bled success, more abuse than reward. If so, I belonged here, dead like this city. Grim, but I was rattled.

We were trapped behind a large black SUV that had failed to signal it was turning left, blocking the entire lane so we couldn't pass. People just didn't give a shit about other people.

"Do they just expect us to know why they're suddenly stopping? They're just totally fucking selfish. Not signaling is a sign of the apocalypse."

"Settle down, Road Warrior," my wife said, smiling. "You need to take it easy, that's what the doctor said. Let's get you home so you can get some sleep."

Then I remembered. The woman from my dream. The housewife, Miranda Goodling. It was as clear as any vivid memory when it finally hit me. In fact, more so. I had a terrible memory. One of the reasons I thought I wrote fiction was to invent stories and characters because I remembered so few from my life. Other writers could remember vivid details of their childhood, stickball in Brooklyn. My own life was mostly bland and eventless. Might have contributed to my enduring faith in the future. I could watch the dream replay in my mind like a movie you've seen several times, committed to memory. I could picture the woman, her kitchen, her name.

"I had the strangest dream while I was out," I told Stephanie. "It was an everyday scene of a woman doing housework. Then I heard my own voice telling me her name and address. It was so strange because it was so normal. What do you think it means?"

"It means you're dreaming of other women," playfully.

But I was intrigued. Recently, I had been struggling with where to take my novel. Part memoir about my own life, part paranoia about the president's life. I considered writing about my family fleeing a war, but that felt hackneyed and done. This dream could be a potential plot. It wasn't much—the image of a woman cleaning her kitchen. But the writer contacts her and finds out that she's a real person. It was a premise.

I kept this to myself. My wife had been through my flashes of enthusiasm before. My promises of a better life. But at least the world didn't seem like it was coming to an end.

5: The Diplomat from Utopia

It is actually quaint that I even had these sorts of problems to deal with—struggling with a novel, struggling with my family. Even though people were screwing and breeding like rats, a trip to the supermarket could kill you, San Francisco was partly under water, life still managed to be normal, like a high—or a low—that came on gradually. People went about their lives eating, sleeping, shitting, breeding in no particular order and if things got rough, people had a tragic aptitude to deal with it and move on. Perhaps if we didn't adapt so well, so many terrible things wouldn't be allowed to happen. In this way, evolution really was against the spirit.

You've gotten what fueled me. Here's what fueled President Winchell: his father.

On the eve of the inauguration, the elder diplomat had a talk with his son. The talk depressed the hell out of the president-elect and filled him with a renewed sense of purpose. The diplomat told him that everything he thought he knew— everything that he had campaigned on—turned out to be a lie. As the president stood at the podium taking his oath, millions of eyes were on him, each person thinking they knew his motivations. Basically, nothing that he said had any relation to what he believed. The presidency was merely a vessel, like the body. What his father had told him was the meaning of life.

"Son, I have news for you," the diplomat began. They were sitting in the library of his father's house on the bank of the St.

Louis River. A fire played in the fireplace. Benjamin Winchell drank warm brandy out of a snifter, leaning back in a thronelike chair which towered two feet over his head. A horribly uncomfortable chair that didn't seem to fit a human body, but Benjamin Winchell looked comfortable, as always. There may as well have been a purebred named Scruff lying at his feet to match the look of comfort in his eyes, the kind of relaxation that only comes with actual power. Charles Winchell sat across from his father in a smaller chair with a lower back—of course—armrests at an uncomfortable height. A mightily expensive chair to be sure—brought over after the French Revolution—but small. Charles Winchell had no problem feeling like a strong man: a feeling as if he'd bed every single woman on planet Earth. The presidency could do that for you. But when faced with his father he was more than just diminutive—a result of being drilled with honor and respect for your elders by the career military man—the president-elect was awed. The hell-like light of the flickering fire, the swirling of the brandy in the wide-bodied snifter as if he was Atlas turning the globe, the look of both amusement and brutality in the man's eyes, which you could never read correctly and so always put you on edge, and, Jesus, just the sheer knowledge the man possessed. He was the only politician Charles had ever known who read *everything*: alternate histories, mainstream histories, classic and contemporary fiction, biographies of jazz men, quantum physics, on and on. It made Charles revere his father with fear, respect, and regret for his own inadequacy. The son was astute enough to realize that this was how you were taught to regard God.

"I've been waiting to tell you this, Charles," Benjamin said. "You've gotten hints, but never all the details. During the campaign might have been messy. Something could have slipped. Your election was an inevitability, of course, but certain information cannot be released to the general public. Not yet. Now that you're in power, we can tell you."

Benjamin paused. He looked at Charles skeptically. "You

ready?"

Charles nodded.

His father looked suddenly at ease. "All right. A major thing I have to tell you is this, Charles: death is not a punishment. It is a release. There are many things that have been hidden from people over the centuries but this is the main one. I have been to the other side, Charles, and it is beyond majesty. Imagine all the sex and knowledge and art ever created in this world felt in one moment, compressed onto the head of a pin. Words can't touch it, so I won't even bother. I won't go into how I got there, just trust me. You'll get to see it too. Do you know what it means if death is not to be feared but sought after?"

"Not entirely," Charles said, which he regretted because it was a rhetorical question.

The diplomat sneered, his eyes almost closing. "Of course not," he said. "Not yet. Imagine if people were to know with certainty that death was not the end, but a pathway to bliss better than any drug. The day after this word got out, there would be mass suicides. People would drop out of work and search for ways to die. In short, it would be the apocalypse. There would be no one left. Do you see? It would mean the end of war. What would war be if we knew that we were helping somebody by killing them."

"You could have a war of torture," Charles said. "You could bring people to the brink of death instead of killing them."

Benjamin looked pleased. "I like the way you think, Charles. Some of the biological weapons being created these days are meant to do just that—disable people without killing them."

"That was just an idea. Why not just put an end to war. War's to be avoided, right?"

"In theory," Benjamin replied. "It is also necessary. Human beings are a warlike species. They like to fuck, fight, love, and hate. All of these things need to exist—and screw the Buddhists—trying to ignore these instincts is just a form of repression. Dangerous in itself. But I'm getting off the subject. We don't just need war to exercise our aggression. It is necessary for the progress of the world. War is progress. Remember that. It is going to be the slogan of your presidency. Charles, you are going to be the last president. Everything from the Sumerians to the birth of Christ and the retooling of Christianity has been leading up to you." He paused, looking almost unsure of himself. "There's a lot I'm not telling you here. So much that I'm not even sure where to begin."

"Tell me this," Charles said. "How do you know about all of this?"

The diplomat shook his head somberly, as if remembering a death, and said, "I'll start there."

The diplomat talked for six hours.

"I'll tell you the true story of what's been going on for the last five thousand years. You want to hear the most terrible thing? The thing that would make most conservatives blush and cry? All the conspiracy theorists are right. There is a conspiracy going back thousands of years. That's not telling you a lot. You must have picked up as much from dinner table conversations growing up."

"Certainly." He had, but even if he hadn't he would have lied. The dinner table conversations about political power and defense contracts had never seemed like a revelation. To most children what their parents do for a living seems like the whole world. If the kid is listening to his father talking about building cars for a living, he thinks building cars is the center of the universe. The difference with young Charlie Winchell was that his father's profession actually was—if not the center of the universe, then at least the center of earth, which wasn't so inconsequential, it turns out, when it came to the entire universe. It may be that every father is God to his son, but Benjamin Winchell actually ran the world.

All of the above was thought in the flicker of an instant, second nature. The diplomat was still talking:

"The UFO buffs are right. There is a massive government conspiracy covering up the entire phenomenon. Sweeping it under the rug with bullshit fronts like Condon and Blue Book.

Poor naïve Vallee thought he was actually uncovering something. Read his journals, the man may have been a prophet and a genius. Let me get to the point though. Roswell happened. Every political action in the last three thousand years has been done to deal with the UFO question. Every religion is a way to describe the infinite, right? People think UFOs are just the latest manifestation of some kind of perennial vision. If this was Fatima, they'd be seeing the Virgin Mary. Not true—UFOs are real and the last manifestation before the end of the world.

"But this is not what gets conservatives all riled up. There's nothing a conservative hates worse than a liberal. Likewise, there's no one more liberal than a hippie. All our plans were almost laid to waste in the sixties when the counterculture discovered LSD. You see, they were right. Everything on earth is bullshit and all that matters is what exists behind matter, blah blah blah, consciousness, God, magick, whatever you want to call it. What they did wrong is they found their utopia too soon. They were undisciplined. Timothy Leary said tune in, drop out, and would have created a nation of raving homeless people if America truly listened to him and dropped out of society. It would have been anarchy. No food getting produced, everybody just lying in bed smiling at the ceiling. That's not progress, that's apathy.

"Which is where we Republicans come in. Our methods might have seemed harsh. Killing students in Ohio. Beating up peaceniks holding out flowers. Cops didn't know what we were up to, and they'd rather beat someone up than not. That's their job, to enforce. But the powers that be knew that we were onto something much larger than putting an end to the small demonstrations to a minor war. Everything we've been doing has been leading up to the big one—the apocalypse. You think you came up with that campaign slogan by accident? Lesson one, nothing in this world happens by accident. He knows when you are sleeping, he knows when you're awake, he knows when you've been bad or good—and we've been bad in order to ensure a long-term, larger good. But it takes time. War is a growing pain, as is ignorance. Am I making any sense?"

"Partially."

"Yeah, I'm trying to tell you the history of the world in a chapter. At least that shows that you're paying attention. We are now at the final stage. The Mayans talked about 2012 being the end and they were right, they were just off by a few years. They were right about everything—even eating each other. Remember, if everyone's immortal what's it matter if your body gets eaten? Now 2020 is here and you're president, which is no mistake. We're going to bring on the end of the world and usher in a paradise. We're going to make this world evolve, whether it likes it or not."

He looked weak for a moment, rare for him. His voice became quiet.

"There are just too many people around for what we want to unleash: spiritual and technological evolution. We've tried to control the population by other means. Wars, diseases, not spreading around the wealth. Keeping some people starving. Hell, we could spread the wealth but it would have led to a worse population explosion. Socialism makes more logical, spiritual sense—the laws of nature made political. But we aren't ready yet. Too often socialism becomes totalitarianism. So we kept it at bay. But nothing we did worked. And now the earth's dying. We need to kill people off to save the planet.

"We've got it: alien technology. We could have had free energy, saved the planet years ago. But the same technology would have killed us off in the hands of dimwitted terrorists. They could have wiped America off the map with one bomb. They could have traveled to other star systems. That's exactly what we didn't want. We've done well keeping major ideas secret. Made UFOs seem like a laughingstock. Created fronts like SETI. What do you think SETI does, sits around all day listening to silence? Of course not. We started wars so we could filter billions of dollars into black projects, the only projects that really matter. Back-engineering technology, building bunkers. If people knew the secrets behind the UFO issue, they would know about the coming calamities. They'd tear us apart. Contact alone would lead to hysteria, daily investigations, people abandoning faith, total upheaval that would be out of our control. If there wasn't such a thing as journalism this wouldn't be a problem. There were two major things that we learned from in the last century: *The War of the Worlds* and Watergate. In short, the media has more power than the Pope.

"It's sad, but the only way to save the species, and to help us reach the next level of consciousness, is to do away with the human population. In truth, it's only sad because people think it's sad. Really, as I said, the billions who need to die will be going to a much better place."

He stopped and looked at Charles with an expression like what he'd just said was normal. Charles felt a creeping sadness. Not about all the people that might die, but about his father's fate. The talk actually strengthened Charles' own faith. He'd found God despite his father and was treated like a rebellious teenager as a response—worse than that, he was ignored. He knew his father wasn't a religious man. An agnostic transcendentalist, he called himself. Charles had found Christ on his own, without guidance, when he was in college his first year away from home. He had spent his days in the college library reading the Bible, the history of religion, none of it assigned. He began going to the college chapel without telling his father, as if he was doing something illicit. This caused his belief to deepen, as it was one of the first and only things he'd discovered on his own—separating himself from the tyranny of his father who seemed to know everything. It had prepared him for this moment, he realized now. His father had one way to describe the infinite, but it was misguided. Of course death didn't exist, that was called heaven. The question was who had domain over the afterlife. Charles peopled his cabinet with true believers because he agreed with only parts of what his father had told him. The apocalypse would come, but on Charles' own terms.

"So what you're saying is the Bible isn't true?" Charles inquired, a shade weakly.

"It's all true, every religion," Benjamin replied. "All true and all false because each religion claims it's the answer. God exists, but it's universal. Believe me, I don't want to see New Agers rejoice, but they're mostly right. Whatever you want to call it— Vril, the collective unconscious, the ether, the Force, or God— it's out there. The problem is religion, the problem is dogma. People think they're different and they're not. We've got to start a religious war so people will give up on religion once and for all."

Charles didn't believe a word of this, but he said, "OK. Let me ask a question. Every religion has some sort of messianic figure. Who is the messiah who is going to usher in a thousand years of peace?"

"We don't know," his father answered. "Of all the questions we have had answered, we don't know what form the messiah is going to take. We don't even know if there is going to be a flesh and blood messiah. The messiah might not even be human. We just know that a major war is inevitable and out of war will come lasting peace."

"Another question: if we instigate a religious war, proving everything in Revelations to be true—why would people abandon religion?"

"Because the final revelation will be—after the war is over— that we are all God, and that is the only religious principle that matters."

"One final question, why not just give people this revelation without a war?"

"Because we've fucked things up beyond measure. People believe in Satan, people believe in horribly grotesque, base and debasing things. Giving them the power of the infinite wouldn't work. This is my one regret: without these people out of the picture, the collective consciousness of the world cannot change for the better." He threw up his hands. "We had no choice. It's what we were told to do."

"I'm sorry, who told you this?"

"They did. The people from the other side. The dead. The Ufonauts. Earth's true allies. They've told us what needs to happen if we ever hope to evolve as a species. We have to burn away the forest in order to save it.

"America is hanging by a thread. Have you watched the news lately? It's a nightmare out there. This was what we wanted to happen, but still. Hard to watch, even if it was the only way for the human race to reach the next stage of evolution. A steady degradation that would make world war an inevitability, a self-fulfilling prophecy. Meanwhile, everyone had to keep living by the insane delusion that this was the way it should be. They had to keep going to their jobs, watching TV, shopping, voting, unaware that the world was disintegrating by design. All leading up to World War III."

Benjamin Winchell sat up and took a deep breath as if he was taking in all the air from the room. "I've got good news and bad news for the conspiracy theorists," he said. "The good news is they're right. The bad news is they're right."

6: Number 2 Dream

A place to get drunk or kill time. It's a dive bar, but without any character, making it a true dive. Paint chipping off the bar from people picking at it absently. Stickers ripped off the mirror behind the bar, leaving a faint trace. Imagine a bar in a strip mall, thrown together so people could just have a place to drink. Except this isn't a strip mall, it's on a street in a northeastern Ohio town called Warren. Incidentally, this was the place of my wife's birth.

So who am I looking for? I focus on the guy at the bar. Not a low-life, just a drunk. Picture Charles Bukowski without any talent. He's talking to the bartender, who would throw the guy out for not shutting up, but the guy spends a lot of money. People listen to him, smiling at first at the eccentric, then shifting and frowning when he doesn't stop. He buys drinks for himself and other people, almost as rent.

He's talking to the bartender, talking through him: "They've got all the power they want, that's the funny thing." He says his s's as sh, so see is shee. I don't feel like transcribing it. "The power is all right there in the middle of the earth. All the magma underground could create superheated steam (shteam), better than any nuclear reactor. Cleaner too, better than wind power. But they don't tell anyone about it. Almost like they want everything to die. It's by intelligent design. That's the funny thing."

Then my voice, the same as before: "This is Bob Banski. 100 Newton Street, Apartment B, Warren, Ohio. Bob Banski."

"Yeah, they're trying to bring about the apocalypse. Prove both

the Bible and the Mayans right. That's the funny thing."

—WW—

Morning, sitting up in bed. My wife was getting dressed. She was irritated, she's late, I was in bed to be there for the rest of the day. No class today. I was borderline unemployed. That didn't stop me, though. It never did.

"That's twice it's happened," I said. "Twice. First the housewife in Irvine and now the drunk in Ohio. Each time I was told their name and address."

I picked up my notebook on the nightstand. On one page I'd written the names and addresses. On other pages, I'd written every detail I could remember from the dreams—embellishing some, I'll admit, but I still wasn't clear about the line between dreams and imagination. They both made up stories.

I checked the names again, like they were friends, or colleagues. "Miranda Goodling and Bob Banski. I remember the dreams clearly. I've never experienced anything like it. A recurring dream with a different cast of characters. Something's telling me to contact these people, like they're significant in some way."

Stephanie was half-listening, still getting dressed, answering distractedly, "What? You think they're real people?"

"I called information for the woman in Irvine," I said. "There's an M. Goodling, close enough. This could be real, Stephanie. Imagine, this could be real."

I wanted her to believe me. To relive the optimism she once had about our future. Something I haven't yet mentioned: she was fading from me. Taking care of me in the hospital was an interruption, but she had come back down to earth. I think catching our daughter online had stripped her of whatever faith she may have had in the reliability of our life together. Sophia had moved out. Not on our orders, but because she couldn't face us. My wife was grateful because her only child had become an example of her failure, as it had for me, but on a deeper level, in that it had affected her faith in me as well. My trip to the hospital wasn't much of a help; it was a reminder.

She said, "Don't you think it could be a coincidence? Maybe you've met this woman before."

"No," I said, too emphatically, as if fueled by doubt. "I've never heard of her before. This means something. It has to."

Even I could hear the desperation in my voice. I regretted it immediately. Stephanie stopped getting dressed and eyed me with concern, like I was breaking. I'd just suffered a concussion, maybe this was the thing to finally make me lose it. But that's probably projection because her concern quickly turned to annoyance, as she said, "I have to go to work," with stress on the word work, as if it was the opposite of delusion.

—∿∿—

I drove to Irvine. Probably against doctor's orders, I couldn't remember. I'd been taking Vicodin, so obviously I shouldn't be driving. And there was question about whether or not my homely white Dodge, named after a cloud, could make the drive. So all in all not responsible. I felt jumpy as I drove the freeway south. Equal parts excited and feeling ridiculous that I was believing my own fiction, a point of no return kind of feeling, like I was being adulterous to sanity. But as I got closer, I became more determined, which wasn't to say any less deluded. It was an experiment, at the very least, and if it turned out to be false I could just rewrite it later as something more interesting.

I pulled onto her street: an average suburban neighborhood, houses with front lawns that blended together. Kids toys, baby swings in front of many of the houses. Formless and functional. I didn't recognize the front of her house because I never saw it in the dream, but it wasn't far off from what I'd imagined.

I parked awkwardly and nervously—the tires hit the curb, scraping the hubcap. A gardener saw this and smiled, a terrible smile. I crossed the street quickly, without looking left to right. As I made it up to her front walk, I realized how poor I looked. Sweating from the drive, unshowered, dressed in old clothes—rushed away from home after days being bedridden. I hadn't thought this through very well. The hem on my right pants leg was coming undone. A faded button-down shirt not tucked in, proof of how I regarded myself. And I couldn't quite stuff my shirt into my pants on her front lawn. But here I was, and I wasn't about to drive home. So I rang the doorbell, careful to not look at my reflection in her front window. I felt like a salesman of a useless product—someone unwanted at every home on the block.

A woman answered the door. Was it her? You tell me. I've described her here, which was just how it felt to me: seeing something imagined, but still lacking clarity. Like trying to picture what a fictional character should look like in the flesh; slightly hazy. Why an actor who played the character from a book never seemed quite right. For one thing, she was brunette, not blonde. I've mentioned how vivid the dream was, but seeing her was not immediate confirmation, as if the dream lost clarity once it became real. Still, I was fairly certain it was her because she was still a woman in her thirties, with a similar expression of ambivalence.

"Are you Miranda Goodling?" I asked.

"Yes," she said.

"My name is Eugene Myers."

I stopped. She stared back at me blankly. I was half hoping that she would recognize me, for whatever reason. That this would be handed to me, and I wouldn't have to work. But she hadn't been expecting me.

Still, I asked, "Do you recognize me?"

"No," she said.

"Are you sure? You haven't had any dreams where I appeared?"

I was objective enough to realize that was a horrible question. Not to mention how sweaty and desperate I looked as

I asked it.

"I'm sorry," I said. "That doesn't sound too good, does it? The thing is, I had a dream and you were in it." I paused. "That doesn't sound too good either."

"I have to go," she said, closing the door, justifiably.

"All right, I'm sorry," I said quickly. "It was nothing racy, believe me. I'm not like that. Something in the dream told me to contact you, a stranger. I know that sounds crazy, but it's true. I'm just trying to make sense of it."

"OK…"

I reached for my wallet, which made her tense up, as if I was reaching for a weapon. A terrible sight, seeing her cringe; I felt like I was raping her day. "Just please take my card. Contact me if you have any strange dreams or anything else out of the ordinary."

I handed her a card out of my wallet—a card from the college with the designation of professor. Looked respectable enough. She looked at the card with unfocused eyes, probably wondering where she could throw it away.

"I'm really sorry to bother you," I said. "Really. I'm sorry," I said again.

I turned and walked the other way, heading back to my car with quick, hard steps, as if to show her I cared enough to leave her alone, but more trying to put this stupid encounter behind me. I longed for sleep.

I got back to my car and looked back at the house. Miranda Goodling was still standing in the doorway, looking puzzled, which was almost encouraging, though she probably just wanted to confirm I was leaving, or to read my license plate number. I waved goodbye. She closed the door without waving back.

—◠◠◠—

I went home feeling like dirt. I didn't feel at all turning what had happened into a better story. Making up a story about

Miranda Goodling seemed like an increased insult to her. I was encouraged that the dream had been right about her name and address, but right now it wasn't going to amount to anything. I just felt uninspired, broke. Nothing good was going to come from this. So I turned on the TV, the news.

The newscaster—an Asian woman who'd rounded her eyes and plumped her lips so she looked like no race—spoke half-smiling about a disaster: "A major typhoon is set to hit China and parts of Southeast Asia. It's said to be the biggest storm to hit mainland China in over 150 years. Already this storm season is the worst on record..."

An idea. I ran to the phone and dialed.

Stephanie answered. "Howard Friedman's office."

"Stephanie," I said. "I'm going to Ohio."

"What? Gene?"

"Yes. I have to take a trip to Ohio."

"Why? What's there?"

"There's someone I need to meet."

She paused. I could hear bitterness in the pause, her breath changing. She said, "This isn't about those dreams you've been having, is it?"

There wasn't a good answer to this question. "Yes," I said.

"Gene, we can't really afford this now, can we?"

"I'll put it on the credit card," I said.

Obviously not the answer she wanted. For some reason I still don't know, she hated debt more than violence. Like her soul was in debt. And we were $28,000 in debt. But it was the only answer I could give.

"It's research for a novel," I said, knowing that was little rationalization, then added, "It could turn into something big. You have to believe me, Stephanie."

"I don't have to believe anything. Enjoy Ohio."

She hung up. Justified, like Miranda Goodling, which I used as my own justification—I needed to do this to prove what these dreams were about and turn it into something that might save our life together. So I threw clothes into a bag and bought a plane ticket I couldn't afford, knowing that by leaving I was breaking totally with responsibility. I was both ambitious and admitting my failure; it felt both liberating and empty. All I could do was move forward.

—⋀⋀—

I've mentioned that I hated flying. On the flight, the weather was bad, the plane was rocking. I clutched the armrests, muttering audibly, begging not to die. The woman next to me was visibly annoyed, more with me than the flight. I closed my eyes, hoping to make myself unconscious. But sleep was not going to come, not here, and I was desperate for it—not just to take me off this plane, but because I was becoming addicted to these dreams. They were like a religious experience. Dreams were normally better than reality, even bad dreams, because they purged your anxiety, while still being only a fabrication. Even though these dreams might not be real, the hope that they could be was more inspiring than the possibility that they weren't. Like when I was writing a book I could ride the illusion that it might turn out well, until it was done and I had to face people's indifference, much like I had faced Miranda Goodling's indifference today. I'd much rather live on hope than face what's real—probably the best diagnosis I've ever given about myself. Each dream renewed my faith in myself. But if I forced the dreams, they never came. If I took sleeping pills, that didn't work. My mind needed to be open and not hung on a desperate prayer about having another vision. I had to not think about dreaming, which was nearly impossible because my hope for these dreams was taking me over.

So instead I grabbed my notebook and started writing, quickly, nearly unintelligibly, trying to lose sight of myself, to approximate a dream, and to create another chapter.

7: Number 3 Dream

A New York apartment. I know it's New York without being told. I can feel it because I've lived in a place like this before. Grates on the kitchen windows that look out on the dirtied brick walls between apartment buildings. I had an ex-girlfriend who lived in a place like this. Almost exactly the same. One of the most romantic periods of my life, six months long. She left me for an ex-boyfriend, then left him soon afterward, never to return to me.

The living room's lit by one candle burning in a kind of translucent rock sitting on the TV—a New Age rock that's supposed to clear the room of toxins. Two girls—early twenties— are sitting on the living room floor. The Velvet Underground is playing "Pale Blue Eyes." The young woman I'm there to see really does have pale blue eyes, shockingly round, like small lights. They're both beautiful—fashion model beautiful—thin and bony and otherworldly. I imagine them to be models because there's nothing else they could be, they seem bred for it. I've never spent time with women like this. Apologies to my wife, who is very beautiful, but these girls are another species, every feature magnified. Their eyes are even wider because they're pinned, high.

I understand what is happening in this room. I've been around junkies enough in my life. Done it myself. The pride in their wide eyes, as if they're accomplishing something. Which they are, partly, but what you learn from dope you learn quickly and the rest is redundant. I don't know where they are in the process, probably somewhere near the beginning. They're still healthy-looking, not pallid, still excited as they snort, don't shoot, another line. They might even be at the stage where they're proud of being dope sick, it's the furthest over the edge they've ever gone. They've become part of a culture and a history, and they're not yet grimly indifferent to how it makes them feel.

I've witnessed conversations like this one too:

Model #1: "I love snorting heroin off a Velvet Underground CD."

Her friend taps out a small mound out of a bag and makes a line with a debit card.

Model #2: "I know. It's, like, so appropriate. He was high while he did all this stuff. You know what's also really good? A Nirvana cover. Did you ever hear him in interviews? His voice was croaking all the time. I heard he even nodded out during interviews."

Model #1: "That's cool. John Coltrane's good too."

Model #2: "Yeah, John Coltrane. But I don't really like jazz. Makes me nervous."

Model #1: "Oh, I don't know. I like the '50s stuff. It wasn't so jumpy. And they were all high."

Model #2, breathily: "Yeah."

Model #1, breathily: "Yeah."

Then I write: "Dominique Blair. 412 East 8th St., Apartment 5, New York City. Dominique Blair."

—⋀⋀⋀—

I looked up from the notebook as if I had been in a trance, surprised to find myself on a plane—the deafening hum in the cabin, people staring straight ahead, wasted with boredom. I felt like I'd just screamed what I wrote. But everyone was silent and involved in their own space, paying no attention to me. I felt slightly high, my head spinning and alive; this was why I wrote. Immediately, I checked the girl's name and address on the computer terminal in front of me. I did this quickly as if to avoid thinking about the possible consequences. Dominique

Blair, New York City. She was listed. Christ, she was listed.

Something's happened. It was ominous, perplexing, but I was comforted, like my future's been decided. As if I've finally gotten the recognition I've wanted all my life, even if I willed it myself. My imagination was finally paying off. At the very least this was proof that I should be taking this trip, and this book was becoming more than I'd hoped. I didn't even feel the plane's turbulence as we headed towards Ohio.

—∧∧∧—

I rented a car and drove to Bob Banski's apartment. The apartment complex looked like a dumpster. A discarded air conditioner, half a tire, how did that happen? The place had a pool but it was empty, filled with a puddle of water and debris. It didn't feel dangerous, just deserted. I walked up the stairwell and knocked on his front door, no answer. I peered into the dark apartment. A newspaper on a coffee table, a beer can in an ashtray, no different than outside the place. He wasn't there, not much I could do. I peered in the window again. It looked like a place no one wanted to live.

A woman, white and fat, walked down the outdoor hallway carrying a plastic bin of laundry, watching me. She stopped at the next door: his neighbor.

"I'm not trying to rob the place," I told her.

"If you were, you'd be stupid," she said, deeply unsmiling. "There isn't anything in there except beer cans and a thirty-year-old TV."

"Do you know where I can find him?"

"Probably at Cutty's, if he's not dead."

Right, the bar from the dream.

"Where is it?"

"Take a right around the corner and you'll see it."

"Thank you."

She called to my back, "If he's not there, try the gutter." She was smiling now, pleased with her poetry.

The bar was right around the corner, as she said, like he'd chosen the apartment because the bar was ten steps away. I hadn't seen the outside of the place, only the inside, but it's what I'd pictured. Not that this type of confirmation was necessary anymore. But I wanted to remember the details. Anything from this point could be part of the book. I really was living my own fiction. It was a purposeful kind of narcissism. As if everything was put there for me, and every detail had the possibility of literature. A couple of neon signs out front, no windows, a black door, pretty grim.

Opening the door poured an uncomfortable amount of light into the bar. Patrons eyes scurried away. It was like night inside. There were fewer people than in my dream. An identical couple wearing football jerseys sat at a table. Bob Banski was again hunched over at the bar.

I didn't have to be as careful with him as I did with Miranda Goodling in a quiet suburb. I walked right up to him. He was staring at his two drinks, a Rolling Rock and a straight whiskey. He didn't turn his head as I approached.

"Are you Bob Banski?" I asked.

He turned his head slowly and took a second to focus on me. He was pretty well drunk. Oddly, it was like seeing a celebrity who'd fallen on hard times. He'd appeared in my dreams, so he had a different kind of light around him, like he was being watched by everyone in this bar.

"I am," he said.

"Could I talk to you for a minute?"

"Funny, I'm usually the one talking at other people," he said with a kind of regret. "Who are you?"

"Gene," I said.

"Gene as in Eugene or Gene as in genial?" He laughed gruffly at himself and continued, "or Gene as in congenital or Gene as in genitals—"

"Gene as in Eugene," I interrupted. I wasn't irritated, he could be anything he wanted and I think he could sense this.

But he was hurt that I cut him off. "So what you need?" he

said, dismissively.

"I'll come right out and say it," I said. "I dreamt about you."

"That's sweet," he said.

"It's true. I had a dream about you that told me your name and address."

"That's strange. Who do I sue for invasion of privacy?"

"I've been having some powerful dreams lately," I replied. "I've dreamt about people I've never met, real people. You were in one of them. So I came to see you. Does superheated steam sound familiar to you? Drilling into the ground for power?"

The bartender stepped into our conversation. He was a young guy, looked like a quarterback who'd taken the job part time and gotten stuck there. He'd been listening. "That's all he talks about lately," he said. "I wish he'd shut up about it."

Banski swiped his hand at the bartender. "Fuck off, *Ken*," with an emphasis on Ken, as if it might not even be his name. The bartender moved away to the other end of the bar, grinning. Banski got quiet. "You've heard about that too, huh? Powerful stuff. We just need to drill a hole in the ground—"

"I dreamt it, Mr. Banski. Do you see? It actually happened in this bar and a voice told me to come contact you."

Banski picked up his whiskey and stared at it. "Well, why the hell do you think that is?" he said, nearly worried.

"I don't know. That's why I'm here. I'm hoping to make some sense of it."

"So you came here to make sense out of nonsense."

I was starting to feel deflated.

"Just kidding," he said. "You've got my attention. Believe me. Here, I want to show you something."

He reached down to the floor and picked up a battered red backpack, stained with ink from pens that had broken apart inside. He took out a wire-bound notebook, much like the one I used, and paged through it. The notebook was almost completely full, front to back, top to bottom on every page. I nearly felt envious. This guy worked. Both our writing was illegible to anyone but ourselves.

He held up his notebook and said, "You know how some people can't throw anything away? They fill their houses with shit. Old receipts, fast-food cartons, junk mail, whatever. I'm the same way with thoughts. If I think something, I've got to get it down on paper. Why else you think I drink? Cause I can't be thinking new thoughts all the time. Look here," he pointed to a section with his dreams: the headings said Dream #1, Dream #2, etc. "These are my dreams, every dream this year. I record every waking and sleeping thought."

He didn't seem proud of this. He seemed relieved to be admitting it to someone. A reminder that this guy wasn't some abusive drunk, he was very deeply wounded. He seemed grateful to be talking to me, which was particularly sad, like I was the first willing audience he'd ever had.

"Have you dreamt anything like this?" I asked. "About people you don't know? Or even me coming to see you?"

He looked up and whispered some words, as if reading something written on the ceiling. "No, I haven't," he said. "All I seem to have these days are apocalypse dreams. Planes crashing, falling from the sky. Bombs dropping, people fighting in cities and fleeing. I don't even have to write them down anymore. I don't record old thoughts, only new ones. And the dreams are the same every time."

"That's interes—"

"Here's the thing, though. I don't think they're dreams at all. The third time I had the same dream, I started thinking: these dreams are real. I think they're about what's coming."

"So how do you think I tie into this?"

"I don't know. But I do know this. Dreams are as real as matter. You've been dreaming about me? Maybe somebody is dreaming about you and everything you see here is somebody else's dream. God or someone else out there in the wilderness." He pointed towards the door like it was looking back at us. "It's just the life that some demented mind chooses to show you. You ever think about that?"

"No. I haven't."

"Of course not. No one does. People spend all day at a computer box. Come home and look at a TV box and live in another box."

"So you think outside the box," I said.

"Very funny. But it's true. You know how people wake up and say, 'I just had the strangest dream'? The strangest dream is being alive."

He grabbed his pen out of the wire binding and found a blank spot in his notebook and wrote down this last thought. As I watched him there, I saw myself—a man furiously scribbling, as if to explain why he exists by inventing something that doesn't, determined to prove that he is sane.

Believe me, I was also encouraged. Somehow my hope for what these dreams might become had turned into reality. But now I had to deal with what that meant. What this may have confirmed was that the chapters I'd written about Winchell might also be true. Maybe I was getting ahead of myself—desperate to be taken seriously. But if my writing about Dominique Blair was real, it was possible the other things I'd written were true as well. Which was a real fucking disaster, not a point of pride. I never wanted World War III to happen. OK, that was a lie—even I thought depopulation might be necessary or I wouldn't have conceived the idea in the first place. But that had the comfort of theory, not reality, and now those ideas were possibly coming to fruition, which was never the intention.

I talked to Banski some more before he passed out asleep right at the bar. He told me he had a lot of money—most of which he'd never spent because he didn't like where it came from—from family. He didn't expand on that. But he did offer to fly me to New York to meet the model named Dominique and get some answers from her. Put all together, my future rested on this drunk and a junkie supermodel somewhere in New York City, both products of my imagination.

I hadn't been back to New York since I last lived there. After Stephanie and I moved to Willamette, South Carolina following 9-11, we went through a withdrawal from city life. We decided on Los Angeles. Stephanie had grown up in Florida. She wanted to move to a place with good weather, but without the rednecks of her childhood. I also remember in there my promises about moving to Hollywood. There'd be more work for me there, I said. I'd gotten the teaching job soon after, not much more.

So this was how I returned to New York, my old life. A crusade to find a junkie supermodel conceived in a stream of consciousness on a plane flight. The city hadn't changed. I'd expected most of the dirt cleared away, as if by leaving I'd taken the dirt with me, but it looked the same. I was glad to be back. We'd never really made a home in Los Angeles. My most creative times were in New York. In New York, you could feel a part of history, in L.A. abandoned by it. I'll spare more talk of process. Probably not much more interesting than hearing about someone else's dreams. Which meant this book had more than a few problems.

Dominique Blair lived off Tompkins Square Park. The front door of the apartment building was wide open. I climbed the stairs to apartment 5, my heart beating weirdly. I was nervous like I was 14 going over to a girl's house for the first time. Which didn't happen as early as 14, but for the sake of argument. Meeting her was more strange to me than meeting the people from the other dreams because I'd willed it myself, it wasn't thrust on me. With her, I controlled my future. I could hear music coming from the other side of her door. Portishead, suicide music for supermodels. I knocked, there was no answer. I knocked again. Nodding out, I thought in a fatherly way. Now what: I wasn't going to go back home. I didn't even have a hotel room yet. So I tried the door and it was open. Did I will this to be or was it open before I got there? Yet to be determined. I thought maybe I could write out what I wanted to be true, but something told me this was a mistake and wouldn't work.

I walked into the apartment. Same scene as before, but now I was inside it. Candles burning, almost dark, music playing. No friend this time, but there was Dominique on the couch, nodding out. I called her name, no response. I went over to the couch and shook her hand, which fell limply. Her eyes didn't open. She was out, bad.

I went into the kitchen and filled up a white plastic bowl with cold water and dumped it on her face. She didn't stir.

"Shit," I said. Then dialed 911.

—\/\/\—

I sat in the emergency room, waiting. Light blue linoleum, fading to gray. The guy in front of me—fat, two chairs wide—was listening to something on headphones and singing loudly, cluelessly off key. No people being carted through, screaming and bleeding, stabbed. It was dull in here, a waiting room. I'd never witnessed major violence firsthand, even during these times, and I was half hoping to see something dramatic. But the room was full of people unanxiously waiting for others who were hurt. It was like the DMV—something you had to get done.

The doctor who'd taken Dominique after I checked her in—riding in a cab behind the ambulance, wondering if she was being revived, a terrible drive that now felt like it was months earlier—stepped up to me. "Are you Ms. Blair's father?" he asked.

That hurt, I hardly felt that old. "No," I said. "I'm a friend. How's she doing?"

"Aside from being a heroin addict, she's doing fine."

"She's not dead, then?"

"Unless she's the living dead. You can see her if you want." His indifference was palpable, an expression like fading fluorescent light, like the rest of the emergency room. "Follow

71
—\/\/\—

me."

He brought me to a curtained-off area with a scuffed floor. Dominique was lying in bed, actually looking like the living dead, as if recently raised from the grave, ashen and damp.

The doctor left us.

"Are you the one who brought me in?" she asked, voice croaking.

"I am," I said.

"You saved my life," she said.

I hadn't thought about that. I guessed I had. I was more selfish—I rushed her to the hospital to save my own life. I was not so altruistic. Just like a junkie to steal from me, I had thought. I was invested in what she could tell me and actually pissed that it had to be postponed. Her resuscitation was for both her and me.

"I've never shot up before," she said. "Really. We just snorted. Everyone told me that was half-assed, not the real thing, so I wanted to try it. I even left the door open in case something happened."

"That doesn't make any sense. What if somebody didn't come by?"

"I didn't think about that. I fucked up." She looked down guiltily. She looked thirteen.

"Do you have any family nearby?" I asked.

"Not in this country. I'm an army brat."

"What about friends?"

"All my friends are junkies. The doctor said I should stay away from them. He's probably right."

"Probably. So that leaves…me?"

"I guess so," she said. "Who are you?"

"I'm Gene."

"I'm Dominique."

"I know."

We shook hands. Her hand was weightless.

"If we ever get married this is something we can tell our kids," she said. "But we'll have to wait until they're at least three or four."

"I'm married, but thanks," I said.

She smiled, some of the life coming back.

"Now what do we do?" she asked.

"Now you go into a methadone program and I'm going to take you out for a cup of coffee."

—✲—

We were sitting in a Polish diner on 1st Avenue. Everything was beige, including the waitresses. Sharing a plate of potato pierogies with fried onions, a hangover meal back in the day when I attempted to be an alcoholic (I thought that's what writers did) but never took to it. Patrons were looking her way, or so I imagined. In the past, she'd be the type of girl to make me feel annoyed and neglected, as she sat with a guy who was beneath her. And now she was sitting with me, older and married, but experiencing something I'd once desired for myself.

She took a bite and closed her eyes, as if meditating. "This stuff is life-giving," she breathed out.

"I've never had a meal with a supermodel before," I said.

"I'm hardly super," she said. "I'm barely even a model. I haven't worked for months. Not since…" She looked around the restaurant. "I hope nobody sees me here. I can't face my life. It's a good thing you came along. I was about to run out of money. Who knows what would happen then."

We ate silently for a bit. She looked stricken, as if finally realizing what had happened to her.

She turned that expression on me. "So, I am grateful and all, but there's this elephant in the room. What were you doing in my apartment?"

Somehow this had slipped my mind.

"Right," I said. "I almost don't want to tell you."

Her eyes widened fearfully, but then she slackened as if she didn't have much fight in her. "You're not dangerous, are you?

The reason I came here is because I sensed you were safe. I normally have a good intuition for these things." Then, dismissively, "Even if I am a junkie."

"I'm not dangerous," I said. "I was coming to visit you for a reason."

I pulled out my notebook and flipped to the list of names and addresses. "This is probably going to sound ridiculous," I said. "But you see this list? I've had dreams about people I've never met. They both turned out to be real. And then I wrote about you. I'm a writer. I didn't dream it, I wrote out a scene where you were doing dope in your apartment and you turned out to be real. That's why I came to see you when I did."

"Are you psychic?" she asked.

"Not usually, no."

"It doesn't sound ridiculous. Not if what you say is true. I've believed in weirder things and had no proof. You've got that list. Let me see it."

I handed her the notebook. She read through it.

"Just three," she said, with disappointment.

"So far, but I'm anticipating more."

"Who's Bob Banski?"

"A drunk living in Ohio. I contacted him and he believes me. Miranda Goodling slammed the door in my face and I don't exactly blame her. Every time I go to sleep I think there are going to be more. If I start writing, I wonder will it come true? I feel like I'm losing my head. I can't quite tell what's real or imagined anymore."

She studied me as I talked, then said, matter-of-factly, "I don't think you're lying. And this would be a pretty fucked-up thing to make up. What do you think it means?"

"I don't know. That's why I came to see you."

"But what do *you* think it means."

"I don't know, that we're part of the list for a reason. That we should all get together. We're connected in some way."

"That's what I think too," she said.

"Do you?"

"Yeah. Part of the reason I trusted you is because I feel like I've seen you before. In a dream, maybe. I'm just crazy enough to not think that's crazy. It's a big universe out there and in here." She touched her temple. "And there's a lot more than we can see with our senses. It's why I started doing dope, you know? To feel God. Because I can't feel it otherwise. But I know it's out there. I know it." She was nearly yelling, desperately. Other customers were glancing over. She settled down some and went back to her food, lifting her fork. "You seemed familiar somehow. Like I met you in another life and forgot about it."

Her response was similar to my own. Looking for answers to unanswerable questions. Why anyone turned to religion. She was a dope addict, so I shouldn't push her too quickly into this, because an addict could trade one addiction for another. But I was grateful that someone else believed me. If she didn't believe what I told her—someone I'd invented—then this was more complicated than I could possibly handle.

—∿∿—

We entered my L.A. apartment, having flown from New York on Banski's dollar. It was a good scenario for Dominique—able to get out of New York and clean out. She packed a small bag and we headed straight to JFK. I hadn't even been in New York a day.

I'd left town to my wife's objection only to return with a beautiful younger woman. No real way to explain Dominique to my wife. I was bringing home a fantasy, in more ways than one. But like I said, Dominique had justified my new life's work; she was proof. This meant I was an asshole because I was going to possibly damage our marriage, make my wife jealous, and she had a tendency for it. But I always did put my writing before my marriage, which was why the marriage was difficult—I prioritized writing and I wasn't successful. Dominique was a kind of proof of success, but she also proved that I was self-obsessed, even if she justified that obsession. Nothing that would make my wife very happy.

"Hello," I called awkwardly as we entered the apartment. "We're—I mean I'm home." No answer. "It's Saturday, I don't where she is," I told Dominique.

Dominique walked tentatively into the living room, looking around at the books, the Persian rug, etc. Stephanie walked briskly into the apartment from a back entrance. Her knees were dark with dirt. It was an apartment and the landlord hired gardeners but Stephanie liked to work in the small flowerbed in back. It was sad, honestly, one of those promises I'd hoped to fulfill—that one day I'd get her a real garden.

She looked up and shrieked when she saw me standing in the front entranceway. "Christ, you scared me. You didn't tell me you were coming home."

"Surprise," I said. "I'm sorry."

I leaned in to hug her, which she returned, and then she saw Dominique standing by the bookshelf. Dominique was still half-eyeing the books.

"Steph, this is Dominique," I said. "She needs to stay here for a little while. We can pull the couch out."

Not much of an explanation.

"OK," Stephanie said, incredulously.

Dominique approached Stephanie. She was a head taller and put out a long arm to shake. "Good to meet you, Mrs. Myers. Thanks so much for letting me stay here."

Stephanie eyed Dominique's hand. "My hands are dirty," she said, holding up a hand that wasn't dirty. "Flowers."

"We met in New York," I said. "I'll have to explain this to you later."

"I guess you will," Stephanie said.

—⋀⋀—

Stephanie and I were in the bedroom, door closed. Dominique was in the living room, knowing full well what we were talking about. Stephanie stood at the foot of the bed, unrelenting, and she hadn't yet said anything. I lay on the bed, over the covers, which was a stupid position to be in—I appeared lazy. I sat up on the edge of the bed, as if this would help.

"She's a nice girl," I said.

"Yes," Stephanie said, bitterly. "Very nice."

"Stephanie, it's not like that."

"Of course it's like that. I know you. Just looking at her is being unfaithful." She was right, of course.

"Nothing happened and nothing will happen."

"That's not the point, Gene. It's all part of this crazy scheme you've got going."

"It's not a scheme. It may be one of the most amazing things that's ever happened. To me, to anyone."

"All I know is that you get hit over the head and suddenly this new idea comes along. You have a tendency to believe in things for sport."

She was right again. But so was I.

"Stephanie," I said. "I've dreamed up three people, all of whom turned out to be real. One of them is sitting in our living room. Doesn't that count for anything?"

She had to concede this. She slumped a bit.

"C'mon Stephanie, welcome me home."

I put my arms out and she hugged me. But I could sense that something had broken in her. She wasn't coming along this time. Maybe because I had finally found some success, she could relent and let me go, satisfied that I'd be taken care of, but sick that it had taken so long.

I lay down on the bed, beat. And I slept.

8: 12-12

A warehouse. It looks like something out of a Jean-Claude Van Damme movie, a fake set. A table in the center of a dark and echoing room. The middle of nowhere. A collection of men—seven or eight—holding guns and looking tough. As if trying to look tough, as if acting out what they'd seen in a movie. They are, after all, terrorists, and not very bright, so maybe they're proud of this posture. The central guy is better looking, better dressed. Frat-looking, wearing a suit without a tie, black hair, blue eyes. His name is Duncan Taylor, but everyone calls him Taylor.

He's laid out a map of the world with tiny red x's for each location—what he calls pressure points. 400 men across the world. Tens of thousands of dollars raised and spent. Bankrolled by church groups, a writer of End Times books, members of the Winchell administration, as well as Russian and Pakistani Islamists—people who wanted their own type of apocalypse, but Taylor didn't care, whatever helped to bring about the Second Coming was fine with him, no matter how alien a faith, no matter how dark.

"It's finally here," he says. "Tuesday."

"Just like 9-11 was a Tuesday," says a second in command, Tim, a man with a neck that's thicker than his legs. He works out on steroids and meth.

"On election day," Taylor says. "People don't remember that. I've been in contact with all our men. They're ready to go, at 9:11 a.m. So people know it's coordinated. Truck bombs on every major continent. Sniper fire will cover the rest."

"Sniper fire's brilliant, Taylor. It'll scare the shit out of people. It'd scare the shit out of me."

"That's the idea. People will be afraid to go outside, go to the supermarket. Like the school shootings all around the world at once."

"Be proud of the plan, Taylor."

He looks like he is, like he's already won. I'm sickened, like humanity's poisoned. It's like reading a true crime book that you hope won't come true, even though you know it will, but you keep reading. This feeling is going to stay with me for months afterward.

I speak the words, as usual: "This is Taylor Veil. 1850 Wright Rd., Plymouth Idaho." But when I do I realize that I'm not watching the dream from a distance. I'm in the warehouse, standing at the far wall. My voice echoes. The men turn around.

"What the fuck is that?" someone shouts. Two men run in my direction.

"Someone spoke over there."

I don't have time to understand what's happening. They're on me.

"Who the fuck are you?" Gun in my face. "You picked the wrong place to be."

They pat me down, each grab me by an arm, and bring me to the table in the center of the warehouse where Taylor is waiting.

Taylor yells at the men, "How the fuck did he get in here? Did you forget to lock the fucking front door?"

"Are you kidding? We have every entrance blocked off and guarded. I don't know how the hell he got in here."

"Where'd you come from?" Taylor asks me.

"I am..." I begin and then I stop, startled to hear the sound of my own voice, confirmation that I'm here. It's not detached like before. I'm dazed—it's both as unreal as a dream and as concrete as waking life.

"What, you can't speak? Who are you?"

"Don't know what this is, Taylor, but he's seen everything," says the guy with the thick neck.

"Yeah, I guess he has," Taylor says, calmly. He picks up one of *the guns off the table, aims it at the center of my forehead, and fires.*

—MW—

I woke up.

"Oh fuck," I said in bed. My hand went to my forehead. My head was damp—from sweat, not blood. I checked my heart rate. Beating quickly like it was running away from my body, but I was alive. The worst experience of my life. I lived through my death.

I got out of bed, legs uneasy, heart still beating terribly. My wife lay unmoving in bed, asleep. The darkness in the room felt threatening. Anything could be lurking in here. I had just entered my dream, who was to say the opposite couldn't happen: men from my dream ending up in my bedroom. I walked slowly, as if to not disturb the air, into the living where the streetlights were pouring in, slightly comforting. Dominique was asleep on the living room couch, jaw dropped, arm dangling off the side. Also comforting—I would not have to face this alone. I tried to wake her and she didn't stir. Dead out—shades of being overdosed on the couch of her New York apartment. She didn't do it again, did she? Nothing seemed reliable. I shook her again and she woke, eyes jumping to see me kneeling beside her.

"I had another dream," I told her.

"What was it?" she said.

"Bad this time. Terrible. I died in the dream. They shot me. They saw me, somehow they saw me. A dream about terrorists. I think something terrible's going to happen."

"You're still alive, Gene. If you know how you're going to die, you can prevent it."

"That's not the point. They're planning something awful. Bombs, sniper fire. Another 9-11. Worse."

"Jesus. Maybe it's just a dream."

"But it was the same as the other ones, except this time I was inside it."

I was beginning to calm down some. Speaking the experience out loud made it more implausible, like I was describing an actual dream. At least I was sharing the burden. As with any dream, it had faded the longer I was awake. Then again, I also wanted this out of my memory and I kept getting flashes of the men, flashes of the possible tragedy, based on images of past tragedies. Up to this point, the dreams had been sort of fun a writer's fantasy of what his imagination could achieve. But I didn't want to see anyone actually die, no matter how many people I might make die on paper.

"I have to tell somebody about this," I said. I looked over at the TV. "But you know what? Who is going to believe me? I dreamt a terrorist attack. It's ludicrous."

"It could still be a dream, Gene. You still have regular dreams, don't you?"

"I hope so," I said.

I spent the rest of the night lying on the floor next to the couch where Dominique slept. Fetal, hardly sleeping, not sure what would happen if I slept again. It was unfaithful to my wife sleeping in the other room. I had woken Dominique, not my wife, after the dream. But I was feeling weak, a target while I slept, and I felt stronger next to someone who believed in me. I was smart enough to get back into my bed before my wife woke up.

In the morning, the light of day was another comfort. The night before seemed like a lifetime ago, cleansed by sleep. Dominique and Stephanie were talking in the kitchen, drinking coffee. I didn't know what to make of that. They stopped talking when I entered, as if I'd broken into a conversation. They looked guilty, I felt accused. I worried that Stephanie had confronted her about where I had slept the night before—which, now that the dark had cleared, I realized I had basically slept in the same bed with another woman.

"Hello," I said weakly.

"We were just talking about you," Stephanie said. "About

this dream you had. How you feeling?"

"Better," I replied. "I was just so worried last night. I think all these dreams are messing with my head. This morning it feels like it might just have been a nightmare."

"That's good, Gene," Stephanie said. "I'm glad to hear it."

She was mostly glad, I imagined, that I wasn't believing my own hype, I was putting these foolish thoughts behind me. No time to be railing against her; moving on. "What's on the docket today?" I said.

"I've got to be at work in a half hour," Stephanie said.

"It's a weekday?"

"Yes, it's a weekday." Darkly.

"I've got that appointment, Gene, remember?" Dominique said hopefully.

Right. She had to go to the methadone clinic. I'd neglected to tell Stephanie that part about Dominique.

"Dominique's on a methadone program," I told Stephanie. "I need to take her to the clinic…I guess I didn't mention that."

"No, you didn't. Well, I hope you're going to be OK," she said to Dominique politely, but stiffly.

"I'm doing much better. Thanks, Mrs. Myers."

"Stephanie," she said, more stiffly.

"Stephanie. I think I just needed to get out of New York."

Stephanie glanced at me, as if nothing more needed to be said than a glance, and left the kitchen to get ready for work.

"Your wife hates me," Dominique said.

"She doesn't hate you, Dominique. She hates me."

—WW—

I still had a job. I dropped Dominique at the clinic and went to the college to teach my one class. It was nearly impossible to concentrate. A girl read a terrible story called "Cat and Mouse," about the "battle between the sexes," and I didn't have the heart or will to criticize her. I was normally a fairly mean-spirited teacher, impatient, taking revenge for my lack of success, as if it was my students' fault. At the climax of the story, someone in the back of the room said, "Holy shit," which was out of place because the story didn't warrant it. There was something in his voice too—fear, sadness, disbelief, everything you'd expect.

"New York is gone," he said. "It's gone."

He was looking at his cell-V (vision/voice) in the back of the classroom. Everyone had one so they turned on their TVs. I pulled one out too. The only footage was from high above, thousands of feet up, clouded by smoke, which made it a little unreal. From high above, obliterating a city seemed less consequential, like killing thousands of ants underfoot. It also made it seem like it might not be happening. The mind had a powerful drive to not believe stuff it didn't want to be true. Especially if there was limited evidence.

There were other reports of bombs at the Tokyo Stock Exchange, the London Stock Exchange, and sniper fire at malls and tourist attractions around the world.

It happened, I thought. Goddamnit. I gathered up some papers—the girl's story—and a book I'd assigned—*The Motion of Light in Water* by Samuel Delany—as if I needed them right now, and headed out the door. "Go home everybody. Go where you need to be."

Some got up and left, but most stayed where they were, watching their TVs, surrounded by their friends, wanting to share it together.

"Be safe," I said and left.

It didn't occur to me at the time that I might not ever see these kids again. I was thinking more of my own family, of getting home.

Outside the classroom I found my daughter, Sophia. She was running up to the classroom, eyes wide and hollow. I hadn't seen her since she moved out. We hugged immediately. It was one of the more beautiful experiences of my life. Just knowing that her first thought was to find me. Recently I'd thought something in our family had died, but it hadn't, which was really a huge oversight on my part—the doubt, the conception that things could die permanently from one act. I was old enough to know that anything faded with time. It was pretty stupid of me to put her recent experience in black-and-white terms. But it was easier and safer to write her off than face her knowing that she'd never be the same. These were the thoughts that hit me in a flash, the gratitude that I still had my daughter. I didn't feel selfish, as if discounting all the suffering that was going on at the moment, just grateful that everyone wasn't suffering. I loved my daughter with the immediacy as the day she was born.

"What are we going to do?" she asked.

"I don't know yet, Sophie. I don't think anything's going to be the same after this."

"Are we going to stay in L.A.?"

"I don't know where else is going to be any safer."

I took out my phone and dialed Stephanie.

She answered, "Howard Friedman's office."

"Stephanie, it's Gene. You hear?"

"Yeah, I heard," she said.

"Sophia is here. We're headed home now."

"Howard wants me to stay here and finish up some paperwork. We have work to do."

"Today? He wants to do divorce law today?"

"Yes."

"OK, please come home when you can."

I hung up. Somehow this affected me as deeply as the news from the world. That some lawyer wanted to finalize the death of a marriage…and that my wife was willing to do it.

On our way back home, I picked up Dominique. I introduced her to Sophia, they shook hands. It was a strange meeting. It occurred to me belatedly that Dominique wasn't much older than my daughter or any of my students. She seemed older. Her personality seemed fully formed, perhaps because she had bypassed college and gone straight to work.

Sophia sat quietly in the back seat, watching the traffic. "I should have told somebody," I said to Dominique. "I should have fucking told somebody."

"Who? The news?" Dominique said. "Like you said, no one would have believed you. And there wasn't enough time."

"I should have tried. People are dead. I just didn't want to believe it to be true. I feel dead myself."

"This isn't your fault."

"Even if it's not, it's a terrible day."

As we were driving, Washington D.C. was hit. The news said, "We regret to inform you…" Most politicians were dead, they said, though some may have been hiding in underground bunkers or had the time to flee. The president and the cabinet, it was thought and hoped, were somewhere underground or perhaps weren't in D.C. at all. He gave a statement about New York from somewhere, speaking nothing but slogans ("We're all New Yorkers now and forever.") Shots of D.C. showed the city devastated, but, strangely, the Capitol Building was still standing, as if it was made out of some other material than the rest of the city.

L.A. was mostly spared. There was sniper fire on Hollywood Boulevard, but no bombs. Maybe they'd failed to work. There was a lot of conjecture and guesswork. The news showed cell phone camera footage of people fleeing the Mann's Chinese Theatre, a person getting shot. After the footage of New York, it seemed slight. The city looked as it usually did on the ride home. People were still sitting at outdoor restaurants, talking on cellphones, driving as if to somewhere other than shelter. They should have all been in mourning, or at least afraid. Pedestrians appeared more apathetic than defiant.

We pulled into my driveway and got out of the car. I looked left to right, up in the sky, as if sniper fire was going to rain down on us, as if we were being watched. It was enough trouble to get my key into the lock. When we got inside, I was the most grateful I'd ever been to be home.

I went to the computer and switched to the news (the

computer and the TV worked on the same network, though mentioning this feels trivial). New images of the devastation were coming in. Imagine New York City after Hiroshima. The city was dead and gray. I can't say much about it. It's like describing a corpse, a soul that's no longer there, and even slightly feels like it never existed. It was like something was cut out of you. You'd get a flash of a landmark, the way you'd get a flash of a person's smile, and just start weeping. This was worse, somehow, than a parent dying: part of the world, something everybody shared, not just part of your life.

The news also showed driver's license photos of the men from my dream: Taylor, Tim, and others who were nameless but not faceless. All dead now. It was confirmation, but unnecessary, almost an afterthought. The news said, "It's now confirmed that the gunmen were part of the same network, a fundamentalist Christian sect bent on bringing about the biblical apocalypse. Strangely, the sect joined forces with Islamic fundamentalists intent on bringing down American interests. More details are emerging."

"This is a nightmare," I said to Dominique and Sophia. The curtains were drawn, the apartment was dark except for the TV. "I almost want to go to sleep again, see if there's any better news there. There might be more logic when I'm asleep."

I looked at the TV again, a repeated image of New York, gray as ash, not even burning.

"Fuck this," I said. "I can't take it. I need answers."

I ran to the bathroom and rifled through the shelves and found an old bottle of sleeping pills, past expired. I took six quickly and swallowed them with water from the sink. Then I got a bottle of whiskey out of a kitchen cabinet and started downing it in front of the TV, as if the images would help me drink quicker.

I started to get blurry and passed out, just as I saw footage of the president making a speech from a press room somewhere in the U.S.

9: Time of the Americans

"Do we know who executed the bombings?" the NSA asked.

"A very organized group of cells. There's possible Iranian involvement. Even the suggestion of involvement gives us just cause."

A group of four were playing golf at a course in the Southwest, untouched by recent events. The course had been cleared of people so they had it to themselves: the Winchell father and son, NSA, and chief of staff. The group walked up the fairway.

"It's terrible that it's come to this," Chief of Staff Whitehead said.

"Terrible but necessary," Benjamin Winchell replied. "Everyone must know that what we're going to do is just. The only way to save the planet, and indeed the human race, is to kill it off. At this rate we're going to die anyway, with the planet dying as well. At least with a new world war we can eliminate major human populations and start over with a more manageable blank slate. Don't worry, everyone. We're talking about utopia, the real American Dream. It's why this country was founded. Francis Bacon called it the New Atlantis. He was more important to this country than Washington."

"You're full of shit, Benjamin," the NSA interjected— uncharacteristic of her, at least in any public appearance I'd seen. "Global warming was done on purpose. It's just that the monsoons, pandemics, and wars weren't effective enough to

control population growth. People just like to fuck too much."
Definitely out of character.

"Yes, Liza, I was trying to save face."

"With who?"

"With myself. If you think killing eight billion people is going to be easy, you're crazier than I am. Even if we know death is not the end, the suffering that's going to be unleashed will be horrible. But let's not talk about that."

There was silence. Benjamin Winchell looked regretful. Not a caricature of evil, human. More startling than if he had been cold and indifferent because it made his plan seem like it was necessary, not diabolical.

President Winchell stayed back from the group, pensive and slightly nauseous. His life was in chaos. He was not a man without a soul. He didn't like to see millions of people and entire cities die. Even if this was by design, it pained him. It cannot be easy to be responsible for the death of millions of people, even if you wanted it to be so. The small amount of footage he'd seen on the news was profoundly distressing—so, like most, he changed the channel. "A thousand years of peace. A thousand years of peace," he repeated to himself. Only a divine being could take this kind of guilt, and Charles Winchell was human, no matter how much he believed he was doing God's work.

Let me make something clear. Winchell was not a bad man. He was not driven purely by malevolence. He was the common denominator of everyone's most basic hope—a little boy's dream of a cowboy or an army man. Charles Winchell had a kind of innocence. Winchell was a child. Appropriate because America was regressing.

His father was the weightier of the two—more practical, less driven by feeling. Colder, unempathetic, Benjamin Winchell did not see the world as comprised of people. He saw the earth, the countries, the cities, the businesses, and the future—with individual people very far down on the list. Except for those he knew personally. Then you were meant to be alive.

Benjamin Winchell chose an iron to take his shot. "It's a shame we're not going to be able to play golf anymore," he said.

"Why not?" asked the chief of staff.

"Even if this course isn't blown away, the roads coming here are going to be impassable. And who's going to mow the grass to such a fine level? This might be the last game of golf we ever play."

"That's sad. Terribly sad."

Benjamin Winchell scoffed, as if at a child. "I hope you realize how decadent it is to care about losing your golf game."

The chief of staff looked immediately contrite. "Yes, I'm sorry."

The NSA took her shot. Not far, but straight.

"Not bad," Benjamin Winchell said. "For a heterosexual woman, you're a fine golfer."

Liza fired back, "For a cancer patient, you're not bad either."

Benjamin laughed appreciatively. He had a recent battle with prostate cancer—a battle that he had won, though it had been humbling. "After this we head to the compound," he said.

"In New Mexico?" the NSA said.

"Ours is in New Mexico. You'll be in Montana."

"Yes. I just got my orders."

Benjamin Winchell stepped up to take his shot. "We'll be in touch throughout the operation. In addition to the remaining leadership around the world. It's better to not have us all in the same location." He shot and made the green. He was always a good athlete, good at whatever he put his mind to. "Really soak in this air. No air underground can ever compare to it. No matter how much climate control or plant life they put down there."

"So what's our next move?" the chief of staff asked Benjamin.

His son was fairly hurt. This was his father's operation more than his own. He rationalized that it made it easier—less of a burden. But they didn't always look to him for direction, even if he was the president, and even if they believed in his ultimate purpose for the war. His father was that commanding a figure.

"We retaliate," Benjamin answered. "Hard—damn the political consequences. We show that 12-12 came through Russia, we bomb Russia. They bomb back. No one will be sure who is doing the bombing, but there will always be blowback. China gets involved. Europe may just come to their aid to make sure we don't go nuts. That's the way we've designed it. This thing has to be complete or it's of no use. If they don't get involved, we'll conduct the war ourselves if we have to. Most leaders are on board. Everyone realizes this is our only option."

"How long do you figure it will take?"

"The war? Not long. War's easy when you're not trying to stop the worst from occurring. They debated bombing Hiroshima. For us there is no discussion. It will be a perfect storm of atomic, biological, and other weaponry. Everything we have at our disposal."

The chief of staff took his turn. His shot sliced wildly off to the left, against the wind. "I'm terrible at this game," he said.

10: Interpretation of Dreams

Over the next week I had a barrage of dreams. Several in one night. I'd wake up feeling like I'd slept eight hours only to see that 20 minutes had passed. Soon I didn't even have to dream anymore. I wrote blindly, just writing names and addresses, confident that this was coming from somewhere other than myself. Yes, I realize how horribly presumptuous this was to consider, but I didn't think I was divinely inspired. It was too practical. This could just as easily have been orchestrated by a teenage alien playing a prank, which may be no less presumptuous. There were people from all over the country— all American for some reason. Maybe people from other countries were having the same experience, I didn't know. All sorts of people—all religions, races, but not all ages. No children, everyone was at least 18. The choices didn't make particular sense. No one seemed exceptional or even exceptionally average. They were just other people: a woman named Janet Friedman, a 4th grade teach in Orlando; Jim Posner, a movie critic in North Carolina; Sarah Baer, another housewife in Duluth; Portia Farrow, unemployed in Seattle; Willard Gomez, a minor-league baseball player outside of Phoenix; Steve Simpson, a bank manager from upstate New York. And so on.

I'm being modest. I was deeply proud of having these experiences. In weaker moments, I thought I might be one of the most significant men alive. I was being given a window into the president's true intentions. I was a kind of prophet. Then I'd sober up and realize that the world was coming to a close. Millions of people were going to die. My faith in myself had only been restored by everyone dying. Another joke by whatever force that liked playing with me.

I kept writing, though. I wasn't looking to sell the book any longer—obviously not, sell to who, for what posterity? Now the book was just a chronicle about what was happening. Getting the events down was somewhat cathartic. Turning it into something better, softer, than it was in life. Somebody had to chronicle this and in a few years there wouldn't be many writers left. Writing was, if not beautiful, then concise. What was guiding me through this was the conviction that I would survive—as would the members of my group. I was writing about these people so I seemed a strange choice to be killed off early. Especially with the chronicle unfinished. One of the reasons I continued to write the book was survival. I told myself I wouldn't die until the major work of my life was done. That's a different ambition than posterity, or even money. I was writing to keep myself alive.

The phone rang as I wrote. It was Banski. I knew this before I picked up—but don't read into that more than you need to. I received very few phone calls. Even though I was connecting with new strangers, I was still detached from the world. Few friends to speak of, few contacts. In some way, I'd invented a social life with these dreams.

"I'm in L.A.," Banski told me.

"We've got to start doing something about all these names," I said.

"That's why I'm here. I got plenty of money. My family's defense contractors. I tell you that?"

"Yes." He had, in another screed about alternative energy. This time about zero-point energy, which could power the world cleanly and save the planet, but could also create a bomb that would destroy half the earth. Information backed up by Benjamin Winchell's lectures. Banski talked for four hours.

"Might make some life out of bloodmoney," he said. "We should get everyone together from that list. Might tell us something."

Call waiting beeped. I didn't predict this call. "Mr. Myers," said a small female voice. Distant, as if she didn't want to be heard. "This is Miranda Goodling. You came to my house the other day? Do you remember?"

It was a shock, but a nice one. "Of course. Mrs. Goodling. Good to hear from you."

She spoke slowly. "You told me to contact you if anything strange happened. You know, dreams or something else. And I've been having some bad ones. Mixed up with everything that's happening, I wanted to call you."

"I'm glad you called," I said.

"Could I meet you somewhere?" she asked.

"Don't bother. I'll come to you. How's today? In a couple of hours."

She agreed. I clicked back to Banski. "Banski, I got something going on. Where can I reach you?"

"Don't worry about me," he said. "I'm sleeping on the streets."

He hung up before I could inquire any further.

—⋀⋀⋀—

I headed to Miranda Goodling's front door feeling very different than the last visit. No longer a broken mess, I was in more control of myself, even with the world falling out of control. I didn't look much better—still disheveled, still avoiding how I appeared, still existing in my own mind. But I was confident, a renewed romance for life, as if it loved me back. Part of me believed the world could still be saved and I might be the one to save it, and this book would amount to something better than myself. Miranda Goodling opened the door looking demure, but grateful. She smiled mildly and wordlessly let me into her house. The dream had faded from my memory so I couldn't entirely remember her home, but frankly I didn't care anymore. These smaller details were starting not to matter.

"Please, sit down," she said.

I sat on the couch in front of a TV that was playing an animated show I didn't recognize. She turned it off with the remote.

"I'm grateful you called," I said.

She breathed in deeply and let it out, as if steadying herself. "I've been having some strange dreams, nearly every night," she said. "About world events. About what appears to be the end of the world. And not stuff that's already on TV." She pointed at the TV like it was a kind of enemy.

"I understand," I said.

"Other stuff's been happening too." Her eyes grew larger and she stopped herself.

"What is it?"

She never met my eyes as she talked. "Well, it's like my dreams and real life are getting mixed up. Like the other day I was looking at our cat, Sam, and his eyes were bright red. I thought it was a trick of the light, but as I got closer it stayed that way." As if on cue, the cat strolled by outside on the porch. The cat's eyes were normal; it looked bored and indifferent. "And then today, I was sitting on the couch where you are now. The wall over there," she pointed to the wall by the fireplace, behind a cabinet with a collection of bells (my grandmother collected bells as well, from all over the world). "The wall just disappeared. And there was a city street. Abandoned, there was trash blowing around. I approached the street and the wall became whole again." She shivered slightly. "Does that sound like anything you've heard of?"

"Not exactly," I responded.

"I'm not crazy. I know that," she said, as if trying to convince herself. "And I think I can tell the difference between a hallucination and real life. I could smell it, you know? The trash. Cold air came into the house. It was real. I'm scared, Mr.

Myers. It was real."

She started crying, hand shielding her eyes, shuddering, weeping with fear. I couldn't imagine how this must have felt to her. The world was falling apart, cities being destroyed, millions of people dead, and now her immediate world was starting to disintegrate. Me, I longed for this. I wanted to hallucinate, wanted the walls to melt away. It was totally alien to her, difficult to confess, and so believable.

I put a hand on her shoulder, which she accepted.

"I'm so sorry about this, Miranda," I said. "This has got to be difficult."

"It is. It's not like I can tell anyone about it. I don't want to be locked up, or have my kids taken away. I remembered your card so I called. What do you think this is?"

"I don't know yet, Miranda," I confessed. "But you're not alone here, know that. A lot of people are having these types of experiences. Our plan is to have a meeting with people from all over the country who are having similar experiences. It could explain what's happening. Do you think you'd be up for that?"

Miranda nodded, shyly, like a girl who'd scraped her knee and was being offered ice cream. I don't mean to be condescending, but being so powerless did make you feel like less of an adult. I was feeling partly helpless too—not answerable to parents, but to some force I couldn't see, even if it was my own creation.

I told Miranda I'd get back to her as soon as we were ready for the meeting. She was appreciative, a weight lifted. The promise of answers was enough of an answer.

"As long as I'm not crazy," she declared.

"You're not crazy," I said. "The world might be, but you're not."

11: The American Cell

President Winchell gave a few speeches that didn't say much of anything. He said he was going to go get the thugs responsible for 12-12, and other things you're probably familiar with. "I will not speculate on who did this until all the facts are in. But we all know the War on Terror never really ended. There will be a swift and deliberate response." He mentioned that Russia was a major target, as were Pakistan and parts of China.

He said one other thing. At the end of the speech he said he wanted to change America's motto from E Pluribus Unum, "Out of Many, One," to Ordo Ab Chao, "Order out of Chaos." The new world will be better than the one before. New money would soon be printed.

The speeches, unsurprisingly, didn't do much for Winchell's standing. People wanted his head. Pundits thought his days in office were numbered. Those on the right said there was no way to stop the bombings any more than you could stop every convenience store from being robbed. Bad analogy, other pundits yelled. This could have been prevented.

They were all wrong. This could only have been prevented if there were other people in office. Winchell's administration were responsible for the bombings. Of course, they had help: the American cell and Russians and Pakistanis who carried out the attacks. Americans weren't the only ones intent on bringing about the Second Coming. There was a wide network of people who were happy to see this come to fruition, even if they died in the process. The pundits didn't know this. For people who were supposed to inform the populace, they were the least informed. They only reported what they were allowed to know, even if their criticism shined a bad light on the administration.

The Winchell family and administration were now at the Winchell compound in New Mexico. It was far away from major cities where most of the damage would likely occur. It was unclear, as of now, how many senators and congressmen and others had left D.C. Though many had been warned.

Even if the current situation was planned, war was unpredictable, even to those at the top. It was a shame too. Even though life after the grave might have its advantages, being alive for it had a greater fulfillment—the difference, maybe, between witnessing a baseball game in person or reading the box score. A fulfillment that would ultimately make life after death that much more fulfilling. Yet another justification: suffering through life would have its reward.

The homestead—which was named Mount Megiddo, but most often called The Compound—had everything they needed. It was the White House nobody knew about. A small underground village. There was a tall electric fence around the property and a surveillance system that ran on generators, though very little of the compound could be seen above ground. Several back-up generators, which weren't needed because the generators ran on water, and they had plenty of water: both an indoor well and rooms full of bottled water, for when the groundwater would be undrinkable. Benjamin Winchell believed in redundancy. The appliances ran on a combination of wind and solar power, another reason to be in New Mexico. It was ironic, really: the compound was a liberal paradise. A sub-basement was stocked with enough canned food to last eight years. Frozen meat that wouldn't last nearly as long, but long enough. Weapons, if needed. Tanks. A private runway and mid-sized plane. It was also a survivalist's paradise.

The underground compound spanned an area as wide as a train station. There were medical facilities, research facilities, a media center, racks of new clothing, even a collection of stores, as if to give some continuity with the world upstairs. There was also recreation: pool, tennis court, weight room, everything you'd expect at a resort; no masseuse though. As more people arrived, so would doctors, scientists, and other types. Though Benjamin Winchell felt that he knew enough about medicine to self-diagnose. This place wasn't meant to be an ark preserving the great men of America—it was mostly a command center, padded with the comforts of home.

Most of all they would be safe and they would be calm enough to make rational decisions. If panic set in, the bunker was equipped with a small pharmacy, including anti-depressants and opiates, which Benjamin Winchell preferred. It was also an easy way to kill yourself if it came to that.

They were sitting in the living room in the main house aboveground. Windows were open for as long as that was possible. The house was something like an overgrown cabin, modeled after Will Rogers' home in Los Angeles. Wooden walls, a Persian rug in the center. The room was fairly dark, as if always being lit by a small fire; it smelled like wood. Benjamin Winchell sat in a thick suede chair, studded with gold. His feet rested upon an Ottoman. Charles was sitting at the edge of the couch, as if waiting to meet his date. His mother, Barbara, walked in and out of the room, separate from the discussion, his wife was sleeping upstairs, and his closest confidant, Chief of Staff Derek Whitehead, sat on the couch next to Charles. The vice president was said to be coming soon. Other people would go to bunkers of this kind, though none as nice as this one. Many were connected to each other via narrow passageways. Mount Megiddo was isolated.

They had spent the last week holed up here—a family together like they hadn't been in years. They ate meals, walked the grounds, even played tennis. It was alternately exhilarating and dull, much like some vacations. The promise of something that wasn't yet occurring. They watched the news, monitored the growing war online. A collection of private satellites could broadcast video when the media was no more. There was a room for this, a theatre with ten monitors, more if needed. His father wanted to monitor everything. Not out of sadism—not completely—but this was war and it needed to be monitored, even one as final and chaotic as this one. He didn't want everything destroyed if he could help it: just the people, not the landscape.

The decision about how to go forward hadn't yet been decided. They would retaliate, and hard, but first they needed to instigate the second phase of the plan: set this up as a religious war. This was going to be a careful disaster.

But the longer they waited, the more it seemed like they could lose control.

"I'm not happy," Charles said. "People hate me. There have been calls for my impeachment and assassination."

"You're here," his father said. "There's no way they can touch you. And there's never going to be an impeachment proceeding."

"That's not the point. I'm afraid it will hurt our plans. No one's going to listen to what I have to say. And I don't like reading about it."

"So don't read about it. Don't watch TV. I'm surprised at you, Charles. Everything they write is based on a fiction. Just remember that. Everything they say is based on half the story. Like monkeys talking about God. No one knows what they're talking about."

"But they think they do. That's what matters."

Benjamin sighed, more like a huff. "Jesus, Charles, did you think this would make people happy? You were prepared for this. You knew this would happen."

"There's a difference between preparing for something and witnessing it. People are suffering out there. Children are suffering. It's a disaster."

"I understand," Benjamin said calmly. "But the next year is a blip in the scope of the universe. We're witnessing the next Big Bang here. Once the world changes over, all of this will be forgotten. Editorials don't matter. They're lucky they still have a newspaper. Even 100% disapproval doesn't matter. Everything's going like we thought it would and no one said it would be easy."

He was right, of course. Charles spoke otherwise to save face. As if speaking doubt out loud was a sort of penance so he could move on. For every death, for every suffering, there was an equal joy somewhere else in the world. His father had taught him that. The greatest tragedy could be turned into the greatest prosperity. He had said that in speeches. We have to be strong now that it's here. This is what He wants.

By "He," Charles meant both God and his father. There was something that Charles Winchell wasn't telling his father: he didn't believe him. Benjamin Winchell claimed that all religions needed to be replaced by a universal, one-world religion: the Bible was the path to make this happen. But if it was the path, it could be true. The Christian Jesus may have been different than the historical Jesus, but belief had made him the one son of God, and belief could transform the world. His father had taught him this as well: thoughts were as real as matter. The idea of Jesus was as real as whoever he might have been two thousand years ago. And so instigating a biblical apocalypse meant that the Bible was the irrefutable word of God.

All of this nonsense about UFOs and hidden technology was just that: nonsense. His father said humanity was seeded by Saurons, evolved dinosaurs who genetically engineered human evolution. Was his father kidding? He had yet to prove it. It would have been laughable if it hadn't come from his father. Charles didn't like defying his father. He wouldn't have become president without his father's guidance. Maybe this was God's plan—to break away from his father and finally become his own man, like Jesus breaking away from the Jews. Maybe his father was being steered by Satan, the serpent. Maybe that's what these Saurons literally were. For the first time in his life, Charles thought his father to be wrong, which was worse than witnessing his father crying. It was a kind of patricide.

President Winchell would follow his father's plans, but only to a point. Benjamin Winchell had said that the president needed to start a religious war in order to usher in a non-religious, universal peace. This didn't make much sense to Charles. Either way, this meant that the Book of Revelations was prophecy. There was going to be a worldwide calamity, fire and brimstone, that led to years of peace. The Book of Revelations was true and Charles Winchell was in charge of making it a reality. He would usher in the time of the Anti-Christ and create world peace.

Many people didn't realize that the Anti-Christ wasn't evil like Hitler or bin Laden. The Anti-Christ is charming and beloved and makes good on seven years of peace. Charles Winchell was this man. Then came Armageddon, the 144 thousand saved and carted away, and finally the Second Coming and new kingdom.

Incredibly, President Winchell was going to play the role of Anti-Christ so the world could usher in the one true Christ. What nobody knew was that Winchell was going through one hell of an identity crisis—probably the worst case in the history of mankind.

12: God Bless America

"My fellow Americans, I greet you from an undisclosed location. These are troubling times for all of us. Believe me, it pains me to make this address, but the world is on the precipice of a major U.S. invasion. It has come to our attention that the attack on our citizens and our allies abroad was the work of men with connections to terrorist sympathizers in the Iranian government, as well as officials in the Russian government. It is the latter that is most troubling because Russia has been an ally since the end of the Cold War. We have reason to believe that munitions are being transferred between the Russian underground, Iranian militants, and terrorist cells throughout the world. We have determined the best course of action is to cut off the munitions supply at its source: Russia. Unfortunately, the Russian president has been unwilling to halt the transfer of arms across his borders. Diplomacy has failed. For this reason, we have no choice but to forcefully stop this aggression from occurring. We will not wait until the worst happens, much worse than the violence we have seen already. I urge people to watch the footage of the recent bombings over again. It may help to strengthen your resolve as we head towards this military engagement. Our goal, of course, is lasting peace. But as was the case in World War II, sometimes peace can only be created through war. Let me close with some scripture." He placed his hands together as in prayer. He said this more deliberately: "In Exodus, it says, 'The Lord is a man of war.' So even though times will be hard, you must know that we are doing God's work. This will indeed be our exodus from humanity's slavish devotion to violence. Our walk through the desert is almost over. I ask you to pray for our country in these coming weeks. Thank you and God bless America."

I turned the TV off. I'd been watching the broadcast with Dominique and Stephanie. I didn't care to hear how the pundits spun the speech. Their opinions were irrelevant. "That last segment is going to fuck people up," I said. "They're going to start believing this is a religious war. Even if that is the point. This is Armageddon."

"You don't know that," Stephanie said. "It might be short-lived."

"Did you hear the man? He referenced World War II. This is not going to end quickly."

"No, it's not," Dominique said, showing some impatience with my wife as well.

"Stephanie, are you going to admit the fact that something very fucked up is going on?"

"I guess I just don't want to believe it, Gene. That the end of the world is upon us."

"Believe it. It's happening."

"OK. I believe it. Now what?"

"Now, I don't know. We try to survive."

"I'd rather live than survive," Stephanie said. "I'd rather enjoy what's left than fear what's coming."

"That's a lovely sentiment, Stephanie," Dominique said.

"Thank you," she said curtly. "I understand what you've been going through. This speech is confirmation of every fucking thing you've been talking about. But what can we do, Gene? What can we do?"

She was tearful and I felt guilty, as if I'd made this worse for her. If she wasn't living with a doomsayer, she would at least be able to live out her life with some hope that things might get better.

"I don't know, Stephanie," I told her. "We can let people

know what the president is up to."

"And if that doesn't work?"

"We can try not to die."

$$-\!\!\text{\large /\!\!\lor\!\!\lor\!\!\lor}\!\!-$$

The next morning I woke up to the radio alarm playing the news, which was never a good idea. Waking up to bad information. The radio told me: "The president has worked quickly since his speech outlining attacks on Russia and Iran. Reports are coming in that Moscow and Tehran have seen bombing in civilian areas, in addition to munitions depots. There has been a general outcry from normally-steadfast allies such as the UK and Canada."

"A nightmare," I said out loud, as if to remind myself that I was awake. Since the dream in the warehouse I had to literally pinch myself to make sure I was awake. It didn't always work. The line between dreaming and waking was becoming blurred. My dreams were as vivid as life, my life more dreamlike.

But then I woke up again. Lying in bed, news playing— same newscast. "The president has worked quickly..." I got out of bed, muttering to myself, "A nightmare," almost ironically, as if ironic detachment would somehow ground me. Dreams weren't big on sarcasm. But really this was terrifying: because if I couldn't tell the difference between my waking life and my sleeping life, then my world really was coming to an end, regardless of whether or not I died.

I walked half-asleep into the living room where Dominique was splayed out on the imitation Persian rug, surrounded by letters and envelopes. She was confirmation that I was surviving, at least, if not awake.

"I've been up all night," she said, excitedly. "I've got it all together. The letter to the dreamers informing them about what's going on. All we need is a plane ticket for each person. Think Banski will come through?"

"He said he would."

"Good. We need to act quick. Planes could be grounded soon. Who knows?"

"Thanks a lot, Dominique. We'll do what we can."

"We'll do more than that," she said, determinedly. She was becoming quite the good foot soldier.

I almost believed her. I had to. If gathering these people together didn't solve anything then I had no other option except to die. I'd kill myself before witnessing world war firsthand. People talked of survival instinct. Mine was negligible. My plan was to break into a pharmacy, steal codeine and other pain killers, and permanently anesthetize myself. Forcing heaven while living through hell.

There was a knock at the door, which was an abrupt and terrifying sound. We never got visitors and I was half expecting government men at any moment, like I was being watched throughout this whole process. It was another possible comfort—that I wasn't alone, if only from a distance. Or I was important enough to be monitored, every paranoid's fantasy.

I opened the door. Before me was a homeless guy, bearded, brown with dirt, staring fixedly at the ground. Maybe this was a person from the list who'd made a pilgrimage here—I'd been expecting that as well. He looked up from the ground and I saw that it was Banski.

"Christ, Banski, what the hell? Are you OK?"

"I walked here," he answered.

"But you look like shit."

"I've been learning about Los Angeles," he said. "Best way to learn about a city is outside, not in any hotel."

This was a man who could afford $1000 plane tickets for 75 people.

"You want to wash off?" I asked. "We've got a bathroom."

"Yeah, I could use a bathroom," he said. He looked down as if seeing himself for the first time, slightly embarrassed. There was a hole, somehow, in the top of his shoe. Fingernails black with dirt like they'd been bruised. He reeked so it stung. "But later. Where we at with everything?"

"We've got the correspondence together," I said. "All we need are plane tickets."

"I'll get you the money," he said.

"Good, thank you. I've also been in contact with a woman who's been having some strange experiences. Like her dream life and her real life are blending together. She's been hallucinating, but they're not quite hallucinations."

"I'm not surprised," Banski said. "I've been working on something."

He rummaged through his bag: past ketchup packets, half-and-half, napkins, and sugar, to his old notebook. "In here," he said, holding open the notebook, which was more battered than before, pages wrinkled and stained. "I see what's happening here. Evolution's coming. The Mayans were right: there's going to be a global change in consciousness. Only they got the date wrong. Actually they didn't, but back in the seventies an alien race helped us divert a hit from an asteroid by changing the earth's orbit. It's partly why the environment's all fucked up, but not entirely. It changed the timeline. But they were right about beginning the Age of Aquarius. The Second Coming of Christ and thousand years of peace amount to the same thing. We're going to enter the dream world where our minds control reality. These dreams people are having are just flashes of what's to come. Telepathy, conversations with the dead, traveling from star to star without moving. Everything that's been kept from us. Our spiritual birthright."

"I hope you're right," I said.

"Of course I'm right," he said, grimly, like I was too stupid to ever believe him. "I've never been wrong about anything. That's my curse. This whole war is about the transformation of the species. The new evolution. Count on it. I'll see you later."

He started heading down the front stoop, his backpack slung over his shoulder, still open.

"Where you going?" I asked.

"To write," he said.

I watched him take a right turn down the sidewalk, hunched

over, nearly dragging his back leg like Igor. A cat passed by his feet in the opposite direction and he paid it no mind. Our neighborhood was full of strays. This cat was fat, orange, and looked pregnant, lumbering. As it passed by our house it stopped and looked at me. Its eyes were glowing red. I looked away and then looked back again. Still glowing red.

"I think I'll ignore that," I told myself.

—WWW—

The meeting of the dream subjects was a week away. Dominique and I took a trip to our local park. People were picnicking, jogging on a track, a Little League game was playing, and so on. I didn't begrudge anyone this. It wasn't entirely apathy to be enjoying yourself while the world was coming to an end. They didn't have the same evidence, though there was plenty of evidence, but what were you supposed to do with your two-year-old child except take her to the park, make believe everything was fine, because to that child everything *was* fine. You couldn't just hole up and wait. In this way going to the park was both comforting and impossibly sad. Evidence of life and evidence of what would no longer be.

We sat on a bench looking out on the playground, as nice a day as there could be. The sky was blue and cloudless, as if to demonstrate that life could still be peaceful.

"I can't believe this is all going to be gone," Dominique said, echoing my own thoughts. Really, there wasn't much else to think about. "People are just living their lives as if nothing's happening."

"Let them," I said. "They can't possibly know what's going to happen. It's almost better that they're hopeful until the very last moment. Fear isn't going to help them any."

"Shouldn't we at least be telling people about what's going to happen?"

"You know that most of them would think we're raving lunatics. People just don't want to believe what we know. So they won't. And if they believe us, then what? They'll be powerless to stop it."

"At least they'll seek shelter."

"You know that nowhere's safer than any other. Believe me, I've thought about this. It's a fucking tragedy. Everyone you see here will be dead. And maybe they won't die quickly. That's the worst of it. Kids are going to die and their parents are going to have to watch. Or the other way around. That's all war is. The worst nightmares made real." I stopped. I was shouting and my voice was carrying. A few parents were looking over, which may have been the intention—some way to tell them and get this off my conscience. "Believe me," I said, more quietly. "I've felt like the whole place needed to be wiped off the map. We're a horrible species in many ways. Strangely enough, this war is a perfect example. But it was only an idea, never a reality. Now I've never felt so in love with the human race."

"It's like that song by David Bowie, 'Five Years,'" she said. "'All the fat skinny people, all the tall short people. I never thought I'd need so many people.'"

"That song's about the end of the world?"

"Oh yeah, it's my favorite apocalypse song."

I almost laughed. We were silent watching the kids play.

"One of the worst things," I said, out of the silence, "is that somehow I'm responsible for the survivors of this stupid war. That our dreams are going to lead us somewhere. Maybe I just want to believe that this war has a happy ending. That I'm capable of something beyond myself. It's exactly like…"

I trailed off.

"Like what?" Dominique asked.

"Like something I used to fantasize about. About being well-regarded. A success. Important. Wish-fulfillment."

It was even in this book. I could no longer tell what was imagination and what was premonition. The book itself was a kind of dream—from a part of my brain I didn't quite understand. I was at the whim of my imagination, just as I was at the whim of dreams. I was never so objective that I knew what I was going to write before it came out. I wasn't that good a writer. But part of me always thought the apocalypse was necessary because the world sucked to shit in so many ways. So much needed to die, if not literally than figuratively, which was half the equation. Perhaps people didn't need to die, but thoughts did. And people were the representatives of thoughts, they made thoughts reality. I am speaking in the abstract here. I am not advocating genocide. The sadness and pain erupting from genocide was strong enough to become like another atmosphere. The indifference to genocide added another layer, so the first layer could never be cut away. At the same time, this world needed to start over. The bad was outweighing the good, which was not pessimism but the absence of repression. I won't say I was grateful for what was happening, but I did think it was inevitable. We'd managed to postpone it for a while and here it finally was. So many thoughts needed to die and it didn't seem like there was any way to rewrite human behavior except by shocking the shit out of it. Humans responded to a kick in the ass. A species that could produce the Holocaust, child porn, war, murder, and rape needed reworking. Our world was a nightmare, a tragedy a second. Something had to be done.

Most every religion had its eschatology, science had made it a reality. I wasn't anti-science, not in the least—but technological progress had built the bomb and killed the climate, helping to prove ancient prophecy. Was that just an accident? Or a realization that came from somewhere much deeper? I would say the latter because I liked to believe there were no accidents—everything is synchronicity, not just interesting coincidences. But that's off the subject, mostly. Armageddon seemed built into the human system, like death itself. It could have manifested itself as an internal rather than external apocalypse, a collective change in consciousness, but that would never happen because people weren't open to the possibility. With fewer people, it might be possible to finally transform the human race. There were just too many people, too many dangerously self-defeating thoughts, like a bad marriage comprised of billions of people—half trying to sabotage the other half out of resentment, envy, anger, and everything else married couples go through. Just look at me and my wife.

All this may have been a kind of demented hope on my part. To give meaning to the tragedy, even to give it a religious significance. Hey, maybe we're going to be in for 1000 years of peace! But that didn't give enough credit to the depth of my belief, or psychosis: you choose. On the one hand I felt like an evil dictator bent on world destruction, on the other hand I thought that the only way to achieve lasting peace was to kill most of the race off. Neither was a good choice.

"The meeting will help answer some of your questions," Dominique told me, by way of epilogue.

"It better or we're even doomed than I thought," I said.

—⋀⋀⋀—

Around seventy people were milling around Miranda Goodling's back yard. It seemed more or less like any party—though these people were different ages and ethnicities, all between the ages of 20 and 50, and didn't entirely seem like people who should be socializing; too many walks of life. It was more like an A.A. meeting, with some nervously eyeing each other, some grateful to be there, some loud laughter, as if laughter would drown out the uncertainty. But everyone was generally in good spirits. It appeared to be most of the people on the list.

No one knew me yet. They didn't know that I'd dreamt or written about each and every one of them. I wanted to keep it that way. It occurred to me, seeing everybody together, that this could become a sort of religious gathering. I had dragged all these people to this place, during war, each having witnessed millions die, and I was the person to potentially save them.

Presumptuous again, sickeningly so, claiming to be a savior, even if their own dreams were proof that this was not all my invention.

I was standing awkwardly by the food table—chips and dip, vegetables and dip, party food. Miranda Goodling walked up to me. She looked radiant. She looked pregnant, like new life was inside her. A totally different person than the one who had been beaten by these experiences. I would learn later that she had literally been beaten by her husband—over this, over everything. He had since moved out, leaving the kids with her.

"It's a good turnout, Mr. Myers," she said. She always called me Mr. Myers, though I'd asked her not to. "It seems strange to have normal party food. This isn't a normal party."

"People gotta eat," I said. "Thanks for all the work you've put in."

"It doesn't feel like work, you know? It feels like survival."

The doorbell rang and she walked assuredly into the house. A man stepped up to me, around my age. Didn't look much different than me, actually, but less Jewish. Sort of like the person they'd pick to play me in a movie. Every feature a little bit sharper, wearing a better suit. I had decided to wear a suit that day, not sure why. The only time I wore a suit was to weddings or funerals.

"Are you Eugene Myers?" he asked.

"I am," I said, a bit hesitantly. "But don't say that too loud. I'm concerned that people might turn this into a tent revival. They're so afraid, they're liable to believe anything."

"I'm one of them," he said. "As soon as I got your letter I knew I had to be here. I've been having the worst dreams. Broken cities. And I know it's real. I can sense it's premonition, not just imagination or paranoia. You normally wake up from a bad dream and think, 'Thank God it was just a dream.' I wake up and think, 'Thank God I've got some time left before this happens.' Your letter, it was like another sign."

"I've had very much the same experience," I said.

"Except you heard names, right? Of all of us? I never got

names."

"I think we've each dreamed something different."

"That sounds about right. I've been talking to people. One guy said he saw himself holed up in the mountains. Like a mountain suburb. And the weird thing is he saw people at this gathering in the neighborhood. He saw me there."

"That's interesting."

"Comforting in a way."

"We'll get everyone's stories together and see if it forms a narrative. Everyone's going to write out as much as they can remember from their dreams. There's a journal in the front hall."

"That's a good idea. Get it in writing. Like we all have a contract together. I'm Geoff, by the way. I'm an entertainment attorney, normally."

We shook hands. Firmly, like this really was some kind of strange business arrangement. Another partygoer stepped up to us. A middle-aged woman with wide glasses, wearing a crystal necklace and feathers from her ears. She looked like a New Age librarian.

"I overheard," she said, "that you're Eugene Myers. My God, I can't believe I'm meeting you." She squealed and slapped a hand to her cheek, dramatically, mouth agape. I got a bad vibe from this woman—a kind of insane earnestness. "In the real flesh and blood," she said. "You're like a prophet, know that?"

"I'm not a prophet," I said, flatly.

"Oh yes you are. You were witness to all our names, saving us. It's like you've got a more vivid window into the other side. You've gathered this flock together. Like a priest."

"I'm just one person," I told her.

"No, you're not. You've been singled out. We all have. Thank you so much for your gift."

She gave me a kiss on the check and gazed at me like no person ever had. Not lust or even love, but a look like she was eating me and ready to be eaten. A lot in those eyes. Both violence and surrender. A kind of self-rape.

The woman named Portia Farrow walked off. Geoff looked at me, smiling slightly, eyebrows raised.

"You better watch out," he said. "You don't want this turning into a religious cult."

"No, I absolutely don't," I said. "I've got to address these people."

Miranda Goodling's back patio was raised up from the backyard by a few warped wooden steps. I got up on the porch and shouted, "Hello, everyone. Please be quiet," and everyone was immediately silent, staring up at me, abruptly at attention. I had been wrong. They knew who I was, but they were keeping their distance. Some were looking at me the way Portia had done minutes earlier, both demanding and submissive. This was the first speech I'd ever given: "Thank you all for coming here. It was courageous of you to come during this difficult time, many of you leaving family behind. But I think all of you know how important it is that we met each other. We are all part of a puzzle that we are only now putting together. And let's be clear about this: no piece of the puzzle is more important than any other. We are all equals here, parts of a whole. So everyone enjoy yourself and get to know one another. We have a lot to learn from each other. Thank you."

I wanted to get the hell off that stage. There was applause as I stepped down. I stood on the faded grass, alone but watched. Was this fame? Is this what people desired? It felt like a violation; of both them and me. I never in my life wanted this kind of attention. Somehow getting external confirmation for something I once desired—people's recognition—felt much less healthy than keeping it private. A man, Indian, wearing wide glasses, walked up to me through the group, a blank smile on his face. The kind of mild smile that seemed like it could become violent. I was limp. He took my hand and he kissed it. I pulled my hand back. My lip twitched nervously. He walked backwards, slightly bowing, as if curtsying. This opened the gates and several more people came up to me. One, a guy in his twenties who looked like a teenager, touched my forehead with his palm, as if this was a kind of prayer.

I backed away and ran into the house. I asked for this, I thought. First thing that came into my mind. This was what I wanted. Effortless, empty worship. This was my fault, my own self-importance becoming manifest. My arrogance and my weakness. I needed to get out of there.

I ran to the front door and startled my wife who was just entering the house.

"Jesus, Gene, what's wrong? You look terrible. How's the party going?"

"Not as well as expected," I said.

"Why not?"

"Some people think I'm a saint."

She shook her head, disapprovingly. "Well, you finally got the adoration you've been looking for," she said.

"I was never looking for this," I said. "I'm not prepared for it."

"No one's prepared to be the center of the world."

"That's real fucking helpful, thank you."

I ran out the door and escaped my own party.

13: Book of Revelations

Charles Winchell needed to get down to work. A select few knew of his personal plans—which he had termed the Revelation Operation. The chief of staff, VP, attorney general, and a host of others. His own generation, not his father's. They all believed the Bible to be as real as God. Most importantly, the plan conformed to what his father wanted—the Order of the Ages declared by America's forefathers. His father would have no idea of the plan until it no longer mattered, at which point he would bow down to his own son.

First, Winchell traveled to Dubai and was instrumental in creating a new Middle Eastern coalition—The Union of Middle East States, a name that could only have American origins. TUOMES, or Tombs if you were cynical. It was a group of ten Middle Eastern countries, including Israel, and, as the broker of the deal, the United States. The world was ready for it—it's like the entire world said at once, Enough of this shit already. We couldn't carry on the way we were any longer. President Winchell was a hero overnight. America was once again a world savior. Winchell had started the war and had just as suddenly stopped it. This was better than retaliation, this was peace. We had turned a corner.

A note on where the Middle East was at this time: several years earlier, in late 2012, a Middle Eastern terrorist named Sahib bombed a synagogue in Israel. 100,000 people were killed. This was thought to possibly bring about Word War III, but the president at the time quelled the violence with diplomacy, much more tenuous than the new coalition. Since then there had been terrible fighting in the Mideast, but it was mainly quarantined—they fought amongst themselves. Believe it or not, things had not changed much in the last 20 years. The degree of death might have been different, but the reasons were the same.

After that bombing, there was a major drive to change the human system, much like there was now. Sahib claimed he had been inspired by a fictional movie about terrorism in which the same thing occurred. There was a push to censor negative movies and negative music. The 2012 president claimed these were a form of pollution, as damaging to the planet as carbon dioxide. He was a proponent of one-world government and a unified one-world religion. A liberal utopia. The plan didn't work. It created a nation of conspiracy theorists. There were revolts. It was called un-American, by both sides, and for good reason. The drive towards enlightenment was met with hostility—people just didn't want to be told what to do. It was this early failure in trying to remake American consciousness that had inspired Benjamin Winchell to install something permanent.

The new situation was much more dire than 2012. More people had died and it didn't seem like a solution was possible. As soon as he started the Operation, Winchell's approval numbers started going up. And why not? He was promising and delivering world peace.

I saw the Middle East coalition as part of Winchell's plan. A ten-state cartel came right from the Book of Revelation. It was one of those things that had to happen. This didn't turn me into a Christian convert, however. Actually it had the opposite effect. I was trying to explain the prophecy in rational terms. Though I had to admit there was always a nagging issue: a person aiming to fulfill prophecy might be the prophecy itself.

There were fundamentalist Christians of all denominations who saw the new events as prophecy fulfilled, but they got the schematics wrong. No two denominations could agree on the Anti-Christ. Some said it was Charles Winchell, but not many, only the fringe who were never taken very seriously. Basically every world leader or movie star had been targeted as the Anti-Christ at one time or another. Not to mention a cadre of New Agers who said this was proof that a new consciousness was coming. The Age of Aquarius was almost here. Let this happen. An institute in California was taking in converts and recruits by the thousands.

There were just too many circulating ideas. The plan could get away from them. President Winchell wanted to give people certainty. The time of interpretation was over.

And so President Winchell gave the speech of his life. He stood in the press room in the Compound, which looked no different than the press room at the White House, except without the press. The speech was co-scripted by Benjamin Winchell. President Winchell looked a little windswept, like he'd returned from a hard vacation, but still presidential. It was watched by more people than any program in the history of the world. It pre-empted everything, even the internet. It showed on every website. Due to Winchell's recent success, people listened:

"The time for hypothesizing is over," he began. "For too long we've had pundits yelling back and forth at each other, trying to gauge the political climate. Predicting elections. Determining how a scandal will affect the voters. What's the next step after a bombing. This is no different than sports commentators trying to predict the outcome of the World Series. They are usually inaccurate, based only on an educated guess, and trying to fill up space. The days of uncertainty are now a part of the past. What I give you today is literal prophecy: for the first time in human history.

"It is time to remake our world population. We have all lived through terrible events. We all have seen that humanity needs to change. If it does not, we don't have a chance as a species. Presidents don't usually talk in these terms, but that is how our world has changed. We are fighting extinction, not just each other.

"Certainly, the peace in the Middle East is an enormous positive. I don't wish to minimize that. But how long do you think that will last? We have proven in the past that we will do horrible things to each other. To think it won't happen again is denial—something we humans are very good at. Take a look around you. Have you led a peaceful life, or one interrupted by suffering and disappointment? Do you despair at the homelessness, immorality, violence, and basic degradation that have overtaken our whole planet? Are your neighbors as welcoming to you as much as you'd like? Are strangers friendly? Or are people sullen and afraid of one another? We have become an ugly people, capable of so much more. It is much easier to be cynical than positive, so that is what we have done.

"My goal for the remainder of my presidency is to change this cycle once and for all. Not through a slow reworking of Middle East politics, or better diplomacy with Europe, trade with China, and all of the other minor issues that have been the distraction of presidents in the past. No, I want to change the human soul. I want permanent peace. Not the tenuous peace written up in a treaty. I don't want to just delay the inevitable war, but bring the inevitable peace.

"How is this possible? you ask. The answer: a Second American Revolution. I am going to say things that no president has dared to say except in the privacy of the Oval Office. I am going to be completely honest and forthright about my intentions. Here it comes. Take a deep breath everyone." He took a deep breath of his own as if to demonstrate. "I am the Anti-Christ."

He paused as if letting this bit of information roll over every single person. You could almost sense waves of thought spreading across the entire globe after he said this. Anger, belief, exultation, fear. A slight, comfortable smile came to his lips.

"That's right. Men on both sides of the aisle—the Vatican, prominent Protestants, Muslims and Jews—have deemed this to be true as well. I don't want there to be any confusion about this. I am him. And what this means is that the Bible is indisputably real. As real as our country and the earth.

"Do you know what is so beautiful about this? If the Anti-Christ is here then that means the true Christ is soon to return. Without one there cannot be the other. That is how the system works. So believe in me. The sooner you do, the sooner He will arrive.

"Look deeply within yourselves. Do you feel like something has been missing your entire lives? The answer, of course, is yes. This is what you have been missing.

"I am the Anti-Christ, the first phase in what will lead to the complete transformation of the human spirit and civilization. True, lasting peace. This is joyous: it is finally here. Thousands of years of history have led to this moment. You are all fortunate enough to be a part of it. Rejoice."

He paused again, now looking serious, but a shade condescending, like a teacher of unruly children.

"I know some people will doubt me. That is healthy. I am not asking for blind faith. This is, after all, an outlandish statement. I realize that. But remember: I am the president. I am privy to information you do not possess. I know the truth of our origins, why America was founded, and where this country will eventually lead. I am not a man shouting about the End Times on a streetcorner. I am the leader of the most powerful country in the world. America is predestined to make the Second Coming of Christ a reality." He swiped his hand as if batting a fly away. "If you want proof, I will give you proof. Look outside. Wherever you are, it will be daylight, bright blue skies. Look now."

The skies were indeed blue, everywhere. It lasted a moment, but it was enough. Like a lightbulb in the sky blew out one final time. It was startling, to put it mildly.

"After this is all over, the result will be beautiful," he continued. "Eden before the Fall. Before we split into the fractured world we see now. Without the violence. Without the environmental degradation. Without the hate. No fear, only love. Heaven on earth. I hope you will come with me for this historic encounter with the Infinite. God bless you and God bless the United States of America."

President Winchell let out a breath as if he had been holding in his breath through the entire speech. The camera was switched off. So were the network of satellites that—somehow—mimicked blue skies. Winchell looked at his audience in the press room: his father, his mother, his chief of staff, and the VP who had recently arrived. They applauded. "I ad-libbed a bit, but I got it across," President Winchell said, smiling.

"You did well," his father said.

—◊◊◊—

It's amazing how words can be apocalyptic. It's also amazing how profoundly stupid people can be. The Anti-Christ of the Bible was a false prophet—someone who steers people in the wrong spiritual direction. Not to mention the Anti-Christ is only mentioned four times and the language is ambiguous. This didn't stop people from following Winchell. Even if he was the Anti-Christ, he would still bring them to the promised land, right? Many were excited. Never mind that he could have been wrong, or dangerous. Never mind that the blue skies could have been a trick of technology. What was worse, living in this world of constant war or the possibility that there could be eternal peace? Winchell was seen, by many, as a savior.

Of course it would be ridiculous to suggest that everyone immediately believed what Winchell was peddling. Including many Christians. He was called a heathen, deluded, insane. Every name in the book, but it didn't matter. Like his father had said, the president was in charge. There was no Congress to impeach him. No laws to stop him. He could claim, and do, anything. The rest of us, no matter how much we protested, were at the whim of his beliefs.

On the other side of the ocean there was more vocal opposition, and talk of military intervention. The feeling was that America was already bringing about the apocalypse, though much more slowly—through environmental destruction, cultural imperialism, militarism, and everything else people complained about. This was merely the end of the line. But other countries were in a bind. I could just picture the boardrooms of world leaders: We can go to war with America and take down the president—where was he anyway?—but wouldn't that just be playing into his hands? Giving him the Armageddon he's after? And if we did that, maybe it means he's telling the truth. It's lose-lose.

Yet many powerful people in government were also on Winchell's side. Even if the Anti-Christ was a fake, the war was something that needed to happen. Christianity wasn't the only religion with an eschatology. Hopi, Mayan, Islam, Judaism, Buddhism, Christianity: they all talked about the end of the world leading to a new consciousness. Winchell's Christian posturing was just a front. A method, not a reality. And so many leaders played along.

For example, Benjamin Winchell talked to the prime minister of the UK: Bradford "Duke" Ireland. Duke Ireland sounded like the name of a porn star but he was liked for many of the same reasons as President Winchell. A straight shooter. Didn't skirt around the issues. He could speak to both the working class and the aristocracy, even if—by some magic force—they were in the same room together. Intelligent enough to be respected, profane enough to be trusted as an equal. Currently, he needed to be appeased.

"What the hell are you doing?" Duke said. He was talking to Benjamin Winchell via a telecam on an internet-satellite link-up. The elder Winchell sat alone in his office in the Compound, as if he was the last man on earth. The room had glossy white walls like wet, white lipstick. He'd meditate on those walls as if they were both solid and melting. A mostly empty room: desk, bed for naps, and his private stash of books—the majority on spirituality, UFOs, secret societies, theories about the apocalypse.

"I thought we were going to do this slowly," the prime minister said.

"There's no such thing as slowly. Either we do this thing or we don't."

"It just feels like too much too soon. Suppose no one believes what the president is saying?"

"They will. Enough will. But even if they don't, it doesn't matter. Those who don't will always be thinking in the back of their minds: what if he's right? People have witnessed cities destroyed. They're scared, unhappy, looking for a way out. Unhappy people believe."

"But what if we're wrong, you know? What if this doesn't need to be a literal war? What if it is meant to be a gradual evolutionary transformation? Forcing people into it doesn't feel quite right."

"Haven't we already had this conversation?"

"Different now that it's here."

"Look, the planet is dying whether there's a war or not. We're taking the war to the planet before it wages war on us. There need to be fewer people if we're ever going to live as a collective and enlightened civilization."

"I realize this, but Armageddon is coming anyway, via environmental collapse. We could just wait for it."

"Then people will feel like victims, forsaken. As if they have no part in it. People debate that climate change isn't man made—there can be no doubt about why this war has started. People have to be in control of the apocalypse or there will be no desire to change the human system. Their beliefs need to be transformed. And besides, do you really want to see another Ice Age? We want to preserve the earth while we still can. If World War II was not the war to end all wars, we need to conduct ourselves differently. We are doing this to save the species, not kill it off. Keep remembering that. It's violent and it will be horrible, but we're in labor here, always painful. We're giving birth to a new human race."

He was very convincing. Not one cell of his body showed any doubt or remorse. He was only here to help. The prime minister signed off: troubled but sated.

Benjamin Winchell was right. Many people did believe in the president's speech. The speech did as much to American society as bombs. Hysteria, as you can imagine. Suicides, mass conversions to Christianity, churches raised in Winchell's name, a rise in lawlessness as if the president's actions justified any bad behavior, a great hostility to the U.S., basically a total disintegration of the past. The nightly news was really just a report on how the speech was affecting the local city, country, and world. There was no other news. The pundits blathered on—some for, some against, but they were increasingly useless. The people who defended Winchell said things like, "It's metaphor," or "It's the best thing to happen to common man." The people against Winchell said: the Bible is a myth, it contains stories of older cultures, don't take it literally. But they were powerless. Opinions didn't matter in a time of such psychotic certainty. We were all spectators now.

—◊—

Charles Winchell stared at himself in the bathroom mirror. He avoided mirrors, normally. Even his reflection in a building window as he was walking by. If this seems like an impossible quirk for someone who was on TV most of the time, he admitted it. Early in his political career, he watched his televised speeches over and over again. He watched how his eyes moved, how the twitch in the corner of his mouth betrayed what he was actually saying. Saw how he was aging. Saw himself through other people's eyes. Hated himself, really. Instructive, but he chose to never watch footage of himself again if he could help it. He rarely watched the news. Instead, he received printouts of important news with pictures of himself excised. This insecurity started in adolescence. At 14 he had contracted acne, terrible acne. He would stare at himself in the mirror, meditating on how ugly he had become. He thought if he could overcome his pubescent self-hatred, he would be invincible. Never materialized. And so he began to avoid mirrors because he was stronger without the reminder. A glance at his complexion was a slap to his soul. The habit never completely wore off, even into his 20's, 30's, and 40's. What this did for him was to not think of himself as a body, but a mind. A soul separate from a body. Not quite entirely living among the human race. It was helpful, in a way, causing him to spend more time looking inward than outward. He believed it had prepared him for what he was doing now.

He stared at his face, the contours, the cheekbones. He was a handsome man, he would give himself that. Women had always liked him. Men less, actually. It was his softness, though that had gotten harder with time. I should grow a beard, then I'd know. He picked up a book he'd gotten from the Compound library—a coffee-table book of Renaissance religious painting. His knowledge of art was poor. It was something he thought he should study, but never did. He started with Da Vinci's *Last Supper*—why not start at the top? Yes, there definitely was a resemblance. Charles was thicker around the face, more well-fed, but he did look like these older pictures of Jesus. That couldn't be an accident. There are no accidents. I am him.

Who was to say that the Anti-Christ and the Messiah couldn't be the same person? After all, the Anti-Christ would be the one to set the stage for the Second Coming; they were two sides of the same coin. A perfect duality, like man and woman in the same body. Anti-Christ and Christ. Charles was the most exalted person to ever live. Divinity is within me and watching me. I can feel it, pulsing like breath. My God, this is so beautiful. So much power I have—over people's minds, over the future. He paused. It's a burden, in a way, the responsibility, but I have been chosen to do important work. Even these thoughts, these words, arrive as if ordained. That is proof enough. I will change the world. Thank you.

He smiled lovingly at himself in the mirror. This was the first time in his life he was comfortable staring at himself for such a prolonged period. Body, mind, and soul had become one—each supporting the other. He was whole. He touched his cheek, his smile broadening. He looked back down at the painting. There was never a picture of Jesus laughing, until now.

14: North of Sunset

"So what do you say in response to the majority of people who see recent events as proof of the Book of Revelations coming true?"

It was an interview show, an interviewer I'd never seen before, bearded and slovenly looking. A cheap set—public access programming gone mainstream because that's all that was left. A priest was talking.

"My only answer is that it is not following the Book of Revelation exactly. And to clarify, it is *Revelation*, singular, not plural, though that's not how it's normally spoken. If events are not following the text exactly, the entire structure falls apart. The president has made his claims but there are other missing elements. Where are the seven years of peace? Where is the rebuilding of Solomon's Temple? Where is the battle in the Holy Land? So while, yes, these events are highly troubling, there are many missing elements for biblical scholars."

"That doesn't seem to be stopping people."

"No, but people have been making these comparisons for years, even welcoming evidence of a new Holocaust. I think if most people look outside, they'll regret ever hoping for war."

We sat at the bar, already past drunk, glaring up at the TV. Dominique, Geoff, and myself. The bartender stood watching as well—gruff, fat, the bar's owner.

"Rock on, Father," Dominique said.

"You mind if I turn this off?" the bartender said. "It's

depressing."

"Whatever helps you get by," I replied.

The bartender switched the channel, past a barrage of bad news—reporters in front of fires, collapsed buildings. Lunatic Christianist fringe groups thought nothing of setting bombs all over America to hasten the Second Coming. Their greatest claim was toppling Seattle's Space Needle with the force of forty times the Oklahoma City bombing. Winchell might have inspired a sense of calm between countries, but he couldn't control average people. I've already mentioned how the world was disintegrating with violence—Winchell's speech gave everyone, even normal people, new license.

"Thanks for staying open," I said to the bartender.

"If there's one thing people need to do now is drink," he said. "And I've got nowhere else to go. Don't know if I'd be running toward someplace worse. Might as well stay somewhere I know. This might be the last time we're gonna stay open."

I was surprised by just how normal this was: drinking in a crowded bar while the world died outside. The events had not changed us totally. Sharing the experience with other people provided a comforting kind of confirmation: that we weren't crazy, everybody else was. It was why the group of dreamers all decided to stay together in Los Angeles—some at my place, some at Monica Goodling's. We actually went out seeking possible danger—not safety. The safe thing would have been to stay at home, never go out in public. But you became sort of addicted to sharing the experience, as well as addicted to the adrenaline and the sense of righteousness when something terrible happened. And you wanted to share that righteousness with other people. I'm not being a prick—we all had this experience. Comforted by communal despair. So we drank in a bar and the atmosphere felt slightly normal.

"Where's Stephanie? Is she coming?" Dominique asked me.

"She didn't want to come. Too dangerous these days, she said. Didn't want me to come either. But I don't think I'm going to die now, unless my dreams are lies. In which case, fuck it." I held up my glass. "More sir, please."

The bartender gave me a refill. He wasn't charging, by the way.

"That party might have just complicated things," I added.

"People need you now, Gene," Dominique said.

"Need me? I can barely stand up straight without my knees buckling. I'm terrified. I'm mortified. I'm no leader. I—"

There was a huge explosion outside. It cracked the glass windows of the bar and sent bottles and glasses crashing off the shelves. It sounded like it was right next to us. My head and body pounded, as if the explosion had broken something open inside me. There was silence like a vacuum in the bar, some faint shouts outside. We walked cautiously to the entrance of the bar, knowing what we would find. None of us wanted to open the door, but knew we had to. As bad as the world was, we hadn't been subjected to violence directly, and now it had finally reached us. The door was opened and we poured outside.

A supermarket across the street had been blasted out—an Israeli market called Glatt Mart. A gaping hole like a mouth in front. Nothing like what you've seen on TV. That's what struck me—the total disaster of this scene, far removed from what had been revealed before, as if my window to the world had always been censored. I'd read about body parts littering the area after other bombings. Disregarded it because I couldn't picture something like that was possible. Didn't want to believe it so I didn't commit it to memory. This was evidence of everything I didn't want to face. Cars burning, body parts, blood—children, men, women, undiscriminating. The scene was soulless and demonic, as if reality itself was dead, or didn't deserve to live. Someone thrown clear so he broke through a manicurist's window across the street. A kind of absurdity: this couldn't actually be real.

We watched, frozen and silent, numbed. Then empathy took over and we ran towards the building.

I didn't know who to help first. As I stepped towards a burned-out bus, I saw Stephanie running up to the scene as well—her eyes wide with a terrible fear, a look as horrifying as the dead bodies lying around her. She ran up to a body and stopped. She hesitated and then turned the body over and mouthed, "No," but nothing came out. I didn't have to see who it was. Our daughter, Sophia. She wasn't overly battered, but she was gone. Stephanie looked up at me as I reached them—her fear turning into a feral kind of judgment.

"You did this," she said.

"What?"

"You made this happen. You did this."

"What do you mean?"

"Writing your book. This wouldn't have happened if it weren't for you." She was screaming at me from somewhere deep within her, as if speaking for all the dead. "You're sick and a coward. You fucker. This is your fault."

"Stephanie, I—"

"Fuck you. I'm leaving. It's over."

She turned and walked in the other direction, slowly, dazed, as if life was draining from her. I watched her go but didn't chase after her. I knelt over our daughter. I touched her shoulder. She didn't move. This was too easy, that someone could die. My mind went silent. I felt strangely indifferent, like I was a coroner. This wasn't registering.

Then my legs stopped working like they were no longer made of bone and I collapsed over her body.

—◊◊◊—

The next morning. I lay in bed periodically crying, overwhelmed by guilt. I hadn't moved us somewhere safer. I was being lazy, always lazy. Her face, her voice. I'd willed her death into being, like Stephanie said. I didn't deserve her and now she was taken away because of my selfishness. Stephanie had left. She may have been killed in that blast as well. She would not survive the loss of her daughter. I killed them. I murdered my own family. That's how I was feeling.

Dominique came to the room and stood in the doorway. She had been helpful throughout the morning, checking in on me, leaving me alone for the most part. I didn't want to share this grief.

"How you doing?" she asked, carefully.

"I keep repeating the night in my head," I said. "Did I really do this to her? Is this my fault?"

"None of what you've written is what you want to happen."

"I wouldn't be so sure about that. Obviously I don't want her gone, but her death makes sense for the book. It makes more sense for the book than for my life. I've done this to her. I'm a terrible asshole. I made this happen."

"I can't believe that, Gene. You wouldn't dream of that happening."

"Even so, she was probably on her way to meet us. I lured her out of the house. She wanted to come earlier—I wouldn't let her because I said it wasn't safe. We fought about it. The last words we had were a fight."

"Those aren't your last words," Dominique said. "What you thought about each other are your last words."

"That's a nice hope, thanks," I said. "We need to get these people out of here. It's too dangerous."

Dominique waved a piece of paper in her hand. "That's why I'm here," she said. "Someone told me about a dream he had last night. He saw addresses of the houses where we should be staying. They've all been abandoned by tenants who were seeking safety somewhere else."

"Do you believe him?" I asked.

"He was told addresses just like you were told names. He gave me the list."

She approached the bed and handed me the list, along with a map with x's on the addresses.

"North of Sunset," I said. "These are all very nice houses."

"We can retire in style," Dominique said.

—◊◊◊—

On the way to the neighborhood, we stopped off at an army surplus store. Geoff and I went. I was grateful for the distraction. I had a project to occupy me. And I was relieved to get the hell out of my house, every crack a reminder. It felt good too, responsible, as if no one else in Los Angeles was showing this kind of responsibility. A sense of superiority was one defense.

The city was still moving, even with yesterday's news about the bombing, one of several. There were people driving in the streets. Stores were open. Some walked. Maybe they were all overcome with a frenzy of terror, but on the outside it looked much like a regular day. Fear had permeated everything, but it didn't make people motionless, and the fear may only have been my perception. Miraculously, movies were still playing in Westwood. Classes at UCLA looked like they were open. Kids with backpacks. Like I said, it was much like any other day. What could you do: sit at home and wait to die? No, you kept being alive. There were a lot fewer people, like the Christmas holiday when many skipped town. But those who were there did not seem to be weighted by fear. It was comforting, even if fueled by denial.

At the Federal Building, a crowd was protesting. Signs in the air: Winchell is Insane, Honk If You Love Peace, The Apocalypse Will Not Be Televised, Impeach Winchell, World War III is Not The Answer, and so on. Some Christianists, far fewer, were also intermingling: HE is Coming, Relax and Let This Happen, Praise Winchell, and so on.

We parked and watched this for a few minutes. Some honking from passing cars. Some screaming between Christianists and protesters. All in all, it was like any other protest, a way to not feel pointless.

We drove on.

We rented a moving truck—one of the few left on the lot—

and bought a long list of items. It was like preparing for the strangest kind of party. Cost was no object because we could combine the entire group's bank accounts, and money might never again mean anything. We got cash out of the bank in case nobody was taking credit. At the supermarket, we bought boxes of candles, water, first aid such as disinfectant, bandages, fever medicine, many vitamins, crates of canned food—every type of bean you could think of, chili, vegetables, pre-made pastas, nutritional bars, powdered drinks, weight-gain drinks, cases of liquor, candy, coffee, and cigarettes for potential trade, something like being in prison. At the hardware store, we bought every type of battery, flashlights, a generator.

At the army surplus store, there were more people stocking up.

A man, by himself, looked like a bank teller, nervously browsed the camping supplies. He held up a jar of something.

"What the hell is liquid smoke?" he said. He looked through me, as if I were a ghost.

"I don't know," I said. "But you might need it."

He nodded, as if a ghost had silently answered.

This was the first fear I'd seen that day—not indignation, fear. At the market, it had been brighter, less grim. People were not shopping frantically, they could have been shopping any day of the week. We efficiently went about our business. I'd load up a cart, pay for it and load up the truck, while Geoff did the same. At the darkly lit, army-green surplus store, with fishnet mesh hanging from the ceiling, as if in a bunker, it was a reminder of what we were trying to avoid.

We bought gas masks, a strange purchase, heavy-duty clothing, an axe, knives—hunting, Swiss Army, I really didn't know what I was doing, camping gear of every kind—I'd never been camping either so this was all foreign. Tents, sleeping bags, portable cookery, more. Finally, I bought the most foreign of all: four guns and ammo. The guy at the front desk, around 50, looking both angry and bored, a lifer, told me, "I don't give a shit about the waiting period. Government laws don't mean a thing anymore. If he's going to go by religious laws, I'm not going to follow federal laws."

"I can follow that," I said.

"You're lucky to be here," he said. "I'm betting you this is all going to be gone by the end of the week. People are too stupid to stock up early."

"Anything else I need?"

"Radiation pills. Weapons. Food. That's all that's going to matter."

This didn't shock me. It was too much to take in. More, this felt like an unfolding cartoon. Stranger than fiction was every other moment.

We filled up an entire twelve-foot truck. Cost us $43,500. Cheap considering it was the best money either of us had ever spent. I realized later not everyone could afford this.

"Do we need anything else?" I said to Geoff as we were driving away.

"Think we're done."

We were both exhausted, like it was the first real work we'd ever done, mentally and physically extinguished. I looked at the people walking on the streets, the cars passing. Someone stepped into a fast food place. Fast food? I thought. You should be stocking up. A woman held hands with her son, as if they were just walking home from school. All these people might be dead soon and they were walking around as if this wasn't a problem.

"I feel like we should do more. Xerox our shopping list or something. Buy people supplies. Help people get prepared. I don't want to see more people die."

"There are fourteen million people in this city," he said. "There's not much we can do."

"It just seems wrong."

"It is wrong. This is a time for people to take care of themselves. If they can't, it's their problem."

I nodded absently.

We drove on.

We drove the truck full of supplies to the Brentwood neighborhood. Dominique was pulling up just as we arrived. She got out of the car with Sam, the guy who'd dreamt about these houses. Sam was wiry and sweaty—creeped me out a bit, like a guy who did too much yoga. They were both looking up at the house like tourists. It was a Spanish style mansion, sunk back from the street, shielded by tall shrubs. In front there was a black gate with a keypad lock.

"We have the combination, right?" I asked.

"Yes," Sam said. "2-3-6-6-5."

I typed it into the keypad. The black gate slid open. We walked onto the grounds—a stone-lined flowerbed, white ivy-strewn trellis, lights in the ground, idyllic—to the front door. Geoff tried the door, it was locked.

"Door number two," Dominique said.

I turned to Sam. "You dream anything about this door?"

"That we have to break in."

"How?"

"Fuzzy. I just remember broken glass."

"Fair enough."

I picked up a small potted plant and smashed a window by the front door. I was able to unlock the window and crawl inside, cutting my arm close to where you slit your wrist for suicide, then let everyone into the house.

The inside of the house was tasteful, but super-rich. Very feminine, flowered vases, pictures of flowers, antique trinkets everywhere, expensive and carefully done. If you had a lot of money and a lot of time.

"A real dream home," Dominique said.

"Very funny," I said. "A lot of us will be comfortable here."

Dominique jumped onto a long white couch, arms splayed out comfortably. "I could get used to this," she said.

"Don't get too comfortable, Dominique," I said. "The

owners of this house are going to die, if they're not dead already."

I walked over to the mantel and picked up a picture from a collection of family portraits. An older couple with their two sons. Other pictures showed young children.

"An older couple with grandchildren. They probably took off to their vacation home. Took the whole family, thought it would be safer than staying in the city."

"That or they're going to come back tonight and be very surprised," Dominique said.

"No, they're not coming back. We belong here. It's time for another dream."

—⋀⋀⋀—

The time had finally come: to figure out why we had all come together. I was still writing, but I'd reached the end of what could be accomplished alone. I even wrote a new chapter where President Winchell died, but Winchell was still alive. Which was actually a relief—it made me feel better about my possible involvement in my daughter's death. I couldn't actually manifest reality. My powers of perception were limited. There had to be a reason why these particular people were all having prophetic dreams. A collection of army cots were spread across the living room. The furniture had been moved to the side to make room. The house was dimly lit, just past dusk, the same night we all moved into the house. We wanted to get this done as quickly as possible. I addressed the group:

"I don't know exactly how this is going to work, but I do know that we have the power to do something extraordinary if we work together. Just concentrate on reaching out to each other—try to be lucid in your dreams. I know many of you have this ability. Try to connect our dreams together. Maybe our purpose will be revealed to us. We all came together for a reason. Let's find out what it is."

The entire group lay down as one on the cots we'd just

bought that day. It was eerie, shades of a suicide cult lying down together. Was I asking them to kill themselves? I had no idea what was going to happen. I had some faith that I wasn't going to kill all these people, that would be too cruel.

Somehow, I was able to sleep in these conditions, we all were...

I found myself in President Winchell's bedroom. It was dark, Winchell was asleep alone in bed. The entire group then began to appear around the bed, one by one, as everyone started to dream, standing in the wings around the bed. Some were flickering in and out, like a lightbulb with inadequate electricity, but most were in the room.

Winchell's back was to me. Geoff handed me an army-grade knife we'd also just bought at the army surplus store. It was lying next to him as he slept. I quietly approached Winchell's bed. Could I do this? Kill someone, thrust a knife into a person's body? I wouldn't have the opportunity to find out because Winchell's eyes suddenly opened, as if he'd heard a sound, or woken from a bad dream. As soon as he woke, we all immediately faded from the dream. I woke up on the white couch. Everyone in the room began to slowly wake up as well.

"Well, that was interesting, but it didn't work," I said to Geoff, lying nearby.

"I think it's time for plan B," Geoff said.

"What's that?" I asked.

"I don't know."

15: The Hot War

Winchell's fragile Middle Eastern peace lasted all of seven weeks, not the seven years of the Book of Revelation. With control of the Middle East, and the oil, the U.S. was accused of despotic imperialism: by allies. A coalition of Chinese, Russian, German, and French forces joined together to strong-arm America into allowing equal control of the world's resources. Winchell knew this was bullshit, and so did the coalition—they had access to advanced technology, both human and alien made, that would make oil obsolete. But oil was what we had at present, and in the midst of a potential world war the world military powers weren't going to suddenly start manufacturing new machinery. There wasn't the time. In addition, cutting off oil would have led to a whole other type of apocalypse: economic—too prolonged, uncontrollable, and uncertain. It would affect the rich as well as the poor.

This was a war of ideas as well. Many Europeans and some Americans thought a literal world war was unnecessary. The apocalypse was only internal not external. The Americans in charge thought otherwise. So World War III was finally waged to stop the Americans from going forward with their plan for World War III. It was a war to stop a war. On both sides this war was about controlling fate. The occultists on one side wanted to reveal information gradually—they had faith that humans could evolve without the trauma of war. The Americans wanted everything now. Two sides to basically the same issue: it was a war over the right way to bring about evolution.

Troops didn't have to mobilized, not like past wars. This war would mostly be fought in the air. No hand-to-hand combat, save what civilians did to each other—which was significant, and factored into the overall war plan. Islamic militants worked with American militias within the U.S. The American rednecks didn't care who they were fighting with, they just wanted the American system to die. A new breed of Weathermen, called the Forecasters—comprised of pro-worker, anti-globalists—were said to have joined the militia. An internal hemorrhage that only helped Winchell's cause. Random bombings of Federal buildings, freeways, fast food restaurants, and even hospitals, actually brought people into Winchell's camp. People with such a disregard for human life must be stopped. These internal acts of terrorism gave Winchell the authority to fight a war within the United States, in addition to fighting the growing threat from other countries.

Meanwhile, Russia was trading arms with Islamic militants bent on taking over Israel. During this period, Winchell preached disarmament for all sides. Israel complied (as part of the TUOMES treaty). In effect, this made Israel more vulnerable to takeover. You had to believe that every bad thing at this point was done by design. But it made Winchell look like a peacemaker and the opposition unruly. Winchell couldn't have scripted it better. The world was a complete mess with people unsure of who they were fighting and why, they just knew it was necessary.

Israel was invaded by Iran using Russian ammunition—considered an act of war by Russia. Jeremiah 30:7—the "time of trouble for Jacob." Winchell read this passage again and again, on the air and to himself. America bombed Russia into oblivion. Russia's allies—Germany and France—joined in defense of Russia. China, which was rumored to have been involved in the bombing of New York and D.C., began mobilizing into Europe. It was World War III.

Given that D.C. and New York were already destroyed, the

Axis Forces—yes, called that again, but more often called the Forces—had to find alternate targets. Bombing D.C. would have been target number one, but it was gone. The Forces had another major problem. A war usually ended when the side with the greatest number of casualties surrendered. But without any ground forces, this was difficult to achieve. Soldiers weren't even located at bases, they were spread throughout the entire world. Many reserve troops hadn't even been called up. Private corporate armies couldn't even be located. So where exactly to bomb? In this war, fundamental strategy was meaningless. More importantly, mounting casualties meant nothing to the Winchell administration: that was exactly what they wanted, for both sides. America had become one massive suicide bomber, every death a martyr and expendable. If there never was retaliation, it wouldn't have been inconceivable for America to start a general bombing campaign—America against the world and against itself. If they so believed in an idea, there was no way they were not going to make it happen. It was more efficient, however, and more socially effective, if the world war was indeed a World War.

What the Forces needed to do most was take out Winchell. Once Winchell was down, a new, less fanatical, government could take his place. But no one knew where Winchell was. The New Mexico compound wasn't a vacation home like his place in the Miami—his favorite place because of the turquoise beaches, so unlike mainland America. The Compound was Above Top Secret. Even if a bomb was dropped on or near the Compound, it could withstand the impact. It was designed to outlast nuclear invasion. The alternate strategy was to level America, as if we all represented our president.

The Forces first bombed Miami and the Keys, most likely because that was where they thought Winchell was located. This so outraged Americans that many Americans who did not support Winchell came to his side. Horribly maddening because this was exactly what Winchell desired. But patriotism and the urge for retaliation go a long way. Even though I knew what Winchell was up to, I thought, *The fuckers, go get 'em!* There may be no way to grow up in a place and not feel this way—just as you felt the insults of family more deeply.

And so there was retaliation. You just couldn't let that kind of aggression stand. It was learned that the Axis Forces were meeting outside Paris. Bombs were dropped, leveling the city. It was seen as a way to end this war once and for all—called a "peace bomb" to kill the warmongers—but really it was more of a kickoff.

The Axis Forces and the U.S. attacked supply depots, bases, nuclear arsenals, and so on. Many military installations were in or near major cities. It didn't do much good because it would literally take a handful of launching pads and submarines to do what they needed to do. The fallout after the bombing would kill as many people as the bomb itself—through disease, hunger and violence.

President Winchell did have something of a conscience. He wanted to minimize the aftereffects of war as much as possible. War was far worse for the survivors than those who died instantly, so the plan was to kill instantly as many people as possible. The bigger the war, the better.

—WW—

Winchell monitored the war with his father and cabinet from the war room in the Compound. They received computer and television data via personal satellites. They had a bird's-eye view of anywhere in the world, down to ten feet off the ground so you could read license plates, or even people's expressions. The uplink showed the war in real time over fourteen different monitors in the war room. To the Winchells, the war was so far a success.

"The war is progressing well," Benjamin Winchell said.

"People are on board," the VP agreed. "You know who's going to survive this? People who don't watch TV. Primitives. People who watch TV are going to panic and demoralize. For some, the world won't be any different."

"We don't care about them. We care about the people whose lives have been altered. Who come from the modern world. Those are the people who will shape the new society. Primitives already have their religion. Moderns don't."

"China is about to get involved," said Defense Secretary Seacroft. "They have a citizen army of a hundred million. They could land on our shores at any time. Word is they want to be in control of the population after the war's over."

(More people had arrived at the Compound since the war started. It was now seven people. Benjamin Winchell, his wife, President Winchell and the first lady, the VP, the defense secretary, and Chief of Staff Whitehead.)

"Let China invade," Benjamin Winchell said. "The East needs to become involved. We need to touch every corner of the globe. If soldiers invade, we bomb them right back. I'm pretty certain China knows this."

"Have you been in touch with Admiral Fu?" the VP asked the defense secretary.

"I have not," Seacroft replied. "This information comes via a satellite intercept. Though it could be a decoy."

"Does it matter?" Benjamin Winchell said with frustration. "Stop thinking like the 20th century. If they invade or if they don't our strategy remains the same. The hint of mobilization is enough reason to invade. That being said, I'd rather not fight them on our own soil. Cleaner that way. I'd rather Americans died with other Americans. Easier to manage after the fact."

"True," the secretary said, "but I think the A.F. [Axis Forces] are going to give up on trading bombing cities back and forth. They are going to want to occupy, rather than merely destroy. Possibly as a way to take the country hostage in order to negotiate. Then we'll have to deploy our ground forces. The worst thing that could happen in this war is for the A.F. to stop their bombing campaign. What happens if we have to fight on the ground?"

Benjamin Winchell paused, pensively. "Then we'll amp up

the bombing campaign. On our own soil. Get it over with as fast as possible. This war shouldn't take five years. Hell, it shouldn't even take a year. This isn't even a war, it's an operation."

"Operation is the perfect word," President Winchell jumped in. "We're trying to heal the sick."

His father looked slightly disgusted. "Kill the slogans, Mr. President. I don't need them."

Charles darkened.

The secretary of defense glanced at Charles, who was stewing like a teenager. "But what if we lose the people?" he said. "What if everyone turns on the American government? More people are joining the militias. That might distort our message in the long run."

"Shouldn't be too much of a problem. Americans believe in America, they'll side with us. The main media centers are down so no one's going to be reporting exactly where the bombing is coming from. They won't know who's bombing and may even think it's necessary. A poll before the war showed that most Americans believe in the Revelation myth—especially now that it appears to be coming true. By the time anyone begins to have doubts, the operation will be over. In the end, they'll believe in God and country like no one has ever before experienced."

—◇◇◇—

Charles Winchell's wife was crying. He approached her cautiously. Amy Winchell had never been the best politician's wife—she was the president's Achilles heel. She was not a woman who spoke her mind too often, who said inappropriate things. It was worse than that: she didn't care. She would rarely sit beside him at speeches. Mostly, she stayed indoors, reading. Sometimes she came with him to speeches, sitting right behind him, looking sullen and bored. She was labeled a depressive and got medication for it, but it didn't seem to do much good. The president and his wife were strangers to each other. Charles liked nothing more than giving speeches and feeling the will of the electorate. She didn't and he couldn't understand that.

Actually, she was well-liked by the voters, just not understood. "Enigmatic" was thrown around every time she was mentioned in print, which wasn't so negative a word. She made clay sculptures in her spare time, some of them nude. She was mysterious, which was better than being polarizing. Women admired her, men saw her as the quiet, inhibited woman that they wanted to know but never would. So, ultimately, she proved to be an asset.

They had married because he loved her. She was so much more alive when they first met. She was out of his league, smarter, even though he was raised by an intellectual father. She was something like his father—deeply intelligent and a great debater. They met in college and he soon moved away to New York to work in business. They started up a correspondence. She was the first woman he fell in love with for her words alone. He fell in love with her letters. She wanted to be a writer and wrote him a novel's worth of correspondence—real letters, not email. He'd kept them, even brought them to the Compound library, like you'd keep the ashes of a dead relative.

She didn't write anymore. She had graduated college, they were married—possibly for the money and security, he thought secretly. She'd grown up upper-middle class, but not regal, not what the Winchell family could provide. This may have been just what did her in, the security. Without the security, she might have worked, but she chose not to—partially out of agoraphobic fear, partially out of the lack of necessity. Picture her like a kept wife in Charles Foster Kane's cavernous castle. She tended to the garden, stared at an empty page, talked to the help, who regarded her with the same sense of mystery as the American public. She puttered, and she slowly faded. Even Charles could see that. She had her moments of energy, but they were bouts, never sustained. Never seeming entirely natural. Together, they set up a sculpture studio so she could bring herself back to life. It worked occasionally. Mostly, her indifference was Charles Winchell's private nightmare, the thing he kept to himself. He was resentful because his fortunes were always rising. If the worst people could say was that she was unknowable, then he was lucky.

Since they'd come to the Compound, she had started taking pills. At first she took some type of amphetamine. They didn't amp her up, they brought her to a normal level, she was that low. Anti-depressants didn't work—they exaggerated her mood swings. Her manic state—wide-eyed and sick happy—was a tragic thing to watch. Recently she'd discovered morphine in pill form. A French drug called Palfium. "They make me feel the God you're always talking about," she told him. They made her docile, at least, but she needed them always.

Right now, she wasn't indifferent or docile. She was crying.

"Charles, this is horrible," she said.

They were in their bedroom in the lower Compound. The master bedroom in the lower half of the Compound was almost identical to the bedroom in the upper half—same antique furniture, same size, but no windows. To counter claustrophobia, there was a greenhouse for indoor plants, a little piece of the outside. It was where Amy Winchell spent most of her time.

She sat in a small wooden chair in the corner. She was sitting, hands clasped, a comatose look on her face, like a frozen photograph of depression.

"What is?" Charles said.

"This," she said, and her face came to life a bit, burning. "All of this. Trapped in a hospital while the world's dying."

"It's not a hospital. It's a refuge."

She stared at him contemptuously.

"Like my father says, we knew this was coming. We can't be afraid now that it's here."

"Do you have no sense, Charles? Do you know what it's like out there? How many people are dying? Mothers crying over children? People in pain? People bleeding to dea—"

She started crying again, in a way that Charles had never heard, and he'd heard her cry a lot. From deep within her, but also above somehow, like she was being marionetted by some force other than herself. Maybe it was the pills she was taking.

"This is necessary," Charles said, trying to sound soothing. "If this war never started, we would have died anyway, but uselessly. Every death is a chance for a new life."

She composed herself and breathed out. "I don't believe it. People could change without being killed."

"They wouldn't."

"What if you're wrong, Charles? You're just a man. Have you considered that? What if you're wrong?"

"I'm not. This has been prophesied."

"By a myth. A myth with many interpretations."

It was Charles' turn to feel hurt. "It's not a myth," he said, deadpan. "There are many other stories that have direct parallels to it, Amy. There's a reason for that. We are fulfilling something inevitable."

Amy pinched her eyes closed. "Yes, you've told me that. Over and fucking over again." She paused, as if seeing how the profanity felt. "It just doesn't feel right. In fact, it feels like the worst thing that could possibly have happened. That we were being tested and failed."

"So you do believe in something beyond us?"

"Of course I do. Which is why I think this is so far beneath us."

She looked slightly pleased with herself, and turned that expression on him. How could she do this to him? Only she could do this to him. Make him doubt the most important moment of his life. She was smarter than he was and she knew how to use it. She sat there, condescending and certain. He hated this hold she had on him. She was doubt personified. The last challenge of his presidency. If he could convince her, his job would be done.

"I have something to tell you," Charles began.

"What?"

"You must be open to this," he said. In a way, this speech was more important than the one he had given to the nation. The nation was gone. This was for the world after the war, when they would rule side by side, finally proving the sanctity of their marriage. "I'm the Anti-Christ," he said.

"Yes, I know," she said, dismissively.

"It's not just a plan. It's true." He stopped. He didn't know how to say it much better than that. You had to really feel it to understand it. Otherwise it was like forcing love on a person. "I don't know how to make you understand this, but it's true. At first it was just an idea—to put the concept into circulation. But the prophecy is real and I'm fulfilling it."

She looked at him blankly, with more exhaustion than judgment. "You're crazy," she said, plainly.

"How can I convince you, Amy? We have been married a long time. You know that I believe in things very strongly. I don't enter into anything lightly. You have to believe me."

"Why do I have to?"

"Because we're married."

She ignored this. "I went along when you said you were the Anti-Christ on TV. I went along because I had no choice. Please, Charles—" she winced and gulped, as if the name was too much of a pleasantry. "If you believe this to be true, then you'll believe anything. And maybe this whole stupid war never had to happen." Tears welled up again. "You could have led by example, Charles. So much more could have been done. We could have gone off oil, stopped killing each other. Promoted peace, not death. So many ways the world could have been changed. You fucking, fucking *moron*!"

She yelled that last one, loud and shrill, out of character. She looked demonic, possessed. Her eyes were both dead and bright. Neck hot and bulging. He'd never seen her like this, except when she drank too much. For a six-month period, immediately following his election—what should have been a time for celebration—she became an alcoholic. Vodka. He discovered discarded bottles under a bathroom sink, as if she wanted them to be found. Drinking turned her into a different person, the person he saw now. "You bastard," she yelled now. Charles glanced at the bedroom door. Sound could travel down here.

"Amy—"

"You've made the world hell. You destroyed the world." More crying.

"You'll see," he said, fearful to see his wife dissolving. "Just wait and you'll see.

Maybe this was a test. A station of the cross. A way to test the strength of his own belief. Jesus went through worse than a nagging wife. Though it cut into him like a whip. He was regretful, but he also pitied her. To not know love as he did, to not realize your divinity. He didn't want to discard her, he wanted to rule alongside her: king and queen. A kingdom with the actual Christ on the throne, not a figurehead. He could picture it perfectly. Her devotion would be the final nail to prove his worth. She would come around, he was certain of it. As certain as he was in the outcome of this war.

"Fuck off," Amy said, as if reading his thoughts. "Just give me my pills."

Charles handed her the bottle on the nightstand.

16: Den of Iniquity

Dominique, Geoff, and I sat in our mansion's idyllic backyard. The entire group was now living in the house. We had other addresses where people could stay, but everyone wanted to stay in the same place together. Miranda Goodling had become a kind of den mother—making sure everyone was fed with a place to sleep. There were 14 rooms for 70 people, so you do the math: it was crowded, but no one wanted to be apart any more than you wanted to lose a limb. It was like our minds were a magnet holding us together. The house also happened to be nicer than the others on the list, especially the sprawling backyard. Brick patio, stone-lined pool, guest house the size of a single-family home, flowers everywhere, though some weeds were starting to get overgrown. Cutting a stark contrast was a shanty-town-like shack resting on the grass: Banski's home. It was a toolshed he'd brought over from someone else's backyard. He exited the house, still looking homeless.

"Banski," I said, "you know there's plenty of room inside. It's got indoor plumbing and everything."

"I don't like it. Too many people living in there. Too nice."

"It's the end of the world. No one's going to hold it against you if you sleep in a bed."

"Yeah, about that," he said. "What are we doing now? We just going to sit it out in luxury and wait for the world to burn away?"

"No. Of course not," I said.

"Assassination is out," Geoff said. "And I think it would amount to killing every world leader. The war is already in motion."

Dominique said, "We could make a video. Spread it online. Tell people what's really happening."

"How many people you think that's going to reach?" Banski said.

"It's a problem, Banski," I said. "Anything we've come up with is insufficient or makes us look like a crazed doomsday cult. Most people aren't going to take us seriously."

A bomber flew overhead, a common sight. Without that reminder, we could almost believe there wasn't a war. "But we need to do something soon or it's going to be too late," I said. "I think we've been going about it wrong. We don't need to kill anybody. We need to save people. Reach out to people in their dreams—tell them what's going on."

"I like it," Geoff said. "Viral dreaming."

"Exactly. Let's do it tonight."

—◊◊◊—

The group lay down as before. We waited until deeper into the night so the entire country would be asleep. It was one of the advantages of being on Pacific time. I nodded to Dominique who turned off the living room light. Again, it was tough conditions to fall asleep, but it was as though our collective sleep brought us to the same place together.

Darkness first and then a blinding white light. Some vague shapes could be seen, and then it came into focus...

I sat in the press room of the White House, just as Winchell did during his last address to the nation when he claimed to be the Anti-Christ. I surveyed the room and immediately knew what to do:

"Hello, everyone out there in the world. Everyone who might be dreaming. My name is Eugene Myers. I know this is a strange place for me to be appearing, but this was the most effective way to reach a large number of people all at once. My main message for you is this: Charles Winchell is mad. He is bent on bringing about worldwide destruction, killing all of us. This war does not have to happen. I have become aware of safe areas that won't be touched by this war. Whatever you can do, go to these places. The closest location will be shown to you, wherever you may live. Please listen to me. This is real, not a dream. When you wake up, write down what you've heard in full and tell as many people as you can. Please remember this and please be safe. Good night."

We woke up together, almost immediately. Geoff smiled at me.

"God, I hope that worked," I said to him. "I don't know what more we're supposed to do. I don't think we're going to save the world."

"I'm sure you just saved thousands of people's lives, Gene. Maybe millions. That's something."

—⋀⋀⋀—

I feel like I've been flip while writing this book. I don't want to seem like I'm making fun of what was happening when describing the ridiculousness of Winchell's story. There was deep pain here, so great as to be nearly unexplainable. Not only my sorrow about my own loss, but the collective loss we all shared together. Putting it into words seems to cheapen it—it was pure feeling. Really beyond comprehension. You needed other tools besides the eyes and the mind. It got to the point where you wished more people would die so it would all be over. Because even if people survived, they'd be left with a ruined world. I was one of them.

I could write about the myriad of tragedies, but it's so exhausting. A cop-out, maybe. But it also reminds me of those old antiques shows where you're rooting for each antique to be worth more than the last. I can feel the same pull here: how bad was it? How tragic? A bloodthirst that can really be comforting—to read or see just how bad other people had it relative to your own life. You'd be watching the news and see footage of a woman holding the amputated arm, cradling it, of her dead daughter. Gray and decaying. A newscaster asking, "How do you feel?" It hurt—the pain, the fear, the anger, the hopelessness. This wasn't funny.

It's so difficult to talk about this war without seeming over the top, or implausible—something that was leveled at me for books I'd written in the past. Too heavy-handed, too unsubtle. I can hear the critics now. This scenario is impossible, couldn't happen. What can I tell you? It's true and it's only inevitable if allowed to happen.

Paris hurt me most. I lived there my 25th year. In Paris, I learned that I wanted to be a writer. James Baldwin said that you never felt as much like an American—as much pride in being American—as when you lived in Paris. The same went for me, all proportions kept. There was real magic in Paris, just as there was real dumb superficiality in Los Angeles. The streets of Paris really did seem to breathe with love and art—striking to someone used to mostly cold and unromantic American cities. So in Paris I found that I wasn't some 25-year-old blindly writing, but I fit somewhere in the history of writing. History liked me. Even if my writing turned out to be shit (which I didn't believe) art was something to pursue and believe in, it mattered. In New York, I'd tell people I was a writer. They'd respond, dismissively, "Yes, but what do you do for a living?" In Paris, the question was never asked. I was a writer.

So this was my relationship to the city. To see it die was truly to see the end of history. It was the first major European city to go down but for me, and many others, it was the worst one. So sad. Worse than New York because it had been alive for so much longer. Even if you had never been to Paris, you knew this was a disaster beyond imagining, the romantic heart of the world dead. More than any other city: Berlin, London, Sydney, Tokyo, Rome, Prague, Brussels, Shanghai, New York, and on, what city could match Paris? The reason people sometimes hated Paris—its snobbery, its too-beauty—were the same reasons people grieved that it was gone.

We spent a lot of our time watching news. Even if it was painful. We kind of blinded ourselves with information, as if we were so overwhelmed the news would stop having any meaning. One after the other, we'd see reports about a city's devastation, usually by helicopter, and then those reports were no more, as if nothing about the city existed anymore. There weren't even reporters to report it.

There was some on-the-ground reporting. Maybe one of the benefits of this war was that news reporters finally became human, became themselves. I remember a reporter standing in front of a burned-out street, I don't remember where. He was surrounded by body parts—he must have been in the outskirts of a city because that was the only place that had a chance of surviving. "The smell is deafening," he said. "What did I just say? I'm sorry my brains are scrambled. This is a disaster. There's no fucking reason this should be happening."

It was refreshing to see a reporter speak like himself, not in the robotic cadence of someone controlled by something other than himself. It took this war to do that. It wasn't an isolated incident.

So the media weren't exactly puppets of the Winchell administration, though they were before the war started. The media became an ally. We were in this together. You might think that Winchell wanted to control the message, but in a war like this the more things were out of Winchell's control. Especially when so many media outlets were being decimated. The war took on a will of its own. Plainly there was too much news for there to be any relevant spin. Before someone could denounce one of Winchell's actions, the Axis Forces would do something terrible. Before long, opinions didn't matter anymore—not just because pundits were dying along with everybody else. Soon news reports were just the cold hard facts of what was destroyed and what was left standing. Nothing more. It was like the Allies and Forces weren't fighting each other, but fighting everyone who was watching TV. Everyone was an equal victim. If one side destroyed Paris and the other destroyed Chicago, no one could declare victory. It didn't matter who bombed a city, just that it was bombed.

Bombs fell in L.A. We could hear them from the house up in the hills. News reports said that downtown, South Central, Hollywood, most of Santa Monica, Beverly Hills, Silverlake, Echo Park, North Hollywood, the Valley, and points further east towards Palm Springs had been bombed severely. I should define what bombing meant. A new vacuum bomb had been introduced in the last five years. It vaporized living things—people, plants, and animals—while leaving the buildings still standing. I have no idea how this bomb worked so I'll make no attempt to explain it. It had something to do with vibrations discovered with string theory. The bomb vibrated matter into oblivion. This would eat away at buildings as well so they'd crumble away as if hit by an earthquake. Like conventional bombs, the point of impact was worst off. The radius from a bomb was five miles. These were combined with conventional bombs—it should be mentioned too that missile propulsion was faster, so the missiles could be fired from anywhere in the world, not just offshore. There were rumors of diseases spreading among refugees. These were the things we feared. The sound of the string bomb was unsettling—like satanic backwards masking heard in the distance. The sound became as common as helicopters flying overhead.

And then the power went out. It wasn't all that bad, actually. We had plenty of candles, lanterns, and a generator. But instead of forcing light, we went to sleep soon after it became dark and woke up early. Better for the spirit than to be suddenly thrust into the 19th century. Washing clothes was something I hadn't prepared for—or else I would have bought 50 pairs of the same pants. But we managed. The practical concerns got worked out fairly seamlessly, without thinking. It wasn't a struggle anymore than it was a struggle to eat food at room temperature.

We didn't open the front door, as if letting in air was an invitation to let in the outside world.

I could write some dialogue here, some conversations. But there weren't many. The silence was—as if to show respect—like a graveyard. Anger had died, and even fear. There were no more dreams either. What had replaced them was resignation. Sometimes we played with Miranda Goodling's kids, Abbie and Daniel, which was a particularly regretful experience—like they were the last kids on earth. But even they kept to themselves, understanding this was a time for reflection. We lived mostly in the world of our own thoughts. Like a freeway sound was blaring, the noise being our pensive thoughts, wiping out other conversation. Someone might open up a can of something in the kitchen. And I'd say, "What's that?" He'd reply, "Baked beans," as if it said everything. At least our shopping expedition had proven to be useful.

I hadn't been to most of the cities that were destroyed. I always figured I would. See most of Europe, tour the Far East. Always kept in mind as an inevitable goal. But as was often the case with my feelings of inevitability—most often exhibited by faith in my success as a writer—it would not happen. There was so much I wouldn't accomplish. So I mourned what I would not do, as well as my memory. I think we all did. We also mourned the human race—not just those who died, but the race itself, for failing. When you're mourning the human race, you mourned your place in it. It wasn't all self-pity, quite the opposite. You thought about how much you loved the human race, how much a part of it you were. Really, this was an intensely positive thing to come out of the war. But it was overwritten by such grief. Our life together did give me some comfort: it gave me the feeling that the war might make some sense. Perhaps because of this the war did not totally kill my spirit. For many, they didn't die by being literally ripped open but just plain heartbreak.

I thought about New York City. I lived there for most of my

twenties, my adult adolescence. I sat in an L.A. stranger's living room and for some reason thought about a time I went to visit the Columbia University writing program. I had a horrible crush on a student there—an Australian girl named Lucy. Perfectly elegant, intelligent, and beautiful. Out of my league, the kind of girl I realized later probably only went out with older men. We set up a time for her to give me a tour of the program. She was a student. We agreed to meet at a nearby coffee shop. I thought this was the girl who was meant to be, I'd found her. A foreigner would understand my passion and talent, everything I held too privately, even if I was not yet a man. I was early. I sat on a church stoop. A homeless guy asked me for money. I gave him a subway token, my fare home. I wrote in a pocket journal that my life was about to change; a prayer. She was late. She ran up huffing, saying, "I'm so sorry. I just forgot." Not disinterested, indifferent. It occurs to me now that that she might have been in bed with someone else and missed the date. I was not very objective at this point. I didn't understand how other people's lives worked without me. I dreamed that she was thinking about our date as I had, as if it was a beginning for her as well. She showed me around the school—comfortable students milling around. I tried to make conversation. I looked down at my thumb and found that it was covered with blood. I didn't realize I had been picking the cuticle of my thumb to shreds. My thumb looked like it had been dipped in paint. How is it so red? Oh. She noticed it at the same time as I did. "Places like this make me nervous," I said. "I don't like writing school. If you can't be a writer on your own, you probably can't be one at all." I wanted to tell her everything about myself. She looked insulted, of course. "Well, why don't we go outside and leave this den of iniquity," she said. Sitting on some steps, she told me the logistics of going to school there, what classes were like, the amount of homework. As if I was anybody, a touring student, which was exactly what I was. She left. I sat dejected on the Columbia steps, imagining judgment from the other students, who looked as elegant as

Lucy. My thumb was still caked with blood.

I wrote a novella about this experience soon afterwards. The story was about a man released from prison after killing his girlfriend during sex. She asked him to tie a belt around her neck and tighten it during climax. He goes to live with his brother's family and begins working at his brother's wife's bookstore. There he meets a British girl, Eloise, who represents everything he cannot have, everything that's gone wrong in his life. He wants to confess to her, tell her everything about himself. If she can understand him, it's as if his past doesn't exist. He tells her that his girlfriend asked him to kill her, it wasn't an accident. The confession doesn't go over well. She storms out, hates him. He goes back to the coffee shop where they once met and he does something that gets him thrown back in jail. It was an exaggeration of my infatuation with the girl and my self-hatred for not having her. The first real autobiographical writing I'd ever done, even if it wasn't, technically. It was never published. I think it got too sentimental.

Why do I mention this now? It's an example of the disparate things that came rushing to me during that time. Not the worst experience, relative to the world outside, and relative to the loss of my family, but maybe that was the point. It was a small memory but it was a reminder of what it was to be alive—these things that seemed to hurt my soul at the time had some purpose. Which led me to think about the war, while a total disaster, had its good side. Never before had I so appreciated life. It was like being high: a revelation which said, You're in love. Fear was eye-opening, unfortunately, as powerful as love but much easier to come by. Our life inside the house—quiet, austere, almost reverential—was peaceful. We knew our lives would never be the same, but our lives were still standing. The books on the shelves, the music collection, our memories, each other. Everything was a reminder both of what was dying and what was alive. You don't normally get to live your life with this sort of appreciation, or this kind of remorse.

There was a lot of time to reminisce. But most of it wasn't spent meditating on dying. As bombs went, the string bomb was thought to be quick and painless. If it happened, it happened. In this world, we'd be as lucky to die as we were to live. Mostly we waited, a limbo state between life and death. Heavenly in its respect for what was good, but closer to hell because of what had inspired it. When we talked, ate, played, read, watched the news, we waited to see if we would die too. Which meant, really, that we had died already.

17: Ice Cap

It was the beginning of the end. Which meant Phase II would now be initiated. It better: the war was almost over and President Winchell didn't feel any different. No prophets had come to greet him. There was no rapture—though he was almost certain the rapture was for those who were left to inherit the earth, the people who would eventually experience heaven on earth, not those who had died or were otherwise taken away. There may very well have been 144,000 people left on earth— the number of the rapture. It was impossible to determine the actual number at the moment, but it was an obvious possibility.

Whatever the case, the war had worked. The population had been decimated and not every region had been destroyed. Many of the nicer areas of the world had been preserved, as had been planned. All the plans in the world and war was a monster of its own. No president was so powerful that he could control how war unfolded, every human mind. At least not yet. People could have decided to torch these Safe Areas and there was little the administration could do, considering most of the National Guard were dead. But the plan had worked beautifully. They had only to check their satellite to see what was still standing— some of the nicer real estate in America and the world. Middle Age castles still standing. The new seven wonders: America's richest neighborhoods, and many tourist attractions. They hadn't saved the Taj Mahal, Mann's Chinese Theatre, others, but that could be expected.

Phase II meant bringing everyone together and beginning the new kingdom. Maybe then, Charles thought, his divinity would finally be ordained. As of yet: nothing. No divine power. Not even a greater warmth of mood, like drinking good wine, besides his own conviction. He'd even spent a moment staring at a rock, trying to turn it into bread, but then felt silly about it and stopped. When would it happen? Maybe there needed to be a ceremony, like an inauguration. A wedding ceremony where he was wed with God. Naturally, he was very eager for this all to begin.

He approached his father in the war room. Benjamin Winchell spent most of his time in the room monitoring the war's progress and relaying orders. Charles didn't do much of anything in terms of strategizing. That was fine with him. The war belonged to his father. The aftermath belonged to the son. He would have liked to be a little more instrumental in tactics and strategy, but it wasn't his strong suit. He justified: his father was good at destroying, Charles was good at creating. Charles was still the commander in chief, his father was a general, so for the time being Charles would use his father like his father used soldiers.

Still, Charles liked to be informed and to interject an idea when he could. Benjamin spent most of his time watching the monitors, aiming the satellite cameras over the globe. It was much easier to watch it unfold in this way, like watching an anthill. There weren't any voices on the ground, no sound at all—like watching an epic silent movie of the earth falling apart. Benjamin could launch missiles from where he was sitting, so the chain of command was hardly necessary. There were not a whole lot of new orders to relay to the field—the theater. If you asked Charles, his father spent entirely too much time in there; every waking moment. He had brought in a cot so he could sleep in the room as well. He immersed himself. No one was going to stop him, but it seemed unhealthy, even if necessary. Someone had to do the dirty work. No one much cared for the actual killing, just the result.

When Charles walked into the war room, around noon, after eating a nice vegetarian meal—he'd recently become a vegetarian because he didn't think it right to eat God's creatures, as if they were his cousins and it was a form of cannibalism—he found his father watching the monitors, bathed in light, with flickering scenes of devastated ground, devastated buildings. Not too many people that Charles could see. He didn't look too long, much like he instinctively looked away from mirrors. The effect of the war was like looking in a medical dictionary at someone's diseased and disfigured skin, cancer of the mouth—fascinating, but worrisome about what you could become.

"Hello," Charles said, breaking the silence of those images.

His father bolted upright and turned around sharply, like Charles had caught him masturbating. This had happened to Charles before, caught by his father. Watching TV as a teenager, his pants unzipped, no way to cover up. For some reason the awkward and mortifying memory shot into him. His father's eyes now showed a similar look of derision and embarrassment.

"It's almost over," Benjamin said.

"That was fast."

"Yes. War's very quick when there are no rules."

Charles nodded. "What's next?"

"In my estimation, the population centers have been destroyed. Every city on earth. But it's not enough. We need to shrink the size of the earth as well."

"What do you mean?"

"Project Burn."

"Project Burn?"

"Targeted bombing of the ice caps, get most land underwater. The problem is that the earth is just too damn big. It cements people's differences. There's no way to start a utopian community on as big a scale as earth. Someone should have thought of that when they made the planet."

This was the first Charles had heard about Project Burn and

he wasn't entirely happy about it. The earth was God's design. This was equivalent to playing God with the planet's surface. Though this could conceivably be the fire and the brimstone of the Bible. But why wasn't Charles told about it? What else didn't he know?

"OK," Charles conceded.

His father nodded blankly.

"And how long after that can we begin the next phase?" Charles asked.

"When it's all over and we make our population assessments—a final census of who's left—we'll start to round everyone up. The survivors will be looking for guidance. That's what I'm counting on. Here come the Americans. Even if we started this thing, they'll be grateful, and familiar with what our country has done in the past. Enough military is left to help start the new world and new government, just as we intended. I've got a name for it too: the New City."

"I thought we settled on New Jerusalem."

"You settled on that, Charles. It's too biblical, too loaded, exactly what we're trying to get away from. I like New City. Pithy, says everything it needs to."

This was getting worse. "What about the revelations?" he asked plaintively. "When do they come?"

"After we get everyone together and establish ourselves—determine how angry people are, or how willing. My guess is that people will be complacent, just glad that the whole thing is over and wanting to start anew. Then we can establish first contact."

That appeased Charles for the moment. He wasn't sure exactly how he would be crowned, but his father's plan made sense with his own. Get the New City together and then Charles' reign could begin, King Charles. Mostly the wealthy had survived, so he would rule over those men and women who had been blessed since birth. To rule over them would be a greater majesty, power over the powerful. Many were actual royalty, blood passed down like an heirloom through centuries.

Many also knew about Charles' plans for the new Christ, in opposition to his father. It would be glorious. Once they came out of their bunkers, they'd fly to the area they'd designated for the future seed of civilization: the luxury homes in the area north of Sunset in Los Angeles, California.

Charles had to admit that he was a bit confused. Where was the battle between light and darkness? Jesus was supposed to descend at the end of the war and there was to be an epic battle with the Light Bearer, Satan. Was it something so simple as America was Jesus and non-believers were Satan? He thought it was going to be something more obvious than that, less metaphorical. He hated when the Bible was reduced to symbolism. His faith was that this war would make the Bible indisputably real, for all people. There was supposed to be a clash of supernatural entities, of which he was one, the first proof of a real God. Certainly, America could represent Jesus, but he wasn't concerned with symbolism or representation, he wanted empirical proof. And that hadn't happened.

But he wasn't doubting. No sir. The war was proof enough that prophecy was coming true. The rivers were indeed flowing with blood. He'd seen it on satellite, actually red. And he was in charge of making that happen. Perhaps the final battle between light and darkness had yet to be waged. Perhaps this Satan had yet to emerge. Yes, that made enough sense, he thought, and his mind was quiet.

All they had to do was wait for more people to die.

18: Descending on Los Angeles

The water rose and washed away Los Angeles. The flats were underwater, the people in the hills were spared. At least the parts that were not also bombed. The Hollywood Hills had burned down and the fire had spread as far west as the 405, where the freeway cut it off like a moat. Beyond that, from what information we could gather, L.A. was mostly leveled. There were barely radio reports anymore. Radio hosts and newscasters had fled, saving themselves. Mostly what we knew were from hearsay accounts from the internet, which existed sporadically, and some overhead images—not in real time—of L.A. destroyed. We stayed away from those images for the most part: too sickening, depressing, and terrifying. Here in our home, still standing, it could appear as if the world was still whole. That illusion was a comfort.

I walked through the house—it was a mess, 70 people living together. I tripped over someone's bag and found Geoff, who was flirting with a young follower. Turned out he was a ladies' man. Insanely—every able woman in the house. She fled quickly when I approached, almost fearfully, as if we had important business and should never be disturbed. I didn't like that was the way people acted, but I couldn't stop it.

"We need to move on to the next phase," I told him. "There haven't been bombings for several days. Perhaps we should get a search party together. Look for other survivors we can bring back here. Before Winchell gets here and does whatever he's going to do."

"I agree with that," he said. "I'll get a group together. Gather weapons. At this point we need to be as wary of other survivors as the military. If there are any left."

"We may have to get everyone together and start our own civilization," I said.

"However that's done."

"Right. However that's done."

—∿∿—

I crossed the threshold of our front door. A caveman going out into the African prairie watching for predators—especially eerie in this neighborhood of mansions and abandoned luxury cars. We had ventured out before in quick bursts to get food or clothing from other houses, but not for a long time, and this was the first time I'd gone out with the idea that it could be permanent. The grass and flowers were overgrown in the front yard. Not really a shocking sight. Actually, it was nice to see it less manicured, to see it come to actual life. Or maybe this was a way to feel less nervous: there's something good out here.

I unlocked the front gate. I expected a loud explosion when I did this, like it was rigged with a mine. But there was just the click of the latch, which to my mind was as loud as an explosion invading the silent neighborhood. The street in front seemed deserted and untouched. Some debris, but that was about it. I can't stress enough how unfair the calm of the neighborhood seemed, privilege upon privilege. Alive and rich. Most people appeared to have left, the street was quiet. The neighborhood didn't seem to be overtaken by strangers. It looked, generally, like any other day. House after house, each unique, unlike many suburbs, each someone's dream home. How many other people were holed up in their houses and how many had fled? At the moment it felt empty.

I walked up to a house and knocked on the door. If someone had come and knocked on our door we probably would have stayed inside, shivering, hands on guns most of us didn't know how to use, and waited for them to leave, or nervously started shooting. But I was here to investigate. So I did.

It was an old rustic house, one of the only remaining older houses along with the place where we were staying, many of the others torn down and replaced by bloodless, three-story mansions. I turned the doorknob and, strangely, it was open. There was no way we would have kept our door unlocked, although it would have been just as easy to break a window. Locking the door was more of a ritual than practical. Maybe the house had been broken into before. I walked into the front room. Light poured in from the large windows in the front and back. A nice house, nice people lived here, not ostentatious. Maybe not even very rich, they'd bought their house decades earlier when prices were lower. "Hello," I called, and then thought of saying, *I come in peace*, felt stupid, and instead said, "I'm your neighbor." No response, no sound, no one was here.

A strange experience walking into somebody else's home. Something, honestly, I always wanted to do—explore people's lives, investigate without being asked. Maybe that's half of writing—exploring what you're not allowed to otherwise, and you can't just walk into somebody's home out of the blue. Much too literary for the moment. It was time to be practical. But my mind was running rampant with all the new input after being stuck inside for so long.

The house seemed peaceful and untouched, like the neighborhood. Dust had gathered, but not an obscene amount, not much more than when you neglected to clean the house. Pictures on the mantel, books, a TV—same stuff, only different. Useless to me now, except as a window into their lives. A thought occurred to me—the new TV would be walking into people's houses and making up stories about them—each house a different channel. There might even be a book in that. Fuck, will you shut up? I could never get rid of that bug, even now. I headed for the kitchen, the useful area.

In the pantry, there were some usable cans of food—tomatoes, garbanzo beans, ketchup, etc.—the only useful thing when you boiled it down, besides the curiosity, which was actually useful, the curiosity, to stay interested, to think about things other than survival.

I peered into a couple more houses, dark and still. I had a fair estimation about what had happened now. People who were unprepared went looking for food and then got caught in whatever happened further south. The remaining family went to look for them and didn't fare better or moved in with other family members if they lived nearby. Maybe they left altogether. Many of these homeowners had second homes in Lake Arrowhead or other resort communities. Maybe they went there. I would have. The end result was that many of the houses were empty. No sound, except for a few birds. It's possible some people were peeking out at me from behind curtains, using me as a scout. But I couldn't sense anyone there. The air felt lifeless.

I got back to the front of our house. We had keys to a large black electric SUV that was parked in the garage. A group of four men were packing weapons and supplies into the truck: Daryl, Jesse, and Kyle, plus Geoff. It was a thuggish group, not too different actually from the gang of terrorists I'd seen in the warehouse. They were the most like military men in our lot. They seemed to be playing the part of tough, or what I imagined to be tough.

I opened the door of the truck to drive us down south. Portia, the fanatic from the party at Miranda Goodling's house, ran up to us, breathlessly. "Dr. Myers," she said—she insisted on calling me this even though I'd never earned a Ph.D. "Before you go, I want to show you something."

She held up a large glossy book of nature photography—*Animals of the South Pacific*. She opened the book to a picture of an orange finch sitting on a branch.

"Now take a look."

She stared at the book intently, like it was one of those old magic eye books that revealed a hidden picture. The small bird suddenly flew out of the page and into a nearby tree. It sat on a branch looking no less confused than we did. In the book, there was no longer a bird, just a picture of a branch.

"Holy shit," Geoff said.

"I made that happen," Portia said. "Just by thinking about it. Something is happening here. Our world is changing."

"Do you know of anyone else who can do this?" I asked.

"No, but I don't think I'm going to be the last."

She handed me the book and then ran back to the house, as if afraid to be outside for too long. I threw the book into the truck and got behind the wheel, awed and feeling a little bit sick. Like I was the bird from that book being watched from above, and someone could suddenly imagine that I'd cross into some other life. Or I could do it myself, which was unsettling enough.

We drove towards the city, barreling down the empty street past other mansions. The rest of the neighborhood was also barren. Kyle sat in the back seat staring at the nature book, a picture of a zebra.

"Hey, don't go releasing a zebra in here," Darryl said, half-joking.

"Don't worry, I'm not doing anything." Kyle slammed the book closed—a mixture of both frustration and relief.

"What do you think about that book?" Geoff asked, sitting in the front passenger's side.

"We seem to be on the front lines of a major shift," I replied.

"Banski calls it evolution," he said.

"Are we so much more evolved? Why the members of our group?"

"Maybe it's random, like any leap in evolution. Survival of the fittest."

"Right, but if we're able to make our hallucinations real it might be like giving an ape a nuclear weapon. What's so strange is this leap was the objective of the war. Only it's happening to us, not the Winchells. Why do you think that is?"

"Because we're not evil," Geoff said.

"We're not God either," I said. I looked in the rearview mirror at the group. "Keep an eye out. Be careful out here. Anything is possible."

The houses rolled by. Not one house was damaged up here.

"Look at all these places," Darryl said. "Empty. Maybe everyone in our group can have their own house."

We passed a strangely-shaped mansion, jagged-modern and colorful.

"I call that one," Jesse said.

Sunset Boulevard was a larger shock. I expected at least a military presence. But there was nothing. Not even the sound of a distant car. Sunset Boulevard without traffic was like a body without blood. I had deluded myself into thinking some life remained. It couldn't *really* be the end of the world.

We crossed Sunset against the light—there was no light at all. Still, it felt like we should wait, as if there was a mystical resonance of all the people who had stopped and waited at that light. I don't know, maybe it was my mind trying to hold on to the old rule of law and routine. It was only a brief hesitation, but meaningful, because after the hesitation came a sense of freedom as well—the ability to do whatever we wanted. I was becoming schizophrenic, trying to rationalize what had happened, trying to create some good out of it, while also seeing the tragedy, the emptiness, as if no life had ever existed, and never would again. It was very much like being part of a waking dream, unreal and could change abruptly.

South of Sunset, where real life began, away from the suburban hills, was just as empty as north of Sunset. We approached cautiously. Twigs and other natural debris filled the streets and sidewalks. I saw what good a simple broom and street cleaner could do. Landscaping, so lifeless and waxen, was very much alive and glad to finally break free. Nature's time to celebrate. We saw only one smashed window in a home. Mostly, everything was frozen still and unbroken, aside from the natural world. The further south we went, the more it began to smell. Not like sewage, more metallic. Like mold on metal.

Finally, when we made it to the supermarket, we saw evidence of people. The front window of the supermarket was smashed in. At least someone was alive here, though this could have been done weeks before. I stepped over broken glass—which once had a mural painting for President's Day: Lincoln and Washington shaking hands. The market was a relic from the sixties, cheap and rundown, but within a rich neighborhood.

We entered the market. The shelves had been mostly looted. A few boxes and cans remained. It didn't smell awful because people had stolen most of the meat as well, which meant that, yes, this had been raided weeks before. The butcher's station was behind glass, I wasn't about to go back there. The verdict was that there was hardly any food left. It didn't seem like foragers had made it very far north. I wondered who could have busted through the window—I imaged a small riot early in the war.

Jesse held up a can of hearts of palm. "The fuck is hearts of palm?"

He put it in his bag.

"Someone was here to take all this stuff," Geoff said.

"This could have happened weeks ago," I said. "We should keep moving."

We left the supermarket and walked east down Vicente Boulevard. The grass median where people normally jogged was unkempt, the only sign of life. Still, somehow, no people. We survived and it really wasn't too much of a struggle, relative to what we'd seen on the news. There had to be other people in this neighborhood. To be honest, it was pleasantly empty. I wanted evidence of people, but it was eerily peaceful—not a dead town, not yet, because the natural world hadn't yet overrun the streets. It was more like time had stopped, like it was waiting.

I've written about Winchell's plans so I had some idea about what was happening, but the novel didn't reveal everything. I still had to live my life, and there was a distinct difference between writing something and witnessing it firsthand. I was still unconvinced that my writing could create reality. I was just reporting on events that already happened, not inventing things that never did. I had to believe that—or risk wanting to kill myself.

We passed a bookstore. It looked untouched. I peered into a bank window, expecting mayhem. It seemed that people wisely realized that money would be worthless, only food mattered. The gourmet market was not as ripped bare as the main supermarket, but maybe people didn't know what to do with dried organic tempeh. Finally, when we exited that market, we saw someone. He stood at a distance. His gun was drawn. Our group's guns quickly went up as well. It was more awkward than menacing. He was a young guy, clean-cut, looked like a jock. He had a similar look of fear mixed with curiosity. He was sizing us up, careful the way you'd be with a stray animal. I decided to approach and he seemed to make the same decision at the same moment. Everyone lowered their guns.

"Who are you?" he said. "Are you government?"

"No, civilian. We're safe."

"Where you coming from?"

"North of Sunset," I said.

"Yeah, me too," he said with some disappointment, as if he hoped we were from somewhere else.

"I expected more people out here," I said. "If you and I survived, there have to be a lot more."

"I'm sure of it. But not if you go south." He pointed. "It's devastated. Broken buildings, flooding, bodies. Everything you'd expect. A nightmare. And for some reason there are barricades keeping people from coming here. I don't understand it. It's like they were protecting this area on purpose. I don't know why it happened but the place you're standing is a fucking paradise."

He said this bitterly, as if it were my fault.

"Where's the military presence now?" I said in response.

"I've seen some at the barricades, but mainly they stay on the other side of the fence."

"How many people are you with?"

"It's just me and my girlfriend. My family is in Illinois. Gone. We broke into other apartments for food. Seems most people got trapped at their jobs or other places south where the worst happened. Who knows why they were fucking going to their jobs. To pay the rent? Jesus."

"Maybe they were trying to get prepared."

"Maybe. It all happened so fast." He paused. "You ever see roadkill? After you see one dead body, another body isn't such a bad thing. A mess of skin and blood. It's so...lifeless. That sounds stupid but it's true." The look in his eyes suggested he didn't believe this. "Anyway, I don't recommend going down there. No point in it. Every usable building is looted or destroyed. The smell is terrible. Just sad."

"You see many other people?"

"A few. Some guy with a six million dollar house who said he lived off wine and movies. That's what he told me. Those are the kinds of people that are left. Movie people. I'm sure more will start coming out, once they get hungry or bored enough."

"What now?" I said.

"I don't have that answer."

We said goodbye and determined to stay in touch. I told him our street name, Bundy, but not the address, as I didn't trust him yet—didn't yet know what made a person trustworthy in these conditions.

He went north back to his place, now living in an abandoned house, and we continued down south. Not seeing what he described seemed liked cowardice. If all these people, an entire city, had died, the least we could do was pay our respects. Our lives and our side of town were so fortunate that I felt I needed to bathe in a little death, almost as penance.

The further south we drove, the greater the devastation. Broken windows, crumbling bricks, whole walls fallen down, victims of S-bombs, some flooding, though not as much as I expected. We didn't see a body until halfway down Barrington on a slope towards Wilshire. It was pushed under a bus stop, eyes a greenish color, flesh purplish with more visible veins, like a withered map. I told myself: the body didn't represent a person any more than a photograph. A representation, a symbol even; made it easier. The real person was somewhere else. I couldn't tell if it was a man or a woman.

The stranger was right. I didn't even get his name, forgot to. Soon bodies became part of the landscape. If it wasn't for the smell, it would have been tolerable. They just looked like debris. The most terrible part was when they died, the screaming, the pain. Now they looked discarded, even lucky now that the suffering was over and death was behind them. We all had to face a harder future.

The man was right about another thing. At Wilshire there were enormous barricades. A tall wall, 25 feet high, hinged together in 30-foot pieces. In some places, the buildings had crumbled making the area impassable. Everywhere else there was this wall separating one corner of the city. We headed west and found that the wall took a right turn at 26th Street, turning north.

Around 20th Street a building had fallen on our side so we could climb up to the top of the barricade without much trouble, like steps. On top of the barricade, we could see a fairly clear distance. Mayhem. Leveled buildings, smashed cars—the city equivalent of the aftermath of a forest fire, charred remains for miles, just useless and burnt. And the bodies. Imagine the pictures of the Jonestown massacre for an entire city. It was too much information to take in at once. It felt like dropping from a great height—something that could stop your heart. One of the guys started crying, or at least covering his eyes with one hand, as if he couldn't look at the city any more than looking directly at the sun. As if it was the only way to hold your head together or you'd break apart like this city. One piece of the world over.

"This is real, right?" Geoff said. "I'm looking at something real?"

"Yes," I said.

The smell was too much. We would have investigated the other side some more, but the stench made it impossible. We should have brought gas masks, but no one could prepare for this. I spotted a group of people in the distance, up Wilshire Boulevard. In this environment, they looked menacing, capable of anything. Monstrous, faceless silhouettes.

"I can hit them," one of our men said, peering through a scope.

"No. No more death. Let's go."

We climbed back down the wall and made it back to Vicente. Like the stranger said, a paradise. Still an insult to the rest of the city that it should be standing. A military helicopter passed overhead, the first such evidence. It continued on. I didn't know if it saw us.

We walked back to the gourmet market. The finest symbol of the northern edge of L.A. Filled with useless ingredients that nobody needed and nobody had yet taken. Part of the reason that this side of the city was untouched was because so much here was superfluous—stores with fashion accessories, a $1500 crib. All of the utilitarian goods, along with all of the carnage, were down south. Yet still, this seemed to be a place where a large number of people would have taken refuge, fleeing the worst of it. But maybe the war was much more abrupt and complete than I had thought. Or those barricades were very successful at keeping people out. The residents on this side of the wall died some other way. There were a lot of questions that I didn't have the imagination to answer. This kind of devastation was unknowable.

I searched the back office of the market and found a backpack. In the bag there was a math book called *Math for Continuing Education*—someone had been trying to get their degree while working at the market. I dumped it out and filled the backpack with what I could find on the shelves—mostly a souvenir to show where we'd been.

With the backpack full of flax meal, hearts of palm, and organic spinach bowtie pasta, we headed home.

—⋀⋀—

We got back to the house looking as burnt-out as the city; assaulted. People rushed to the door to greet us, led by Dominique.

"What was it like? Are you OK?"

"Yeah, we're OK. Somehow. We are."

"Is it safe?"

"Here? It's a fucking paradise. The news tells you nothing, Dominique. Nothing. It's a barrier like that fucking wall."

"What wall?"

"We're terribly privileged here. I'll tell you about it later."

I trudged into the house.

"Where are you going?"

"To get some sleep."

19: Marriage of the Lamb

Charles came into his wife's room. She slept in a different room now. Smaller, not as comfortable, meant to be a guest bedroom for someone who had never arrived. Everyone in the Compound knew they had separated. This was not something that could be keep secret, especially since they were never seen together. It shamed him. It was against nature and—more importantly—against God.

"It's over," Charles said, trying to sound reassuring. "The war is over. You can stop worrying."

She was sitting at the desk writing. She seemed to spend all her days writing something. Writing what, he didn't know. *This*, he supposed. Their marriage, her take on the war. Nothing to look forward to.

She smiled a little at the news. Was it relief? Was she finally going to let up on him? "Congratulations," she merely said, with no sense of praise. "Now what?"

"Now we're going to move our operations to Los Angeles— the section that still remains. A great location in the Santa Monica Mountains. You'll like it there. It's all been prepared for ahead of time."

There was nothing that came out of his mouth that did not make her sneer, like the sight of him was causing her pain. This was clearly the end of their marriage. She despised him, totally unforgiving.

"You are free to do whatever you want. Stay here if you

like," Charles said, though he knew she hated it here more than anywhere.

She didn't sneer at this. She looked inquisitive. "No," she said. "I want to come with you, I think. I want to be there when this all blows up in your face. It's the only hope I have right now."

"Perhaps you're curious if I'm right and we're going to enter into a beautiful reign of peace?"

"Oh please, Charles, leave. I think you're a fucking idiot."

"OK," Charles breathed.

He closed the door to her room gently, as if she might judge how he closed the door. Every one of their conversations went more or less like this. He felt horrible afterwards, but also determined. How much of a vindication would it now be when his prophecies finally came true? He was giddy with anticipation—like a child on Christmas. He smiled at the double meaning and felt good again.

Outside the room stood his VP Chris Duncan. The VP looked regretful, as if he'd been eavesdropping. Charles' relationship with his wife was making him distrust everybody.

"Chris," Charles said, dully.

"Is there anything wrong?" the VP said, glancing at the First Lady's door. "Problems with Amy?"

"Yes," Charles conceded and slouched. "Have you talked to her? It's impossible."

"I keep my distance, to be honest. She's been hostile to most everybody. You have to remember, there will always be non-believers. Consider it a test of your strength."

"I try to remind myself of that. I just wish it wasn't my wife."

The vice president nodded awkwardly, offering little consolation.

"How about if we change the subject?" Charles said.

"Fine by me. We're just about ready to make the move to L.A.—or should I say, the New City."

"Good."

"I don't know about you but I'm ready to get this ball rolling."

"So am I." Charles pictured his wife frowning, dead with rage. He couldn't even picture her smiling anymore. No memory of the past washed away who she had become. "God, am I ready," he said.

—ᐯᐯᐯ—

The second phase was put in motion. There was no media, so there was no way to contact many people. TV was down, the internet was down. But not for everybody. There were satellite web servers that connected bunkers across the world—those who knew the reasons for the war, those who sanctioned it. It was determined that these well-connected people should try to find as many survivors as possible. If you survived this war, you were meant to. A major revelation was to come—even Benjamin Winchell thought this—so it was important to have a large number of people to witness the revelation. This was supposed to be the beginning of a great new civilization and it would be much harder with 10 or 50 or even 1000 people. Especially people who were well past breeding age.

Centers were set up all around the world to bring in refugees. There were calls put out on giant loudspeakers from helicopters all over the world. Word spread quickly. And so planes full of people made their way to an Arizona airport, a Protected Area. Survivors were then shuttled to their new home. Somewhere around 40,000 emigrated to the New City. That's all that was left, aside from those who never made it to the transportation centers, who would likely die off or create small primitive colonies of their own, if they could manage. At the transportation center, people were tested for radiation poisoning and other diseases. If they tested positive, they were turned away and placed in a camp run by people who were also infected. If possible, or necessary, some refugees would be picked up later—located by automated satellite sweeps that could pick up human or animal movement. This was no Noah's Ark. For all they knew, many nationalities, and most animals, had been destroyed. There were genetic storehouses, but not actual people. Due to the state of the terrain, it was impossible to find everybody. Again, if you made it to a transportation center, you were meant to. 44,000 people was a pretty good take, though more than had been initially estimated.

This process took several months, wherein each person was given access to a luxury home in the Brentwood area of Los Angeles—those that were left after the people from the bunkers (referred to as the Connected) got first choice, the largest homes. It turned out that 80% of the original residents of the neighborhood fled or were otherwise killed—many more than had been anticipated. They could not have known that it was one of the safest places on earth. The neighborhood had been monitored and guarded throughout the war and then blocked off with a great wall before flooding began. Of course they couldn't entirely control what the enemy would do, but real estate casualties had been kept to a minimum. L.A. had it all—temperate weather, even with the warming, and some of the nicest homes in America. They had wanted to stay in the U.S., rather than heading south of the equator. America would be the new Atlantis. L.A. was its new capital. The plan was working fine. There was no radiation poisoning in the city, only flooding. And now there were thousands of vacant homes. Beautiful homes, especially north of Sunset. Some families had to double up, and they converted several office buildings into makeshift apartment buildings, but generally people were comfortable.

How could the residents complain? Not only had they survived, but now they were being placed in the lap of luxury, with free food. For many, this was a step up. To Charles it was appropriate for the new society to be in a place where people had achieved the American Dream, famous and celebrated and living as well as one could. One could even say better than human. It was one of the richest neighborhoods in the west, already the richest part of the world—with saunas, Jacuzzis, tennis courts, and everything else that made the neighborhood like a five-star resort. The survivors would be at ease. And if they lived in luxurious homes, they'd be less prone to revolt. Winchell's dream had almost arrived, as if the entire neighborhood was his dream home. The wall safely keeping the neighborhood intact was the white picket fence.

Sure, things weren't playing out exactly as in the Bible, but they didn't have to. He realized that now. Israel had been destroyed, so that was not going to be the land where Revelations would play out. Instead of the old Jerusalem of the Middle East, he—privately—called the new community the New Jerusalem. As Jesus was supposed to ride on a white horse, Charles chose himself a nice white Mercedes. The keys were on the kitchen counter at the home where he was staying. How appropriate that the home he chose to be the new White House would have a white car—400 horsepower, he snickered—parked in the garage. The house also had a black gate guarding the grounds like a fortress. Everything was as it should be.

Moving in was enjoyable. Charles got rid of everything that was a reminder of the past inhabitants. He threw away every photograph, but kept most of the paintings. The house itself was beautiful—modern, circa 2007. Not enough windows for his taste, but this was good for security, and it was the most unique house on the block. Imposing—filled up an entire lot without space for a front or backyard. Blinding white, appropriate for the new White House, though more angular than classical. It looked like a kind of modern cathedral, appropriate too. He said a prayer for those former tenants who had martyred themselves for him. He didn't bother to say a prayer for his wife and he didn't know where she was staying.

It was from here that he could finally declare heaven on earth. Now all he could do was wait for that glorious moment to arrive. True, he couldn't ascend to the throne with his wife as he had wished. But maybe she could be converted once she witnessed how powerful he would become. That he could be worshipped, not just elected. The Marriage of the Lamb would be a "glorious church, not having spot, or wrinkle, or any such thing; but that it should be holy and without blemish." (Eph. 5:27)

20: The United States of Sumeria

There was a knock on the door. We had been expecting it. Recently there had been more activity in the neighborhood—more helicopters flying overhead and even cars driving. We were still tentative about connecting with people. We knew, of course, what was going to happen, but not the how. When someone knocked on the door—not impolitely, not a pound, a regular knock—it felt like an invasion. So much silence up to that point, just the group. But we also had a new sense of both bravery and resignation—what happens happens. Geoff and I looked at each other when the person knocked a second time, both of us thinking, all right, we've hidden long enough, let's begin what's next.

I opened the door and everyone else hung back. Who knew who was out there? Bandits with guns blazing come to take over our house? Someone with disease? Maybe just a friendly neighbor. Instead it was a military man.

He was dressed in army green and looked about eighteen, didn't look like he shaved. He could have been pointing a gun at us, but he still looked harmless. We were relieved to see a boy.

"Sir," he said. "Are you the resident of this house?"

"Of course I am. What else would I be?" I said. I think this was instinctive annoyance at anyone from the government, no matter how innocent-looking.

"What I mean is, are you the original owner of this house?"

"I see. No."

"But you were staying here during the war?" He asked this with amazement.

"Yes."

"You're lucky. This was a designated Safe Zone. You might have picked the best place on earth to hide out."

Everyone was inching closer to the front door. Things were moving forward, a relief. He explained what we already knew: that people were being flown into this neighborhood to begin a new community. He took down all our names—which was unnerving, giving our souls over to this government plan. But we didn't have much of a choice. And even though we distrusted the government, it was heartening to see that something was being done. There would be no chaos.

"So what's going to happen now?" I asked him.

"We're working on getting electricity and plumbing up again. And getting the internet back online. After everyone has arrived there will be a New City meeting to get everyone acquainted with the process."

"New City?"

"That's what this is called," he said, proudly. "The New City."

I knew this as well but it still continued to be strange to get confirmation.

"How many people are left?" I asked.

"By our estimation, around forty to fifty thousand." He did not say this proudly.

You could almost hear everyone's stomach drop. It was an incredible figure, billions dead—an unfathomable number. Extermination. We were all the richest people on earth and the poorest.

"Did you fight in the war?" Geoff asked him.

"No. I survived in Illinois." He began tearing up, almost without thinking.

"Your family gone?"

"Yes." He turned stoic and stopped tearing. "I was in junior high during the war. They couldn't use me." He tapped his clipboard. "OK. Wait for your orders. I'm your *liaison*—" he pronounced the word slowly—"so I'll be in touch once we begin Phase III."

"What's Phase III?"

"The community meeting. I'm not sure what it's all about. It's supposed to be something important. Just to get everyone acquainted, I guess."

—◇◇◇—

Dominique and I took a walk around the neighborhood. There were cars on the road. New residents sat in beach chairs in their front yards. Some people walked dogs. It was like summer camp for everybody. Like the neighborhood was the park or a beach. Everyone had been beaten by the war and now they were comfortably retiring. It was a weird sense of relief—almost aggressively happy.

We passed a couple walking a dog—forties, midwestern. The man did a double-take and stopped in front of me. His wife stopped with him.

"My God, it's you," he said. "Cherie, it's him."

She studied me, as if looking past my eyes.

"It is you, isn't it?" she said.

"From the dream, you mean?" I said.

"Yes," the woman replied.

"We saw you. We both did. That's how we knew it was real. What are the odds that we'd both dream something with the same story? Impossible. The dream told us to head to Grosse Pointe, so we did."

"It's the only reason we're alive," she said. "We owe you everything. Thank you so much."

She hugged me. I accepted this reluctantly. Believe me, I know how this looks: the self-love and self-inflation. I agree with you. I didn't want this to become like our dream group writ large, with me as the figurehead. I was no hero. If my novel somehow brought this war into being, I killed more than

I saved.

The couple walked on.

"If you ever wanted to be famous, you're now in everyone's heads," Dominique said.

–∿∿–

The electricity went on soon afterward. It might appear the wrong time to go this route, but it seemed biblical: let there be light. This was the war's V-day. Gave back some hope that humanity could be whole again, that humans could achieve things and wouldn't be overrun by wolves and weeds. Yes, absolutely the wrong point of view—our desire to control nature by controlling light was partly responsible for the world falling apart. We owned the world so we could mess with it as we pleased. But that's the glass half-empty. All technology wasn't rape and that small taste of the old world still being alive filled us all with joy. The day the lights suddenly sprang on it was like a piece of heaven had returned. Seeing the world bombed to ruin might just have led to bombastic statements like that one.

"Thank God," Dominique said, as she tried the lightswitch in the dining room.

I turned on the TV—no channels. The radio, the same. It was an odd experience too. An abrupt reminder of how things had changed. Living by the light of the sun and candlelight, sporadic light through a generator, made it easier to face the future. With the lights on, there was clarity. The dining room looked the same—same too-expensive $5,000 table, same artwork on the walls, same cupboard with china—but outside it was irretrievably different. This piece of the past—light—was the final proof that the future was here and the past was dead.

That's the philosophical take. Mostly, it was great to have the full use of the house.

As the soldier said, the internet also came back to life. There was no new TV programming, though we could now watch old movies, which was an odd experience to even consider. There was so much hope in movies, faith that the world would stay the same. Putting on a movie made even two years earlier seemed to me like looking at cave paintings. All those actors were probably dead.

An online forum was set up so people could converse with each other: find relatives, trade goods that other people might need. The rest of the web was able to come online as well. Seeing the web was both tragic and exhilarating—a museum-like storehouse of everything we had achieved, no matter how insignificant, but also static. The brain of a civilization that was now on life support. In the forum, there was a thread simply called "Dream." A member asked, "This may sound crazy, but did anyone have this dream?" and went on to describe my appearance. A handful of people were participating.

"Does anyone know how to reach him?" a poster asked. "Do we even know that he's still alive? I looked him up and know that he was teaching somewhere in Los Angeles, but maybe he got caught in the south like everyone else."

"I hope not."

"Yeah."

It warmed me like crazy, I'll admit. I thought about responding, but I didn't. A strange cult was forming around the dream, at least with these people. They were believing in it more than they should have—in a way that I had always wanted to avoid. Ironic, really. I'd created a new wing of fundamentalism. I felt uneasy. Like a recluse suddenly famous for something he didn't accomplish. I decided to keep my distance.

We got a notice pinned to the front door, after a knock, that there was going to be a city meeting on the golf course at the Brentwood Country Club. President Winchell was going to make a speech, the invitation said—gold script lettering on a hard piece of card stock, like a wedding invitation.

The entire town was at the club. Forty thousand people spread out on overgrown greens and sand traps. A large stage was set up with massive PA speakers on either side, something like a rock concert. Men and women sat in chairs at the back of the stage. Before entering the course, everyone was stamped—a simple permanent tattoo, without a needle—with the words "New City," on the right or left upper arm, your choice, so newcomers could be picked out of the crowd. Everyone was showered and dressed in clean clothes—even if the clothes weren't their own (I guessed people had been knocking on doors looking for clothes of their size and gender, if they were put in a house with mismatched tenants). It was good to be with so many people again, to see that a crowd was still possible. They did look weary, but they didn't look too much like refugees, clean as they were, standing in a golf club. There was as much gratitude for being alive as the fear of being displaced. People were mostly friendly, exchanging names, hometowns. Most looked under fifty and most were white, not too many children. Some couldn't speak English, but the majority appeared to be English or American.

A man stepped up to me, smiling wide with thick, blinding-white dentures. "How are you? I'm Ronald Corbin," he said.

"Gene."

"Hi, Gene. Glad to meet you. I'm from Arizona, not far from here. Pretty nice digs they've got us set up in."

"Why are you so happy?" I said. "The world just died."

Ronald looked hurt. "I don't know. I'm just glad to have made it through, I suppose."

"Well, have some fucking remorse."

Ronald cowered off.

"I guess everyone doesn't recognize me," I said to Dominique. "I almost feel gypped."

I knew we were in for a lot of trouble as soon as the speech started. Winchell stepped up to the mic and began: "In Revelation 19, it states, 'Now I saw heaven opened, and behold, a white horse. And He who sat on him was called Faithful and True, and in righteousness He Judges and makes war. His eyes were like a flame of fire, and on His head were many crowns. He had a name written that no one knew except Himself. He was clothed with a robe dipped in blood, and His name is called The Word of God.'"

Christ, how about a hello or a welcome? I wondered if he had dipped his clothing in blood.

Geoff said the same thing, out loud, "Christ."

There was a stirring in the crowd. I couldn't tell if people were indignant, like us, or if this was going to turn into a religious ceremony.

Like a good politician, Winchell quickly got more reasonable. "Welcome," he said. "I hope you have found your accommodations comfortable. Congratulations on making it this far. Los Angeles, the City of Angels, is said to be a place where dreams are made. Fantasies come true. It seemed the perfect destination for the new seat of civilization. People, I give you the New City."

He stopped as if waiting for applause. There was a pathetic response, mostly from those on stage. The rest of the audience were still waiting for more of an explanation.

"Eventually much of the city will be cleaned up, as well as the entire country," Winchell continued. "America is now truly the center of the world. But America is an old name, for an old way of life. The first seat of civilization was in Mesopotamia and the Sumerian civilization, which sprang up, remarkably, seemingly out of nowhere. Which is what we are doing— springing out of the wasteland of man's past ignorance. And so officially we are dubbing the new country Sumerica, with the New City as its capital. We are starting with a blank slate, a profound improvement on our former civilization."

He paused again. A little more applause this time.

"This will not be a country without a rule of law. Yet these laws are universal. In this new civilization I will still be your president, the commander in chief of God's army. As it says, 'In righteousness He judges.' I am so much more than an elected official." He raised two hands in the air, palms facing us. Then he said, "Ladies and gentlemen, I am the Messiah."

I thought back to the last time I heard him speak: "I am the Anti-Christ." We were in my old apartment, watching TV. All of us cynical, muttering anger. Here I was standing with 40,000 witnesses and it was a horrible spectacle—a quick shocked breath from everyone at once. Then some shrieking, as if possessed, some people falling to their knees, others crying—out of holy joy or renewed fear, I couldn't tell. I saw one person throw up. People had been through the worst event in human history. They didn't know what to believe anymore. With all they'd seen and suffered through, it would not be surprising if they suddenly believed in Winchell. They were vulnerable enough to surrender to anything. Given what they'd all witnessed, each with a more horrifying story than the next, it would be no surprise if their vulnerability turned to worship. They'd watched children die, more shocking than this revelation.

Thankfully, there were dissenters. A man nearby, thick, looked like a mechanic, yelled, "You're no Messiah. You're responsible for this. This is all your fault. Jesus would never do that!"

Which is what I hoped most people were thinking. The man couldn't be heard over all the other noise—shouts in both praise and anger. Most of those around us were stunned and quiet, as if there was more information needed.

"Like I said before the war, this is good news," Winchell said. "A dream come true. Now, now," he said. He pointed at someone in the front of the crowd and spoke to him or her off the mic. I couldn't hear it. "Please settle down," he said back into the mic.

"Let the president speak!" a woman yelled nearby, which scared me. Our world was about to be controlled by lunatics.

"I understand there will be disagreement," Winchell said. "That is natural. At first. Eventually, nothing will have to be taken on faith. The entire history of civilization has been leading to this moment. This is the new kingdom and I am your king." He pounded his fists down on the podium, which was slightly overdone, as though he was trying to force us to pay attention. "You are fortunate to be a—"

He was stopped mid-sentence. Someone behind him was taking him aside and talking to him. Maybe it was an assassination warning. I didn't mention that we'd all been checked for weapons before we entered the golf course, as well as being branded. I don't know what was said to the president, but Winchell was taken off the stage and the speech was abruptly over.

There was some confusion on stage, people chatting with each other, the crowd waiting. Someone came to the mic and said, "Thank you for your time. Please continue on as you have been. We will give you further direction in the future," and the stage was emptied. The spectators looked at each other, more confused than they were before. Soon people started filing out of the country club.

"Praise Jesus," someone shouted, but it sounded like a token gesture, alone in the crowd. "Jesus is Lord," said quickly.

"Can you believe this?" a young man said in front of us, eagerly. He was met with somber silence by those around us, as if this was a funeral and no one wanted to dignify enthusiasm.

I heard, "If he's Jesus, then good, things will be easy. If not, won't be any different than before."

Most were silent. I think everyone was just tired of fighting.

"Once a lunatic, always a lunatic," Dominique said, concisely, as we left the country club gates, and we didn't say anything more until we got back home.

21: King of Kings

"What the fuck are you doing?"

His father was talking. Red-faced, shaking, as if his skin couldn't contain his rage. Charles felt like a teenager whose grades were failing or who had stayed out too late. Still, he felt some measure of righteousness—also like a teenager.

"This is not what we talked about."

No, it wasn't. But he couldn't tell his father about the speech beforehand. He would never have let it happen. So Charles let his father know about his plans right along with everyone else.

"Do you realize that you've systematically fucked up our entire plan? How can we ever think about establishing first contact when people are all mixed up with this Jesus business? This is exactly what we didn't want to happen. What did you do with the speech I wrote?"

He read it and then burned it—another small case where "He judges and makes war." His father's speech said the very opposite of what Charles wanted to say. It was an apology. An admission that there was no one true religion. Who better to help organize this new society than the person who was the most repentant man on earth? The man responsible for the war would also be the man responsible for cleaning it up. A new utopia could be born—without the prejudice, without the differences of religion, without all the old world problems. What more proof did anyone need that we should change our ways than this war?

It was a well-written speech, he would give his father that.

Just off base. Charles used elements of the speech in his own, but not the heart of it. Christianity was the one true faith. He could concede that Jesus was a representation of a larger, universal system—perhaps like the president of Earth, and each planet had its own spiritual leader—but the Messiah was very real. As real as Charles was himself.

The main thing that was troubling him was not his father's criticism. It was that he had crowned himself king and nothing had happened. Instead of emanating a great white light, arms aloft, as he had pictured, his father's assistant—in from a Wyoming bunker—had whisked him off the stage before he could complete his speech, on direct orders from Benjamin Winchell.

Maybe that was precisely the problem: Charles wasn't able to complete the speech. Though he had said the most important line: "This is the new kingdom and I am your king." He was hoping that would crown him in everyone's eyes and the new church could begin.

He supposed, again, that more needed to transpire. The battle between the Lord and Satan. Yes, that was it. He had to defeat Lucifer. Was his father Satan? Could this be his challenge? He really didn't want that to be true. Partly because he didn't want to take on his father, but mostly because he didn't want to see his father humiliated, disgraced, banished. Charles wanted to keep him a part of the new kingdom—to have his respect and adulation, to win him over.

If his father was not the Satan of the final battle, then who was? That had yet to be determined. For now, he would have to weather his father's scorn. It hurt, deeply, because he was still human; he had not yet ascended.

"You retard," his father said. "It was all an act. A path. None of it true."

Charles glanced at his wife, who was standing nearby. They were all grouped behind the stage. Most of the crowd had filed out, except for a hundred or so who had stayed to pray—more proof. Seeing his wife hiding a smile, gloating, was worse than what his father was saying.

"You just don't understand," Charles fought back. "You don't know what it is to believe."

"Believe? Believe?" His father looked like he might die suddenly. He looked unhealthy. The absence of grace. Sweating profusely, arms flailing. He couldn't take it anymore and stormed out of the country club, muttering anger to himself.

Charles' wife wasn't trying to hide her smile anymore. She laughed.

—⁓—

Charles was sitting in the den, the TV room of his new home. A ten-foot screen came down from the ceiling by remote control. He was watching footage of the war—saved on the TV's harddrive before everything had blacked out. Charles hadn't seen much actual news footage with newscasters, only satellite surveillance footage that looked at everything from above. There were some cameras on the ground, but those eventually were destroyed. Camera drones were shot down. The satellite photos were objective—none of it seemed like it was literally happening. The eye-in-the-sky satellites, which only he had access to, appeared benevolent and detached, without judgment or commentary, Godlike. They were not much of a witness, not like a real human that could think and feel, a different cameraman choosing what he wanted to see. The war was horrible, he saw that now. He had known of war's horror, but only in the abstract, as if a story being told. He saw babies bleeding, starvation, crying, anger, every hostility.

It filled him with anger and resolve of his own. How dare his father let all of these lives be lost in vain. His father wanted to continue the same old path that would inevitably lead to disunity and more warfare. The more Charles watched the news coverage, the more he became convinced of this war's divinity, fire and brimstone proof of the Bible. There was something devoutly religious about so much suffering. Even the Buddhists said that. This was earth's crucifixion. Without resurrection, there was no hope for mankind. The resurrection had to be led by Christ or there would be no salvation. His father mentioned how the final revelation would be that all humans had an inner divinity. But this negated Charles' faith. No, not faith—conviction. Humanity needed guidance. A priest class of leaders who strictly followed the laws of the Bible. Humans contained only elements of the Christ—like a power station that sent electricity throughout a city, it could not be done without the power station, a central generator. Charles reminded himself that there were always those who didn't believe in Jesus. After all, Christ was crucified. But not this time. To not end this war in resurrection was an insult to all those who had died.

Fortunately, there were others who believed in the cause. The doorbell rang. There was going to be a major meeting of the minds: the Connected. There hadn't been a chance yet for everyone to meet. Too much busywork getting people in homes, electricity up, and preparing the speech. Despite the criticisms from family, he was emboldened to know that so many believed in him—many in his administration, and many he'd never met.

The party filled out to ninety. It wasn't everyone who supported the Revelation Operation, but those who had the most influence. Elegant missionaries. Most were fifty or over, and most had lived a life of privilege that even Charles couldn't fathom, even if he was American royalty. People from all over the world who had survived the war in remote castles, bunkers, or military installations. Some, he heard, had died, unfortunately. More reason that they should not die in vain. The group stood beneath a jagged modern chandelier in his living room, eating canned foie gras, caviar, and other delicacies set aside for this meeting (though unfortunately no cheese). There were congratulations given to Charles about the country club speech, even if it had been cut short. "It lays the groundwork, a strong beginning," a British woman said, the Duchess of something. "I've never liked the occult practitioners like your father. There is a reason that Christianity is the most powerful religion on the planet: because it is true. These aliens your father is always talking about are mentioned throughout our Bible—they are called demons. Further proof that we are right. I am so proud to be a part of this, Charles." There was no speech by Charles, only mingling.

It took on the tenor of any cocktail party—the women well dressed in jewelry they'd brought from homes far away; the men dressed in suits, some in tails. This was a formal evening. There was only one topic of conversation, like the party after a premiere—some elation, but mostly it was a time to breathe out, the hardest work already done. "I'm so relieved this war is over," someone said. "I know it was necessary. In my bones I know. But I could not wait for so much suffering to be over."

His companion nodded solemnly.

"Hogwash," another partygoer interjected. "All life is suffering. This was a way to compress many lifetimes of suffering into a few months. The worse it was, the more we were successful."

People nodded solemnly at that as well.

An Indian man, 40, attractive, walked through the group towards Charles, then got on his knees and kissed Charles' hand. "My Christ," he said. Soon, most others did the same—as if they needed the opening, or it hadn't occurred to them yet that Charles was indeed the Second Coming. The idea had been disseminated among the Connected and there weren't many dissenters. Some said, Oh, he's not the Christ we know from paintings and movies, but he will be possessed by Christ's spirit because he's the world's most powerful leader, in a position of the highest authority. There was some underlying uncertainty about what would happen next—based, still, on faith. No one would admit this outright, but it was human to doubt, right? It proved their humanity. Yet at the same time they wanted certainty. The war was a shock to them as well—they were, after all, human. And they desperately needed to make certain the war had a purpose. So it only took a slight push to turn them into pure believers. Many people had been debated to be the new Christ over the years, but how appropriate, and how plausible, that it should—literally—be the most powerful man on earth.

The partygoers all got on their knees, closed their eyes, and said, "My Christ," as if marionetted by each other.

Charles stood in the center of his living room surrounded by this crop of humanity on their knees. All this power—these men and women of fantastic wealth and ancient bloodlines— were bowing down to him. If the speech at the country club did not elevate him to the rank of the divine, this was a vital step. Vindication at last. He could feel the love; the presence of love, as if it were an entity. Pure, sexless love. He nearly wept, but kept his strength. He should not show weakness. He loved every cell in every body. This was what it would be like for all eternity, for everyone. It was the finest moment of Charles' life.

People slowly stood up. Slight, embarrassed smiles went around, as if they had all fainted and were surprised to find themselves in a crowd of people. The mood soon turned professional. A group of 30 remained in the living room and got down to logistics. First: how to overcome his father's beliefs and bring the many non-believers on board. Next, there was the issue of the final battle with Satan.

"I don't believe it has occurred yet," Charles said. "I mean, of course it hasn't, because I haven't fought him face to face."

"It's most likely your father. The leader of non-believers," Chief of Staff Whitehead said.

"I've thought about that," Charles replied. "But it doesn't feel right. He seems so, I don't know, *mortal*. I think I can trust my intuition."

There were nods of agreement.

"He might not be Satan, but we definitely need to take over his reign," said a man who had something to do with South African wine.

"A coup?"

"Yes. It may come to the point where we'll have to kill all

non-believers. If they haven't come around yet, they may never. It's not ideal, but it may be necessary."

"I agree," Charles said. "We need complete control of this situation. We need a willing foundation."

"If not your father, who do you think Lucifer could be?"

"I don't know," Charles said. "But not until after the battle between Christ and Satan can the prophecy be truly fulfilled."

The party members agreed.

"Until then, we will have to be in a kind of limbo. Better than earth but not quite heaven. We've waited this long."

"Of course, and there's still much to be done," his VP said. "In preparation. Bring in those who accept Christ and try to convert others. Whoever they are: Benjamin Winchell or a farmhand from Iowa. So when the meeting with Satan does occur we will already have a good number of people who accept Christ as their personal savior. We don't want a new war to take away half our population. Think of it as another campaign."

"Precisely," Charles said. "That's what I'm good at. And like my presidency, the outcome has been pre-determined."

22: The New City

Life in the neighborhood was relatively normal. Winchell declaring himself Jesus hadn't really affected our everyday lives. We still lived in the real world, not a post-apocalyptic kingdom. It was much easier for the members of our group. We hadn't been uprooted. We were living where we'd been for months. There were pockets of believers, pamphleteers passing out booklets saying "Jesus Is Lord" and stating how the current situation paralleled the Bible, etc. No different than before the war. The heavily religious people kept to themselves and out of sight. There were no secret police demanding our allegiance. Maybe people were sane after all. It's possible I just wasn't seeing it, or I saw what I chose to see—because it was totally heartening, not living among 40,000 converts to Winchell's new religion. I have no numbers, but just from talking to people it appeared the ratio of believers to non-believers, or at least agnostics, was the same as when the war started.

If I saw anything irritating it was some arrogance, a sense of entitlement, among those who had stayed in our neighborhood through the war. The guy we met in the streets of Brentwood—who I never saw again—had mentioned another survivor with a six-million-dollar house. I met him. He directed terrible action movies that made a lot of money in the pre-war world. In the old life I would have also found him distasteful, if not slightly demonic. Rewarded for something that shouldn't exist. Now he let his success go to his head even more. Large, decadent parties were thrown at his house, a bacchanalia, a sexual de-evolution in his six-million-dollar house, with cocaine to spare—he kept mounds of it in his wine cellar. Boasted of stocking up before the war. Am I a prude? No, but the rumors about that house bothered me, almost as much as non-converts bothered Winchell. I wanted to see us evolve just like Winchell did, and, yes, I saw this new community as an opportunity; an opportunity potentially getting wasted.

But that house was on the other side of town, a neighborhood of much more ostentatious houses. This neighborhood was middle class in comparison, a suburb. Around us, it was more domestic, like a daily block party. Most everyone I met was glad to be together, sharing stories—not so much about the war, though there was some of that, stories of heroism or how they survived. People traded stories about their old lives, each an eager listener to the other, with no sense of impatience, as if talking was the best form of entertainment. Mostly there was an authentic sense of enjoyment, a scene that would never have existed in isolated and competitive L.A. It was no wonder people spent their time in the open streets and didn't want to be cooped up inside. The fear of the old days was gone. Not just about the war, but the years leading up to the war as well. The safety and freedom were exhilarating.

Another reason people collected in front of their new homes was because there wasn't much else to do. There was abundant food—canned and boxed. Much of the canned food were delicacies taken from L.A.'s remaining gourmet markets, restaurants, and storehouses. The military, for the moment, were handling food distribution. Food was rationed out, but there was plenty—an entire city and country's worth of canned food for only 40,000 people. There would be no need for farming for a long time, or factory workers to work in canneries. There was abundant clothing too—not just in each and every home, but in stores too. Some stores had been burned out, but many were still standing. Beneath the rubble, a lot of usable items remained.

So there wasn't a lot of need for workers, except the young men and women who joined the military to go on foraging expeditions—their main job. A woman from our group joined the service, out of boredom. The expeditions were more like school field trips to specialty stores. She came back telling us stories about the city—cars piled on top of each other, buildings toppled on buildings, so much mayhem that you could hardly devise a story about what had happened. The corpses that were more like mummies, like shells, dead leaves off a tree. Keeping the peace was not yet a priority. She didn't even carry a weapon.

When it came down to it, all people really needed was food, clothing, and shelter and all that was taken care of, cost free. There was some worry that Winchell might start a Christianist insurrection, but so far that hadn't occurred. We were, for the most part, left alone. Some more people did recognize me, but not a huge number, or maybe they only had a hazy memory of my face; they just remembered what I told them. I remained quiet about what I'd experienced during the war. I wanted some peace of my own. I still wrote about my life and the president's plans, but I didn't see Winchell as that large a threat. In a way, we were all equals here, all equally famous and equally powerful, no matter what Winchell believed about himself.

Every day there'd be potluck meals in a cul-de-sac near our house. There weren't many cars on the road—mainly military vehicles, or young military men driving Mercedes. There wasn't very far residents could travel either. The road was still cut off a few miles west. The beach was sealed off until parts of Santa Monica could be cleared of debris, disease, and anything else that could hurt us. Whereas before we were entirely expendable, now each life was precious, especially the women, the womb of a new civilization. All in all, there weren't many places to go.

Obviously, there was sadness too. People had lost young children, everyone they loved. But the war was over, a new life had begun and the eulogies I heard were positive, not somber. Being happy now was, for some people, a way to celebrate the lives of those who had gone.

Generally, it was the time to breathe out. Not to worry about one man's megalomania. Of course I wasn't that deluded. Anyone in history who'd professed to be Jesus was out of his mind, dangerous. Yet oddly enough, Winchell seemed a relic of the past. Instead of fearing the future, his subjects rejoiced. The meek really did inherit the earth.

—W—

At one of these block parties, someone took me aside, a married woman of fifty whose husband had died. "I won't call myself a widow because of the unnatural way he died: this *war*." She said it like it was cancer, worse than cancer. She was a portly woman who managed to keep her heft through the war. She told me she hid out in the basement of a farmhouse in England, an American living abroad, and lived off a storehouse of canned jam and wine. Her husband had gone off to look for candles and food and never returned. She didn't look like someone who could survive war, or even run a mile. She was wide, breathed heavy, but cheery, even when talking about death. She sat out the war mostly in the dark, except for a small, thick basement window, and listened to the sounds of war. When she finally stepped outside, she found that the entire surrounding countryside was devastated, burnt to the ground. Many others had stories like this—a sort of supernatural occurrence of surviving amid total devastation.

We talked over canned salmon and crackers. Forty or so people milled about a table of food. Some ten-year-olds passed an electric Frisbee. Children were much more restless than adults, even though every day was recess. No school for now. The woman talked as though repeating a story she'd told many times before—but like a theatre actress who recites the same monologue fresh every night. A baffling talent, to my mind.

"One night I crept upstairs. It was pitch black. I was as quiet as possible. I didn't know what could be outside, or even in the house. Though I hadn't heard any footsteps from the basement. I was just so terrifically bored. It's amazing how boredom can sometimes trump survival. The things you learn. I just needed something to *read*. There were so many books upstairs. My husband was a collector. There were none in the basement because of the flooding. I'm telling you, I was afraid to move in that basement, but I couldn't help exploring. They say solitary confinement is not very healthy, it can ruin a person, like not dreaming. I couldn't sit there grieving for my husband. I needed other voices than my own. So I went upstairs and got a pile of books—quickly, I wasn't even sure what they were, and some new clothes. I spent the remainder of my time reading those books, reading a couple more than once. One book really stuck with me though. I mean, really."

"Which one?" I asked. I was transfixed by her monologue. In another time, this would have bothered me—someone talking and talking without stopping for a question, or to see if the other person was interested. But of course I was more forgiving now. She wasn't narcissistic, but energetic, like she was compelled to talk.

"*The American Book of the Dead,*" she said and my heart jumped. I actually felt a sudden pain in my chest.

"I'm sorry, which book?"

"*The American Book of the Dead*. A novel. Written years ago."

"By who?" I asked.

"It's about the writer, Eugene Myers. He became my best friend. Because the weird thing is, the weird thing," she sidled up to me and spoke quietly, "he predicted everything that would happen. Everything."

How was this possible, I thought. But how was it possible that a bird had flown out of a book a few days earlier? A book I had yet to finish had already been published, meaning it was written by me when I was much younger. The past and future were coming together. The world was becoming timeless and limitless. The initial shock lifted and it felt...inevitable. This was, after all, the point of the book itself. And now it was a reality.

"The book kept me sane. I've been waiting to..." she said and trailed off.

"Waiting to what?" I asked.

"Waiting to meet the writer," she said quickly and caught herself. "That sounds silly but it's true. I've been telling everybody that I'm in the book even though we've never met. They look at me like I'm crazy. Some though, mention seeing someone in their dreams just like the novel. The book's about dreams. There's a section in the book about a woman holed up in the basement reading the book who survives. There was so much else in the novel that came true, I thought maybe, just maybe it was me. Even if it was a delusion, it was comforting, you know? Anything to keep you going. Have you read the book?

"Yes," I answered. "I wrote it."

"What?"

"I'm Eugene Myers."

"Oh my God, it's happened," she breathed. "Just like the book."

"Yes."

"I've been trying to track you down for the longest time," she said. "I thought I was mad. I had a feeling when I saw you, but I didn't want to let on. I've been obsessed with having our meeting unfold just like the book." She didn't look cheerful anymore, she looked overcome, but also determined. "We need to do something about this."

"Do what?" I said.

"Tell people who you are. Anyone who will listen. Anything to counter what Winchell is peddling. I mean, I'm a Christian, but I'm not his kind of Christian." She put a hand to her mouth. "Oh my God, that's right from the book. Do you remember?"

"Not exactly," I said. "Do you have a copy of the novel?"

"Of course," she said. "It's become like a Bible to me."

I felt slightly nauseated. Not about her reverence—if I'd written her into a book without knowing her, she had reason to be overwhelmed. But this woman had a book that would predict my own future. Everything I did from this point forward had already been written. I felt powerless. As if I had no control over my life—it was decided for me. It was not a good feeling, no matter the pride about predicting my future as a young man.

"I've met other people who knew about the dreams," she said. "But I needed to confirm that I was really in the book. Thankfully, there are other people who want to get the word out about what you've done as well."

She reached into her purse and handed me a flyer. It had a recent picture of me taken without my knowledge like a private investigator photograph—with words underneath it like a sign for a lost dog: "Have you seen this man? Dr. Eugene Myers, writer and seer, will speak Friday evening, 8:00 p.m. Please join us."

"Who gave you this?" I asked.

"That woman over there." Charlotte pointed to Portia, the zealot.

"Can I have this?"

"Of course. I'm passing it out to everyone I see."

I stomped over to Portia and held up the flyer in her face.

"What is this?" I demanded.

Portia was undeterred.

"It's an invitation," she said.

"You consider asking me about this before you advertised it?"

"I wanted to make sure you would come. Otherwise you might have avoided it, Dr. Myers. Without you, none of this would have happened. It's time for you to take responsibility for that. People need you."

"Where have you posted the flyer?" I said.

"Oh, many places. On streetlamps, in mailboxes, handing them out. Many people from our group are helping. It's very exciting."

I slumped, worried about what was being asked of me, but powerless to fight it. I knew the outcome was inevitable—just as the ending of a book can't be different each time you read it. I had written my own fate.

"I should have been asked," I said, dimly.

—◇◇◇—

Dominique and I sat in the living room, alone in our house.

"What's the worst that could happen?" she said.

"The worst is that people could believe I'm something I'm not. These are fragile times. People have had their lives overturned. They're looking for a savior, and I'm no savior."

"They're looking for some answers, that's all. Who knows, if you don't take the initiative, Winchell could turn this into an internment camp. And if your book is accurate, you have nothing to worry about." She smiled thoughtfully. "After all, this scene is in the book too. The scene where we talk about your fears about giving the speech."

"Yes, but I still have to live my life. And if it's been pre-determined then I have no power at all. I'm just a puppet of my own mind." I put a hand on my head, as if to feel my brain. "Jesus, this is eerie. Do I really have no free will whatsoever? That seems a strange fate for someone who invents things that turn out to be real. I'm a nobody, do you remember that? I'm a failed writer."

"Not any longer, you've become—"

The doorbell rang. I went to get it. A young couple, college age, were standing at the door. One held a clipboard—they looked liked canvassers for a candidate; optimistic, malleable.

"Yes?"

"Sir, we would like to invite you to a gathering on Friday night, led by Dr. Eugene Myers."

The girl held out a flyer. I grabbed it from her hand.
"Yes, I know about it." I closed the door.
I looked back at Dominique. She laughed.

23: Coup de Grace

"Charles," David said. "I have some news."

David was his father's assistant. He looked like a newscaster and could have been one. He had always followed the news religiously, on the left and right, a true political junkie. Benjamin Winchell had once told Charles that David reminded him of himself, like he was a second and more likable son, with no regard for how this would hurt Charles. Remember, David was the one who carted Charles off the stage at the country club. Just reluctantly following boss's orders. In reality, David was in the Charles Winchell camp. He had become a trusted advisor, in a perfect position to spy on Benjamin Winchell.

"There's talk of a coup attempt," David said gravely.

"Of what?"

"Of killing you."

Charles took this in slowly. Somehow, he was not hurt. Actually, it pleased him. Sure, this was his father talking about killing his own son, but you only assassinated important people—people with power. Others were just left to die. He was one of the American immortals, like the Kennedys.

"I assumed something like this would happen," Charles said.

"You did?" David said, meekly, like a son who'd found out his father was dying.

"Yes, it is inevitable. It always happens when someone becomes too powerful. When do they intend on doing this?"

"I'm not certain. I'm sorry. I only heard the conversation

about deciding to get you out of the picture. I'm not entirely sure they've decided on a time or place. But you better be careful."

"That's OK. I'm very well protected. We've planned for it."

"I'm glad to hear that because I've been increasingly worried. It's getting harder for me to be impartial. I don't know how much more I can take while still holding my tongue."

"Thank you, David. You've done fine," Charles said calmly. He put his hands on David's shoulders, which seemed to calm him down immediately. Charles was falling very well into the role of a wise old sage—unaffected, unlike earlier in his life when every slight hurt him. He was becoming more Christ-like with each passing day. Peace flowed through him. David seemed to notice this because he lowered his head reverently, bowing slightly, and left.

There was little cause for alarm. Since he moved to Los Angeles, Charles had an active secret service detail, comprised of those who knew about the Revelation Operation. He admitted they did not quite have the skill of his Secret Service before the war. Most of his old Secret Service were dead. This group were young men, mostly 18, some as young as sixteen, who kept watch over Charles' house—the children of the families who believed in Phase III, Winchell's divinity. An army of Christ. Charles could feel the momentum building in the new community—he was told of mass rallies of Christianist survivors, raising signs that said "Winchell is Lord" and "The Beginning is Near." As with any presidential election, they needed a mandate so there could be a smooth transition. And they required an army that could enforce their rule over whatever non-believers remained. His group of vigilant young men were up to the task, bred for this. The Winchell youth. Until it was proven that Charles was the Second Coming, they were still at war.

Which was why it was necessary to determine who was the Beast so all this could get underway. In the meantime, something must be done about his father. Charles didn't revel in the idea of killing his father. He despised the idea, as much as he also despised his father's point of view. That was the forgiving God within Charles coming forward. Perhaps he could just put Benjamin in jail. Lock him in a basement. The actual jail—at the local precinct—had been flooded and needed repair. Unfortunately, a number of people were in his father's camp as well—as many as in Charles' own. David had shown him a list of names—some of whom hurt Charles, former allies in his administration and abroad. Benjamin was the figurehead, the architect, so taking him down would be a crucial first step, but it wouldn't be the end.

There was a knock at the door of his office. A young guard came into the room and said, "It's your father at the front gate. He's alone."

Charles mused at the coincidence. His powers were growing still. "It's OK, let him in. But be wary, keep a lookout."

Charles walked to the front door and opened it himself. There was his father laboring up the driveway. He looked tired, whiter, as if his hair had gone more gray in the last week and his skin was losing life. They had stopped talking since the speech at the country club a few days before. This was part of the reason David had been enlisted to spy on his boss. There was no way to gauge his father's actions from a distance.

"Father," Charles said with his hand up in a half-wave.

"Charles," his father said sternly when he made it to the door. "We've got a problem."

"I know," replied Charles.

Charles brought his father into the living room, where David had told him about the plans for a coup minutes before. Was it possible that his father was coming to do the deed himself? Charles was disgusted by how far his father had fallen, but he was restrained. "Please have a seat," Charles said.

Benjamin Winchell fell back into the couch with a groan. He looked so defeated—normally emanating confidence and arrogance. It was eerie, ghostly, but also good news. The battle was already being won.

"What is it you need?" Charles said.

"I've been very pissed off at you," his father replied.

"I know."

"An entire world we've destroyed," he said. "And you sabotage our hope just as we're ready to begin a new life. You've had me doubting the war, Charles, terribly. You should have told me that you had other ideas. This moment is too important for there to be secrets. Not between people in our position."

"You wouldn't have believed me," Charles said. "And I didn't believe in your side of the story."

"That's fine, but humanity's at stake here. A lot of people have died and a lot has been destroyed, irretrievably. It's nothing to play around with. The aftermath shouldn't be determined by one man's ego."

Charles sat back comfortably in his seat. "Well, that's the problem, isn't it? Ego—you know you're right and so do I."

"Charles, there is so much you don't know. So much information you're not taking into account. I can't even begin."

"Like what?"

"Like the Bible is only part of the truth. It takes stories from other cultures, it's part of a perennial philosophy. Does it really make sense for one human to be the representation of God in the entire universe? The universe is big, comprised of other dimensions, other worlds, the afterlife. Jesus is a great idea, I'll grant you, but God is so much bigger than one man." He paused. "You know, I don't really want to debate theology with you, Charles. And I don't want to see you get hurt. I'd like to talk some sense into you. You've got a lot of people very angry at you."

"And I've got just as many that believe in me."

"Yes," Benjamin said and sighed. "This is becoming unmanageable. Who thought that forty thousand people could be so difficult to govern? I thought after the war would be much easier, it would run itself, a collective sigh of relief. It's almost as if all this—" he gestured to the house as if it represented the war—"should never have occurred. It's such a shame. And now there's a new problem."

"What?" Charles said with some alarm.

His father reached into his jacket pocket and Charles feared he might be taking out a gun. Charles looked in panic at the dresser in the corner of the room. In every room there was a gun. He was about to call out and run. But his father merely removed a folded stack of papers. "Here," he said.

It was an invitation on a simple xeroxed sheet of paper. At the top it said, "Come see the author Eugene Myers discuss his book, *The American Book of the Dead*, a book which predicts many—if not all—of the things we have recently been through. Included here are sections of the book that parallel all of our lives, word for word.

"He saved thousands of us by appearing in dreams—chronicled in a book written years before the war. What does it mean? That's just what we aim to find out.

"This is no joke. *The American Book* was published in 2009, well before Charles Winchell was even elected.

"We can't trust the government anymore. Look where they have brought us.

"Come see us if you are interested in the future. Be sure to read the attached sections of the book. It proves everything." It then gave a date and location.

Charles turned the page and read the attached pages while his father watched. There was a description of his candidacy, including the Apocalypse Ticket. More importantly, there were excerpts from his speech declaring himself the Anti-Christ that were nearly verbatim, as well as he could remember. Scenes about the war. Scenes about the new community. And, finally, a scene where the president reads the flyer that he had just read himself. It was chilling.

Charles looked up from the pages. "Do you know this writer?"

"No. I've never heard of him. We've been looking for a copy of his book but we can't find one. There wasn't one at the local bookstore and the library's been flooded out."

"What does this mean?"

"I don't know, but it makes things a lot more complicated. And things were pretty Goddamn complicated already. From what I gather about the book, he was against the war, which means people could turn against us. If people start believing in this guy, or in this book, it could start an uprising against what I'm trying to accomplish. What we're both trying to accomplish."

"But Benjamin," Charles said mockingly. He rarely, if ever, called his father Benjamin. "I thought you were trying to create a utopia in which people live as an enlightened species. In your way."

"Yes, but they need to do it collectively. There are rules to follow, as you know. This *American Book* could turn into a cult. People are looking for something to believe in and all these divergent ideas will just make the utopia more difficult, no different than before the war. Fragmented and adversarial. Which is why you screwed up the plan so much. Got people off the same page. I was counting on everyone to start working towards the same collective goal, and now everyone's in competition."

"So what are you going to do about it?"

"We have people going to this meeting and see if it amounts to anything. If we kill him, this could just make him a martyr. Word about the book might spread more quickly. An assassination is on the table. But Charles—Charles, I really need you to stop your crusade. It could have terrible long-term consequences. We could just be starting over with the same civilization, but with no chance for evolution. Just in much smaller numbers. We can't have that. I want to be one of the evolved. I'd like to see you become one of the evolved as well. Not just part of a new primitive civilization."

It was so sad to see his father like this—but unsurprising, a man of so little faith. Tragic, seeing the pillar become weak. He didn't want to see his father left behind either. Charles *was* evolved. Throughout this conversation something had been formulating in Charles' mind. What his father thought was a problem, Charles realized was the best news he'd heard since the war began.

Simply put, Charles had found his Satan. This Eugene Myers, author of *The American Book of the Dead*. Myers was the man who would turn the new masses against Christianity, and against Charles himself. A man with a parlor trick of predicting the future—hypnotizing people into believing he was worth attention. This was Charles' greatest adversary.

His father was fading, hardly a threat. Charles still had to be on guard against a coup attempt from his father's side—especially with this new confusion. His father might want to eliminate one wing of the confusion. Charles would start wearing bulletproof protection again.

But really all this was a technicality. With Eugene Myers, Charles had a spiritual problem, predicted by a book thousands of years older than this *novel*—he spoke the word bitterly to himself. It was perfect: one book that had predicted the future against another. A good book against a vile one. With Myers gone, the thousand-year reign could finally begin. Charles was nearly dying with anticipation.

These thoughts on his mind, Charles said goodbye and closed the door on his father.

—⋎⋎⋎—

Charles relayed this new information to his team. They were equally as ecstatic. Only one step in the process remained. Charles recited 1 Timothy 4:1—"In the latter times some will depart from the faith, giving heed to seducing spirits, and doctrines of devils." Eugene Myers was clearly the false prophet. The final showdown would be between a president and a writer: who do you think had a better chance?

"But what if in the book it's written that you lose the showdown?" David inquired.

Charles shot him a look of such derision that David might have died instantly—once the battle was over and Charles had actual power.

"A lot of the book did come true," David added, as if the derision meant nothing.

"The information contained in that book is a trick, the work of the devil. Of course there is some truth in the novel, as the devil has some degree of power. But the power of good will always outweigh the power of evil. We have no room for doubters here, David. We will banish you from this place if you are not a follower."

That silenced him.

"What we must do is kill Eugene Myers," Chief of Staff Whitehead said, glancing scornfully at David.

"Correction," Winchell replied. "*I* must kill Eugene Myers. You can be there as back-up, and as witnesses, but I must kill Eugene Myers myself. It is said to be a battle between the Lord and Satan, not a battle by committee. As it says in Revelations, 'The armies in heaven, clothed in fine linen, white and clean, followed him.' They followed him, not side by side."

They all agreed, nodding silently.

"One thing does concern me though," Charles said. "In the same scripture it is written, 'Out of his mouth goes a sharp sword.' What do you suppose this means? That I'm supposed to bite him? Or that I carry a knife in my mouth?"

There was quiet while they mulled this over.

"It could be your words," David said, trying to get back in good graces. "That you are supposed to strike him down with your words, a biting tongue."

"That's not strong enough," Charles replied sharply.

"Maybe it just means a sword," Whitehead said. "A sword and words together."

"Yes, I like that."

"And because it was written in ancient times, before guns existed, a sword was selected as the weapon of choice. In the present day, you could very well use a gun, much like this war used weapons of the future not mentioned in the Bible."

"I think I would prefer that," Charles said with some relief. "A gun would be easier, and cleaner. Wouldn't want to mess up any of our fine white linens, would we?" He snickered.

There was laughter.

"A gun it is then."

The group kneeled and prayed to be victorious in the battle between light and dark.

24: Second Crucifixion

The meeting was coming together. The woman named Charlotte was a big help. She told me that she had been an HR manager for a large software-development company. She had also headed charities. "Cancer and animals," she said. Some of these old skills were springing into action. I did none of the organizing myself. I was unavoidably worried about making this thing so public. Part of it was stage fright and part was that I knew that Winchell had heard about it. If you knew ahead of time that someone was going to come after you with a gun, you'd be fearful, even if it gave you time to duck. And who knew, maybe being so hyper-conscious of the future could alter it in some way. Just as you didn't want to go back in time and kill your parents when they were children, you also didn't want to know how your life played out. There were many possible futures—maybe the book had become real because no one believed it, and now that many did could it alter the fabric of the future? Or increase its inevitability? I couldn't say. The book was turning me into a neurotic.

When I began writing the novel, initially, I was lost, a failure, struggling as a writer. And no—I didn't remember writing it when I was younger. These ideas were somehow sent from me to my younger self, both of us writing at the same time. An open line of communication between a young writer imagining himself as an older person, and an older person imagining who he wanted to be. I suppose I could have seen this all coming, but this plot point was not part of my original conception. Even so, I could remember who I was twenty years earlier and what my purpose would have been for the book. The same as in the present. I wanted to write something that would force people into thinking the book was important. I wanted to feed my family. The book was a product of an overactive ego, still clinging to oversized hopes for my future. Back then I wouldn't have to face the pain of real events. I could just dream about what I would become, while being careless about what had made that possible. I could never say that I wasn't proud that the book had come true, but it was unhealthy: vindication of a person who was self-involved to the point of isolation. I was older now and realized the infinite things I did not know. I was less prone to arrogance, so I was able to better weather this realization. Twenty years earlier and I might have started a church.

Irony, of course. Because that was exactly what this meeting could turn out to be. Far different from any literary reading or book group. This was going to be a service. I could feel it, apart from anything that had been written in the book. People were hopeful, they thought this might be an answer. I wasn't sure what all I could give them. If I just read straight from the book, like any reading, that would not reassure them. Memorizing passages wouldn't be very effective either. Too nervous, too much emotion. I was terrible at learning a new language; this felt something the same. I was a natural introvert, an anti-actor. This would not come easy, except on paper.

Charlotte gave me a copy of my novel, which I had never seen—a cover that wasn't far off from what I'd envisioned. I read it to the end, which was a singularly disturbing experience, almost traumatic. A memoir of something yet to happen. The book was identical to the book I was currently writing—down to the point where I continued writing the book even after I discovered it had already been written. I kept writing because that seemed to follow the rules of the book. You might think I'd check the book to see if every action I made was reflected in the novel. I didn't. I started to do that, then stopped. I didn't want to use the novel as a manual for how I should live: memorize what I said in dialogue and recite it as if it were real. That felt wrong, too restrained, even inhuman. I needed to live my life naturally, not as if pre-determined—fateless. And besides, if the book was accurate, it didn't matter what I did. It would be in there. So I left the book alone. My final justification was that the character in the book makes the same decision as I did—to leave the book alone. That was the last thing I needed to read.

But I would have to come up with something for the speech. The meeting was this evening. At Charlotte's house, at the top of our block. Or, rather, in the street outside Charlotte's house, which sloped downward in a fairly straight line like an amphitheatre, so a large number of people could converge and still be able to watch. Charlotte had tracked down a P.A. in the basement of someone's house.

I showed up four hours before the meeting was supposed to begin. Several audience members had already arrived, milling about or spread out on blankets. I walked past them, feeling strangely like an imposter—like they belonged here and I didn't. Charlotte ran up to me as soon as she spied me. "I'm so glad you're here," she said, anxiously. "I think we're going to have a great turnout. Already fifty or so people have been up here. Unfortunately we don't have a lot of refreshments to feed all these people. We don't want to use up all of our rations for one party."

"I think it's going to go well," I said.

"Of course it will. But I still have to do the work, even if it's inevitable. I always feel like there's something I've forgotten."

"If the book says everything went fine then don't worry about it."

I didn't quite believe this but it made her comfortable.

"I feel it's so odd to check the book to see what is going to happen or what I should do," she said. "As if it's against the laws of nature."

"I've had the same experience."

"Like I have no free will."

I nodded.

"So I don't check the book very often," she said, apologetically.

"That's OK, neither do I. What happens happens. Let's just hope that I wasn't right about everything except what happens tonight."

I regretted that one as soon as it was out.

"I don't think that will happen," she said, as if saying, Please, I have enough to worry about.

"It'll go fine," I amended.

She nodded blankly and turned to the stage, which wasn't much of anything except two large P.A. speakers and a microphone stand. Much different than Winchell's earlier address at the golf club, which was professionally set up like it had been prepared for months.

"What would you like me to do?" I asked.

"Nothing," she said. "You just rest up for tonight. You're the main event! This is so exciting." She said this with more trepidation than excitement. She touched my cheek with her palm and walked determinedly toward the stage.

I didn't have anything to do for the next four hours. Standing alone, not talking, was making me nervous. At past readings, I'd take a drug for stage fright—taken by the entire New York Philharmonic, I was told. Otherwise, my heart would pound in such a way that I could barely speak. My hands would tremble embarrassingly and sweat. I didn't have that luxury right now, and this would be the biggest presentation of my life, in front of the largest audience.

A young couple were sitting on a blanket on the grass median between the sidewalk and street. The grass was now four inches high. Some people were mowing their lawns, but not everyone. I approached the couple.

"Hi," they said, brightly. "Sit down." As I mentioned, people were much more welcoming these days. But this couple might always have been. They were in their twenties, attractive, and optimistic-looking, like this could be a college lawn. Strangers who had found each other quickly in this neighborhood. They were wearing hand-me-down clothes from wherever they were staying and blended well together.

I sat down on the blanket. They were sharing a can of peaches.

"I'm Gene," I said.

"This is Greg," the girl said. "And I'm Jannifer."

"Jannifer?"

"Yes."

"I'm curious," I said. "How did you hear about this meeting?"

"Oh, we got the pamphlet like everybody," Greg said.

"I see. And were you convinced about the writer right away?"

"Sure, what's not to believe? Everything in the book came true," he said.

"And living through this war has shown us there's something else out there," Jannifer said. "Many say it's evidence that there is no God but, I don't know, I think it must have happened for a reason."

"This book might be a key," Greg added. "He appeared in people's *dreams*." He said this as if the word itself couldn't be believed.

"So what do you hope to learn tonight?" I asked.

"I'm not sure," Greg said. "I just hope to make some sense of all this."

"So do I," I said. "What do you want Myers to say?"

"I guess something about how he came to write the book and what all this means to him." He said this with no reverence, as if it was a fact: "He's like a God: he predicted the war and saved people's lives, that's pretty incredible."

"He's a prophet," the girl added.

"OK, thanks," I said, feeling weighted. "See you tonight."

We said goodbyes and I walked on, more or less feeling the

same as when I arrived: responsible for too many people's hope and fearing battle with a psychotic president. I didn't know what I was going to do that night.

"Are you him?" I heard called to my back as I walked away. "Are you the writer?" But I pretended I didn't hear. I didn't want to lie and I didn't want their attention.

—MW—

The time had arrived. I'd spent the remaining hours walking around our neighborhood, jotting down notes, refining what I was going to say. I wanted to be alone. I went back home, where Geoff said, "Ready for the big night?" with a tone like I was woefully unprepared, or maybe I was imagining that. I paced the streets some more and then made my way to the meeting area, walking on my own.

As I approached Charlotte's neighborhood, it was madness. Two miles back I could see a great number of people making their way up to the stage, some holding hands, some holding printouts, all expecting something. My heart pounded sickly-deep the closer I got to the stage so it was getting tough to breathe.

There was a crush of people nearly a quarter-mile back from the stage, pressed close together. I pushed my way to the front and was relieved to find that Dominique and the group had already arrived. They were a comfort; at least I wasn't alone in a crowd.

"You always said that you wanted to be a wildly successful writer," Dominique said. "Now the entire world knows who you are. All of them." She laughed.

"God, I hope this goes well," I said.

"It will go fine, Gene."

"And what if Winchell comes here to kill me?"

"We have a group of people on the lookout. You've got your bulletproof vest on, right?"

"Right."

"Then relax. Everyone is here to see you."

"That's the problem."

Charlotte greeted us with widespread arms, face flushed with happiness and anxiety.

"Eugene, my Eugene," she said. "I'm so glad you've arrived. Not bad, huh?" She beamed proudly. "Better than I expected."

"Maybe they're just bored. Nothing else to do."

"Oh, Eugene," she said teasingly and hit me on the shoulder.

"There's someone I want you to meet," she said, prouder still. "Someone important. Amy, Amy," she called. "Could you come here for a moment?"

A woman walked our way and I recognized her immediately as the First Lady, Amy Winchell.

A shocking sight, even now, someone as famous as she was. Even if I'd written about her, she had more presence in person. I didn't dislike Amy Winchell. She was intelligent—in a different league than her husband. I did, however, blame her for not leaving him when all this began, for not speaking out. What I'd written about her was perhaps more sympathetic than what I felt.

Still, she was here, in some way my guest.

Charlotte said, "Gene, I want you to meet the First Lady."

"I'm not the First Lady anymore," she replied. "I'm just a citizen."

"Fine to meet you," I said. We shook hands. Her eyes were bright and warm. There was a light about her, as if her skin glowed. It was odd—like her fame and her position made her stand out physically from all these other people on the dimly-lit street.

A stranger stepped in, gruff, bearded, an old hippie. "Hello, First Lady," he said abruptly. "I just want to say to you that I hate your husband."

She didn't appear struck down by this. More, she seemed pleased. "I don't like him either," she said. "Actually, I think he's a fucking idiot."

Everyone laughed and we were all immediately won over.

"In fact," she said, "I'm hoping this meeting will be the thing to help counter his lunatic ideas. There are other people who are against his line of thinking as well, so take heart."

I nodded.

"I hear that you wrote about me in your book," she said. "How do I appear?"

"Fine," I replied. "I just wrote about the problems between husband and wife. Something I know well about."

She smiled.

Charlotte stepped in. "Should we begin? I was thinking that I could give a brief introduction, then maybe the First La—maybe you could say something, and then Gene can go on."

"Hard act to follow," I said. Somehow, my heart was no longer beating as hard. The presence of the First Lady, a professional, experienced, was calming.

"OK, let's begin," Charlotte declared. She just about ran to the microphone.

"Hello, everyone," she said into the mic. "Hello. Can everyone hear me?" Most people started quieting down and faced forward. "Good. Thank you so much for coming here tonight." She cleared her throat nervously. "I had no idea how many would show up tonight. Then again, we're all looking for answers after what we've been through. We've either dreamt this man or heard about his story. It's kind of magical, but also a profound responsibility." I groaned inwardly at the heavy-handedness. "Let me tell you something about how I read this book because many of you haven't read it yourselves."

She launched into her story about discovering my book. I looked out on the crowd. They were listening, interested. This felt insane—like an inaugural address for a writer. Too much, but I had no choice. The crowd's expectations were pushing me on. I was a reluctant leader, having never been much of a leader in my life. Hell, I'd hardly had any friends for most of my life, from high school on. After being a well-adjusted child, adolescence hit me, and my parents, like a brick. Then my life in New York City, up to my time in L.A. teaching, where I had acquaintances but few friends, few people to count on and who counted on me. Regretted it always. I had a terrible capacity for solitude. Stephanie had been the same—which was why we were exactly right for each other and exactly wrong. Ironically, my total alienation from people was how I could write about the genocide of humanity without a second thought.

Next, Charlotte introduced the First Lady. "This woman needs no introduction. I am sure she is familiar to all of you. I'm certain you are going to want to hear what she has to say. Please give her a warm welcome. Ladies and gentlemen, the First Lady."

Charlotte conspicuously left off the First Lady's name. Hearing the name Winchell again would not have been received very well. As it was, there were some boos in the crowd, and only polite applause.

"Hello, welcome," she said. "I heard some boos when I came up to the mic and I don't blame you. I would have done the same. I have been ashamed. I have been unable to look myself in the mirror. I wanted to stop this war but I could not faced with the machine that was already put in motion. I have cried most nights. I hate my husband as well." She paused to let that drift over the crowd. "Let me make clear, I don't hate the concept of Jesus. Christ is a beautiful idea when not corrupted, which is too often not the case. But my husband—my ex-husband—is deluded and dangerous. This war is all the proof you need. It should go without saying that extermination is not the path to God. Nor is an inflated ego and megalomania.

"But we must make do with what we have now. We will make the best of it. I don't know all of the implications of the book by Mr. Myers, but I do know that the novel makes more sense than literal genocide. I also know that this moment in history is not about establishing a cult or new religion. The universe is much larger than one book. I don't mean to devalue a man who may have been prophetic, I just want to argue against blind worship. Blind worship has gotten us to where we are today. If the book can be one avenue towards stopping the violence and mindlessness that have led us here, then all the better.

"I don't want to say too much. This is Mr. Myers' night, not mine. So here I give you the man you've been waiting to see. Try and not let this go to his head."

She looked over at me and smiled warmly. I walked on stage and there was loud applause—though I imagine this was for the First Lady who was departing the stage, and not me, who was entering.

I looked out on the crowd. The streetlights were dim so I could only see the faint outline of anonymous heads and eyes, not much more, as if they were all one person. My nerves had drifted as the First Lady spoke. I felt alone in a room. I was as blind as when I wrote, not really looking for words but letting them come, good or bad, obsessed with getting some ideas down on paper. I had to get this done. It was involuntary.

"Hello, everyone," I said, my voice sounding hollow, and I began. "This is not a position I'm entirely comfortable with. I've never been one of those people who could carry a room with a story. Always looked up to people who could. I'm somewhat of a private person. Not a born leader by any means. Some of you have read parts of my novel. Some of you had the dreams chronicled in the book. The novel was written tongue-in-cheek to a degree, a way to resuscitate a faltering career. It was also a kind of prayer about what I wished I could be—not to be ultra-famous, but, on some level, to have an impact. I imagine that's every writer's dream. And then the book turned out to be real. Believe me, I'm a humble person—I was merely looking for a story to tell. I was looking to exorcise my fear about the current situation." I stopped myself. "Forget exorcise. Nothing religious, like the First Lady said. I was venting anger, fear, and maybe some hope that we could live differently. That this all came true is bad news. None of this should have had to happen."

I paused. That said enough, I thought. They looked up at

me expectantly. Even if I couldn't see them, I could feel it. I hit a short block but I moved on.

"This is hard for me. I'm not exactly sure what you require, and what won't come off too much as praise for myself. The war has been a shock to my system like all of you, this meeting is yet another shock." I didn't want to be too negative. "On the other hand, it is very good news that the book has come alive. We have a lot to look forward to. The war, the novel, are all a catalyst." I stopped again. A catalyst? Jesus, that was presumptuous. "The future is up to all of us. Just rest safe knowing that together we can help create a utopia."

"You're a liar!" someone shouted.

There were sounds of "ssh" from the crowd, and "Sit down."

I couldn't see if the person was sitting or standing. I knew who it was, of course. And what would happen. Things would unfold just like the novel. He had somehow made his way to the front of the packed crowd. He stood ten feet from me.

"Everything he says is a lie." He looked back at the crowd. "Can't you see, people, that he is a false prophet, leading you down the unclean path with trickery and magic? He is Satan."

This wasn't entirely effective because Winchell didn't speak into the mic, so only those in the front could hear him. I almost wanted to say, for the benefit of the people in back, "He says he thinks I'm Satan."

Instead, I said into the mic, "Ladies and gentlemen, the president of the United States."

Some people instinctively started applauding, but that quickly died off. Then there was a hushed silence as the crowd wondered what his appearance meant.

"You are the Anti-Christ," he said to me.

"I thought that was you," I replied.

There was some laughter.

"Of course you have them on your side," Winchell said, bitingly. "You are powerful. But not nearly as powerful as I am."

"I don't believe in God or Satan being represented by one

man," I said. "It is overvaluing one man that devalues others."

There was applause after that one. I was falling into this role quite quickly.

The First Lady stepped up. "Charles, you have to stop," she said.

"Be quiet, Amy," he snapped. "This is partly your fault."

He seemed as much hurt by her as anything I'd said, or all these people turned against him. Weakened by the sight of her. He took out a gun then. There were some shrieks. I looked out into the audience and could faintly see men with rifles or other weapons scattered throughout the crowd, keeping everyone still.

"I come quickly," Winchell said. "All authority has been given me in heaven and on earth."

And then he shot me. It hurt like hell and I fell. There were screams, a terrible sound, as if everyone got shot at once.

I stood up slowly. Bulletproof vests work, but it still hurt, like the echo of a real gunshot wound. There were some gasps, as if people thought I'd risen from the dead.

"It's OK," I said. "I'm fine." I brushed myself off, as if this would alleviate the pain.

I looked back at Winchell. He aimed the gun at my head. He fired and missed, then looked at the gun as if it were broken. His mouth was agape, speechless.

The whole place suddenly lit up like it was daytime. There was a blinding white light in the sky—some kind of craft hovering above, as big as the neighborhood. Hard to make out any shape. It was like the sun had descended from the sky. The light made all color diffuse and indistinguishable, but it didn't hurt the eyes.

Winchell looked stricken—the worst expression, as if his life was ending before his eyes. He raised his gun like he was going to shoot me again. But then he put it to his temple and fired. Blood sprayed out from the wound like bits of light, as it reflected the blinding light above. There were no screams. Winchell fell limply to the ground.

I ran to where Winchell was lying on the pavement. He was still alive, gasping, bleeding out the mouth. His eyes looked like they were trying to keep him alive, wide and forceful. I bent down to hear what he was saying. Very broken, but he wheezed it out. "I'm Satan. I'm Satan. I'm Satan." Then it was done.

The crowd stood there, waiting. So many people, it was hard to move, unless everyone did. The men with guns, from what I could see, were stunned and silent. I sensed everyone needed something from me.

"Charles Winchell is dead," I said.

There was only silence, no applause. "He is dead."

I looked back up at the craft. It made no sound, as if it was taking sound from the air. Most of the crowd were pointing at it now, bathed in white light, but not fearful. Actually, most were grinning, amazed, even grateful. All gazing up like it was some peaceful joke, a benevolent God with a sense of humor hovering above us.

The light above became more solid—definitely some sort of UFO. Here's the punchline: it landed.

Epilogue: A.D.

The craft landed on the hillside. Or rather, it was too big to land anywhere else so it kind of molded to the shape of the mountain. There was a brief stand-off between the people on the ground and the beings who exited the craft—not out of any type of door but they suddenly appeared outside the craft onto the suburban street. First the greys, as expected, the stereotypical little grey men, then came a kind of bipedal dinosaur, a human-sized praying mantis. It was fantastic, but it also felt perfectly natural. Like seeing a relative you thought had died. Next came many mythological characters documented throughout history: faeries, leprechauns, chupacabra, as well as blonde humans from another world, a Noah's Ark of once-fictional characters. Sounds ridiculous, but you also felt like they'd always been here, trapped in our minds, and now we were finally seeing them.

Were these real beings or a projection of our imaginations? The difference no longer mattered, but the answer was: both. All of us were the product of self-perception and the perception of others—watched and read by beings of our own invention, some of the stories tragic, some uplifting. We were the universe's entertainment. And now these different realms of imagination had come together.

That's fairly abstract and there were pragmatic concerns as well. Such as how were we going to start living together, what our new society would be like. A grey came up to me, looked exactly like the others—four feet tall, skin like a suit, wide and unreadable eyes. I was a temporary leader, though there would be no leaders anymore. But I was the one currently documenting it. He (really it had no gender) told me they were from the future—what we would eventually evolve into being if we were forced to live underground, as would have been the case if the war had ended another way. Technologically rich, but emotionally dead. They were waiting for us to evolve, he said, before they could make contact.

"Couldn't we have evolved by learning about you earlier?" I asked. "This war could have been averted."

We spoke without talking.

"If first contact was made with eight billion people living as you were, violent and hating each other, it merely would have led to a world war for different reasons—led by people holding too tightly to their beliefs. Overturning a belief system is not guaranteed to be constructive."

"Then this war was necessary—in order to diminish the population to make the situation more manageable."

"No, this is just one possible way contact could come about. You have conceived one possible outcome. Every possible storyline is happening at once."

"That's fine, but the suffering was terrible."

"True, but that's only because you were at a point where the suffering was overwhelming and unavoidable. As you wrote, if people knew that death was not the end, but a beginning, they would rejoice any time a loved one died, and not mourn. Mourning death is one of the hallmarks of an early civilization."

"Physical pain is physical pain. Watching a child suffer is not a primitive feeling."

"Of course, but imagine a world where death did not matter: war would lose its utility and the pain of losing a loved one would take on a different meaning. People would be less dissatisfied with their current condition if they knew paradise was attainable. Each person would determine what could be learned from suffering, rather than feel forsaken. It would change the fabric of human civilization. A utopia isn't alleviating pain, but knowing that pain is a necessary part of the human system."

"All right," I said, plainly. Maybe this kind of New Age manifesto would have once been met with cynicism, and with doubt, but you try doubting when a grey alien is telling you the nature of reality.

"So what happens now?" I asked.

"Whatever you want," he replied. "Anything you imagine will now become manifest."

"I don't want you to exist," I said, challenging him, half-smiling.

"But I want to exist, so that is not going to work. There are rules, even here."

I looked down at my hands. I imagined a small tree sprouting out of my left palm. It happened like time-lapse photography, fruit growing on the branches, and I picked it with the other hand, where it quickly evaporated.

"This will take some getting used to," I said.

"Yes, it will. Any step forward in evolution takes practice. This world will have as many fits and starts as the old one, just without the unhappiness."

"Sounds like heaven. Something you wish to exist."

"Doesn't make it any less real."

I could see that he was going to have an answer for everything. I looked back at the group. Some were beginning to discover what they were now able to do. Talk to each other without speaking, levitate, converse with the dead. I saw an older woman reverse her age and then become old again. Some vaporized, then returned. Others were taking it slowly and mimicking my trick with the tree. There was no shock about this—more like curious kids with a new toy they'd just opened. I wanted to take this new power out for a spin as well.

I pictured what I wanted. And the idea spread through all of us at once. Nobody wanted to live in a ruined world. The world sprang back to life...

Picture the burnt-out neighborhoods of L.A., east to west. A city being built in reverse—crumbled concrete, shattered glass becoming whole. It's exactly how you'd see it in a movie: morphing into a new form. Maybe because movies were our only frame of reference, this was how the world was rebuilt. Broken-down buildings and smashed cars were put back together. Glass, metal, concrete, and wood moved like water. Wounds were healed, people rose from the dead: they gave a brief look of confusion before moving on as if nothing had happened. The entire city was alive again.

Now picture the same scene transpiring all over the world: the Eiffel Tower, Taj Mahal, Big Ben, the Louvre, the world's great cities, and humanity's greatest accomplishments, became whole again. It happened because you're imagining it happening.

—◦◦◦—

Dominique, Geoff, and I shared a drink. It was a bar frequented by survivors. We were living in a time right after Winchell took office. Why then? I had a feeling we were meant to live this life over again, see if we could get it right this time. Sophia was alive again. It was both exhilarating and strange. She remembered nothing of her experience because it never occurred. I apologized to her. She asked why and I had no other explanation except to give her a copy of my book. My wife and I were back together as well, living in our same little home. I had no need to live in a larger place, but money was no longer an issue.

One major thing remained from the aftereffects of the war: my novel, *The American Book of the Dead*, was on the shelves, published years earlier. My wife and daughter could read what I had written about them. As a young man, I had predicted terrible things about my daughter when she was just a toddler, and now she could read about her demise and resurrection.

Even if it was fiction, it was unsettling. I explained to her that the novel was a prolonged worst-case scenario, the archetype of my worst fears, not something I actually thought would happen. Yet even if the novel never came true, it was something I imagined, which was its own kind of reality. Maybe this doesn't need to be said, but my daughter was young when I wrote the book initially and she wouldn't understand the implications until now. I was writing about the best and worst elements of my life, which meant putting my family in jeopardy.

But what was done was done. I wasn't going to censor myself by rewriting the book—something that was in my power. I couldn't erase catharsis: what I'd purged by writing about my worst fears. No matter what I'd achieved, I was still a writer and had to face the consequences about the novel. Mostly I was at peace with what I'd written, the hardest work behind me and better life ahead.

There was some sense of distance between those who survived the war and those who didn't. The survivors shared something impossible to describe—something alien to anyone but ourselves. So we hung together in places like this bar. We liked the comfort of being with each other where we didn't have to hide. Possibly reprehensible—like celebrities who only married each other, but we shared something that couldn't be explained. We knew this was something that needed to remain private. What would happen if it was revealed that the majority of the human population was unevolved, and the only way to evolve was to die? It could turn into a disaster. People might think life was even less worth living. We were smart enough to keep silent. The bar was full of people—most liked the familiarity of the old world. They traveled to far-off planets, via remote viewing, only to come back to earth again, like coming back to family.

And the full story of humanity hadn't been written yet. On the surface, the world was the same it always had been, with all of the same problems. If you're wondering, we couldn't wish the new evolution on everyone else because it needed to be gradual. That was one of the rules of the new system. If eight billion people suddenly had this power—without the humility of seeing the world destroyed—it would have led to destruction and madness. In any evolutionary leap, the entire species didn't evolve at once, only some did and the others died off. But for humans, it was different because this was an evolution of consciousness, not of physical strength. Part of that evolution was coming to the aid of those who hadn't yet made the leap. There was still work to do. So our world was a mixture of the surreal and the normal: the survivors hanging together in bars, homes, or other locations. Not abusing our power, we wouldn't think of it, but planning how to use this power for good, quietly underground.

"Bartender, another round please," I said.

The bartender looked our way and smiled. Our glasses were filled without the bartender raising a bottle or moving.

"Thank God you can still drink on the other side," Geoff said. "I like it, even if I don't need it."

"Hear, hear. And there's no hangover," Dominique added. "It almost seems too easy."

We all drank.

"You know what's troubling me though?" I said. "The president started the war to change the human soul. And he did."

"Right, he did," Geoff said.

"As if world war is inevitable and necessary."

"I don't know about that," Dominique said. "I think this could happen even without a World War III."

"You want to see if that's true?" I asked the table.

A look went around. Everyone agreed.

"All right. Let's go stop a president."

—∿∿—

In a blink, I woke up a year earlier, in bed, before all this started. Before the "Apocalypse Ticket" was even an idea. I looked over at Stephanie, who was sitting up in bed reading a book—rereading *Alas, Babylon*, one of her favorites.

"Good dream?" she asked.

"Strangest dream of my life," I said.

But then I woke up again—at my desk, my head lying uncomfortably on my laptop keyboard. On the screen was a draft of *The American Book of the Dead*. I scrolled through the book and could only find the first two chapters. Almighty, that wasn't all a dream, was it? That would be incredibly disappointing. Not only to me, but anyone reading this book. Shit, such a clichéd way to end this. I remembered: I'd passed out with despondency and loathing after writing the chapter about catching my daughter online. At least the novel had already been conceived for me. And now that I knew what was going to happen, I could change the ending.

But maybe not. Maybe I had to finally face reality. This wasn't heaven where I was beloved and immortal. Where my self-indulgence and isolation were rewarded. Where the earth became one with the universe and the future justified everything that came before it. No, this was hell where I remained unread and forgotten, while the world slowly died without purpose and all my hope was fiction.

Stephanie entered the room, carrying laundry in a blue basket.

"You fell asleep, I didn't want to wake you," she said. She studied me. "You look scared, Gene. Bad dream?"

"A nightmare," I said.

Henry Baum is the author of the novels *The Golden Calf* and *North of Sunset* and has published work in anthologies with Another Sky Press and 3 AM Magazine, as well as stories in Scarecrow, Identity Theory, Purple Prose, Storyglossia, and others. Currently, he's at work on the second volume of *The American Book of the Dead,* as well as writing and recording a song for each chapter in the novel. He lives in Los Angeles. Find out more information at <u>theamericanbookofthedead.com</u>.

Bibliography

Constantine, Alex. *Psychic Dictatorship in the U.S.A.* Feral House, 1995.

Craft, Michael. *Alien Impact.* Tor, 1997.

Davies, Paul. *The Mind of God.* Simon & Schuster, 1993.

Dick, Philip K. *The Shifting Realities of Philip K. Dick. Selected Literary and Philosophical Writings.* Edited by Lawrence Sutin. Vintage, 1995.

Goldman, Emily, and Carol Neimann. *Afterlife: The Complete Guide to Life After Death.* Newleaf, 1995.

Greer, Steven M. *Disclosure: Military and Government Witnesses Reveal the Greatest Secrets in Modern History.* Crossing Point, 2001.

Hall, Manley Palmer. *The Secret Teachings of All Ages.* Tarcher/Penguin, 2003.

Horn, Arthur David, and Lynette Anne Mallory-Horn. *Humanity's Extraterrestrial Origins: ET Influences on Humankind's Biological and Cultural Evolution.* Silberschnur, 1997.

Huxley, Aldous. *The Doors of Perception & Heaven and Hell.* Penguin, 1961.

Kaku, Michio. *Visions: How Science Will Revolutionize the 21ˢᵗ Century.* Anchor, 1998.

Keel, John. *Our Haunted Planet.* Fawcett, 1971.

Kinney, Jay, and Richard Smoley. *Hidden Wisdom: A Guide to Western Inner Traditions.* Quest Books, 2006.

Klimo, John. *Channeling: Investigations on Receiving Information from Paranormal Sources.* North Atlantic Books, 1998.

Lewels, Joe. *The God Hypothesis: Extraterrestrial Life and its Implications for Science and Religion.* Granite Publishing, 1997.

Lindsay, Hal. *The Late Great Planet Earth.* Zondervan, 1973.

Mack, John E. *Passport to the Cosmos: Human Transformation and Alien Encounters.* Kunati Inc., 2008.

Marrs, Jim. *Alien Agend*a. Harper, 2000.

———. *Rule by Secrecy: The Hidden History that Connects the Trilateral Commission, the Freemasons, and the Great Pyramids.* Harper, 2001.

Mishlove, Jeffrey. *The Roots of Consciousness.* Council Oak Books, 1995.

Pinchbeck, Daniel. *Breaking Open the Head: A Psychedelic Journey into the Heart of Contemporary Shamanism.* Broadway, *2003.*

———. *2012: The Return of Quetzalcoatl.* Tarcher, *2007.*

Shaw, Eva. *Eve of Destruction: Prophecies, Theories and Preparations for the End of the World.* Lowell House, 1996.

Talbot, Michael. *Mysticism and the New Physics.* Penguin, 1993.

Thompson, Keith. *Angels and Aliens.* Ballantine Books, 1993.

Titor, John. *A Time Traveler's Tale.* Instantpublisher.com, 2003.

Vallee, Jacques. *Confrontations: A Scientist's Search for Alien Contact.* Anomalist Books, 2008.

Walvoord, John F. *Armageddon, Oil and the Middle East Crisis.* Zondervan, 1991.

Wilson, Robert Anton. *Cosmic Trigger.* New Falcon Publications, 1991.

Wyller, Arne A. *The Creating Consciousness: Science as the Language of God.* Divina, 1999.

CPSIA information can be obtained at www.ICGtesting.com
Printed in the USA
268484BV00001B/52/P

9 780578 026930